BURIED TESTIMONY

AN ALEX HAYES LEGAL THRILLER
BOOK 3

L.T. RYAN

WITH
LAURA CHASE

LIQUID MIND MEDIA

Copyright © 2025 by L.T. Ryan, Laura Chase & Liquid Mind Media. All rights reserved. No part of this publication may be copied, reproduced in any format, by any means, electronic or otherwise, without prior consent from the copyright owner and publisher of this book. This is a work of fiction. All characters, names, places and events are the product of the author's imagination or used fictitiously. For information contact:

contact@ltryan.com

http://LTRyan.com

https://www.facebook.com/JackNobleBooks

THE ALEX HAYES SERIES

Trial By Fire (Prequel Novella)
Fractured Verdict
11th Hour Witness
Buried Testimony
The Bishop's Recusal

CHAPTER ONE

THE LOBBY of the U.S. Attorney's Office reeked of fresh carpet cleaner and bureaucracy. Everything gleamed with an unsettling sterility—polished floors, neatly framed portraits of past Attorneys General lining the walls, the eagle seal mounted above the security desk watching, judging. I adjusted my blazer, reminding myself that this was a step forward. A fresh start.

Not that I felt like celebrating.

The elevator ride to the Criminal Division was quiet. I kept my eyes on the numbers blinking above the door, half-expecting someone to step in and ruin my moment of solitude. No one did. When the doors slid open on the seventh floor, the quiet shattered—phones ringing, the distant clatter of keyboards, hushed voices exchanging deals and case preparations. I wasn't just a state-level assistant district attorney anymore. The U.S. Attorney's Office was bigger, grander, and the undercurrent of tension here pulsed with a more palpable intensity.

I tried applying logic to my nerves. At least here, I wouldn't have to worry about everyone around me gossiping about how I'd exposed corruption in the Martin case. Or about how I'd single-handedly revealed the rot in the mayor's office while tanking the trial that should have been my career-making moment. Here, I was just another new hire, effectively invisible.

I followed the hallway signs to "Criminal," passing offices with glass panels that revealed their occupants—some deep in conversation, others buried in files. The place hummed with the cold precision of machinery, every cog turning exactly as designed.

I found my assigned office, surprised to see my name already mounted outside the door in a temporary placard. *ALEX HAYES, AUSA.* The letters swam before my eyes, refusing to solidify into something that felt like my reality.

Inside, the office offered little comfort. An ancient government-issued chair squeaked in protest as I brushed past it toward the plain wooden desk. The tall bookshelf loomed in the back of the room, the *Federal Rules of Criminal Procedure* and this year's Sentencing Guidelines staring down at me like sentinels. The essentials.

Dropping my bag on the desk, I eyed the computer that had a "Welcome to the Department of Justice" login screen glowing at me. I was about to sit when a sharp knock sounded at the door.

Erin Mitchell leaned against the frame, arms crossed, her signature half-smile firmly in place. "You look like someone who just realized they joined a machine bigger than they can break."

"Nice to see you, too," I muttered.

I still considered Erin a friend. At least, in the way you could be friends with someone who'd once used you as a pawn to take down a dirty cop. She'd had her reasons—I understood that now. But it didn't make it any easier to forget the way she'd maneuvered around me, steering me right where she needed me while keeping her own agenda close to the vest. It had worked. Andrews had gone down. But I'd been left to pick up the pieces with a bullet wound in my shoulder. These days, it only ached when the weather drastically changed. Which for Houston meant basically every day.

Erin had apologized, in her own way, and I'd accepted it as much as I could. The trust we had before the Martin case? That was gone. Now, I kept my guard up at all times, even with people I liked. *Especially* with people I liked.

She stepped in and took a slow look around, nodding in approval. "Not bad. You're already ahead of where I started—my first office didn't even have a window."

"I get a stunning view of the parking garage, so I think we're even." I folded my arms. "What's my first case? Racketeering? Drug cartel?"

Erin's mouth curved into that familiar, knowing expression. "Oh, you sweet summer child."

She handed me a file.

I flipped it open. Habeas petitions. Post-conviction appeals. Inmate filings from prison. My stomach sank.

Habeas corpus—the so-called last hope of the damned. In theory, it's a noble concept. The great safeguard of justice, the mechanism by which the wrongfully convicted could claw their way out of a prison cell and back into the world. In reality? It was ninety-nine percent bullshit.

Most of these petitions were just stacks of wasted paper filed by inmates who had nothing but time and a battered copy of *Federal Criminal Procedure for Dummies*. They'd scrawl out half-baked claims, including ineffective assistance of counsel, constitutional violations, and evidence that conveniently hadn't existed during their trial. Some even argued that the court had had no jurisdiction over them in the first place—rambling manifestos peppered with legal jargon, written in all caps with red ink, as if that somehow transformed them into valid arguments.

I'd seen it before. Back at the DA's office, these filings were all the same: desperate, sloppy, and almost always meritless. An endless cycle of grasping at legal technicalities, hoping some poor overworked judge would be too exhausted to deny it outright.

I flipped to the first page. Some guy out of USP Beaumont claiming his defense attorney had been incompetent—failed to investigate witnesses, to object at trial, to present mitigating evidence. Classic. Every inmate swore their lawyer was an idiot after the fact.

I looked back up at Erin. "You're kidding, right?"

"Welcome to the big leagues," Erin said, clapping a hand on my shoulder. "Hope you like reading handwritten legal filings on notebook paper, because you're about to drown in them."

I closed the file with a snap, my own temper starting to flare. "I didn't leave the DA's office to do post-conviction work."

"You didn't leave the DA's office at all. You were recruited out of it.

Now you're here, and guess what? Everyone starts in habeas. Even I did."

My fingers tightened around the edges of the file, my disappointment burning in my chest. "How long until I can actually do real work?"

"That depends. How fast can you prove you're not just another former state prosecutor trying to play federal?"

Before I could give Erin a piece of my mind, another voice cut in. "Hayes?"

I turned to see a man in his early forties standing in the doorway, sleeves rolled up, tie slightly loosened. The type who'd been here long enough to know everyone's mistakes before they even made them.

Erin straightened slightly. "This is Nathan Callahan. Your new supervisor."

Callahan cut straight to the point. "Just making sure you found your office."

"I did." My expression remained neutral. "Thanks."

"Good." He glanced at the files in front of me. "Habeas cases. Get through them fast. We'll see where you land after that."

His tone made it clear—I was here to prove myself.

"Understood," I said, thumbing the files on my desk like I hadn't already considered tossing them in the trash.

"Welcome to the USAO." And just like that, he was gone.

Erin let out a low whistle. "You passed the Callahan test. He didn't look like he wanted to murder you."

"Is that the benchmark around here? If your supervisor doesn't immediately fantasize about strangling you, you're doing great?"

"Pretty much," Erin said, her eyes crinkling with amusement. She checked her watch. "I've got a debrief with Organized Crime in ten. Want to grab drinks after work? You're gonna need them."

I stared at the box tucked around the side of my desk, stacked high with desperate pleas masquerading as legal arguments. I was pretty angry with Erin. If she had told me I'd be stuck doing habeas petitions, then maybe I wouldn't have moved to the feds. I took a deep breath and tried, for once, not to get ahead of myself. Today was only day one and I was here for a reason. Making an enemy out of Erin probably wasn't going to help me advance. "Yeah, alright. And what happens when I finish this nightmare?"

Erin's eyes glinted. "That's the spirit." She eyed me with the smug satisfaction of someone who'd been through this gauntlet before. "Don't worry—when you finish those, they'll just bring you more."

"Of course they will."

Erin strode off, leaving me alone with my not-so-glamorous first assignment—and the soul-crushing box of appeals waiting to remind me of my place in the system. I sat at my desk, flipping the file open again. The words "Petition for Writ of Habeas Corpus" stared back at me. Not exactly what I'd envisioned for my first day at the U.S. Attorney's Office.

But if they wanted me to prove myself?

Fine.

I'd play the game. For now.

CHAPTER TWO

I LOOKED at the first file on my desk, cast in a blueish glow under the fluorescent overhead light, and braced myself for the mind-numbing legalese inside.

PETITION FOR WRIT OF HABEAS CORPUS
THE UNITED STATES DISTRICT COURT
SOUTHERN DISTRICT OF TEXAS

I skimmed the first few paragraphs. The petitioner—one Jerome L. Barlow, Reg. No. 48219-179—served forty years for drug trafficking and firearms offenses. According to him, his entire conviction represented a miscarriage of justice. His attorney had been incompetent, the judge biased, and the government had conspired against him.

The usual greatest hits.

I flipped to the next page and saw the real reason I had to deal with this mess—a court order directing the government to file a response. Lovely.

Here's how it worked. Any inmate could file a habeas petition, arguing their conviction or sentence violated the Constitution. Most of them were summarily denied, meaning the judge tossed them without bothering to ask for the government's input. But every so often, a judge decided a petition warranted further review—hence the order on my desk.

That meant I had work to do.

I skimmed the court's directive:

ORDERED that the United States Attorney's Office shall file a response within 30 days addressing the petitioner's claims regarding ineffective assistance of counsel.

Translation: *Alex, welcome to the USAO. Here's some homework.*

The judge hadn't determined whether the claim had merit, just that it deserved more than an immediate dismissal. The threshold for that remained painfully low. If an inmate managed to string together a few coherent sentences and reference the Sixth Amendment, the court practically had to take a second look.

I returned to Barlow's actual ineffective assistance claim.

The man claimed his lawyer never objected to certain testimony at trial, and if he had, the jury might have ruled in his favor. According to Barlow, a key witness—one of his former associates who had flipped on him—had misrepresented their own plea deal while testifying. Barlow argued that his lawyer should have called this out, that the jury had been misled, and therefore, his entire conviction deserved to be thrown out.

According to Barlow, it didn't matter that he had been caught with twenty kilos of cocaine, a firearm, and enough cash to buy a small island. He pinned his hopes on one witness's apparently faulty plea agreement description.

I checked the docket number and pulled up the case history on my computer. The trial transcripts would tell me whether his lawyer had, in fact, screwed the pooch or if this was just another inmate fishing for a loophole. My money rested firmly on the latter.

Before I could dive in, a soft knock at my door pulled me out of my haze.

A woman stood in the doorway—blonde, early forties, polished but no-nonsense. She held a travel mug of coffee in one hand and a stack of marked-up case files in the other.

"Alex Hayes?" she asked, glancing at my nameplate, then back at me.

"That's me," I said. "And you are?"

"Maggie Cohen, Appellate Division." She gave me a once-over, assessing. "You're coming from the Harris County DA's office, right?"

"Yeah."

Cohen's lips curved into a knowing smile. "Welcome to federal. Hope you like paperwork."

I motioned to the stack on my desk. "I'm getting that impression."

She chuckled. "Here they always start newcomers on habeas petitions. But you'll get the hang of it. Let me know if you need any help deciphering the nonsense. Most of these cases have been appealed and denied so many times, they should come with a greatest-hits playlist."

"Duly noted."

Raising her coffee in a mock toast, she walked off.

The parade of introductions continued throughout the day—a stream of faces and names swimming together, most of which vanished from memory almost immediately.

Before I knew it, my stomach growled in protest, and my inbox overflowed. I glanced at the time and realized I hadn't left my desk once today. Not even for lunch.

I logged out of my computer, stacked the files into something resembling order, and grabbed my bag. Time to meet Erin for that drink.

I swirled the last of the scotch in my glass, watching the amber liquid catch the dim bar light. Erin leaned against the counter, elbow propped up, her expression expectant.

"Are you gonna keep brooding, or are you gonna tell me what's eating at you?"

I exhaled through my nose, setting my glass down with a dull *clink*. "It's not that bad, really. I just … this isn't what I thought it would be."

Erin raised an eyebrow. "You mean you didn't dream of spending your days drowning in habeas petitions? I could have warned you, but would you have believed me?"

I shot her a look. "You spent years trying to recruit me to the federal side, talking about the 'big leagues' and 'important cases.' Instead, I'm sifting through stacks of long-shot appeals, filing response briefs no judge will actually read, and pretending that this is important work. I have a right to be pissed at you, Erin."

"This *is* important work," Erin said, tilting her glass toward me. "It just happens to be soul-crushingly boring."

My lips twitched reluctantly. "Exactly."

Leaning back against the bar, she studied me. "But that's not really what's bothering you, is it?"

I hesitated. Erin had manipulated me during the Martin trial, and she definitely wasn't stupid.

I rubbed a hand across my forehead. "After everything that happened with the trafficking ring, after finding out what happened to my mom—I thought maybe this job would give me more resources, better access to continue that investigation. Instead, I'm checking boxes on paperwork while the people responsible for what happened to her are still out there." *There. I'd said it.*

Erin's expression didn't shift, didn't turn patronizing or dismissive. Instead, she nodded, her gaze steady. "I get it."

I looked up at her, surprised.

She shrugged. "Hell, that's part of why I wanted you here in the first place. You want to *do* something. You want to pull at the threads, continue Katherine's investigation before she died. But instead, they've got you shuffling through procedural motions like a glorified law clerk. That's frustrating as hell."

"Exactly." I let out a breath, staring at the rim of my glass. "Finally I've got my foot in the door at the feds, but I'm still stuck on the sidelines."

Erin tapped her fingers against her glass, thoughtful. "It won't last forever."

"Easy for you to say." I scoffed. You're working real cases."

"That's true. But you *will* get there, Alex. I should have been clearer that the USAO doesn't operate like the county DA's office. They test everyone this way, even someone who cracked open a major trafficking ring. You've gotta prove yourself here first. Which, let's be real, you'll do *annoyingly* fast."

I snorted, shaking my head. "That's generous."

"But it's the truth." She took a sip, then gestured toward me with her glass. "Look at it this way—this is the first time in years you don't have a huge trial breathing down your neck, no hearings to sprint to, no cops demanding arrest warrants like you're some kind of vending machine for probable cause."

The image pulled a genuine smile from me.

"I know it's not what you expected," she continued. "But for now, you get to breathe. No pressure, no public scrutiny, no media outside the courthouse waiting for you to screw up. Just you, some badly written petitions, and time."

"Time," I echoed, the word tasting foreign on my tongue.

The bar hummed around us, glasses clinking, conversations blending into white noise. The scent of whiskey and polished wood mingled with something fried from the kitchen. I traced a water ring on the bar top, realizing Erin had handed me a perspective I hadn't considered.

"Time to dig, time to put your own pieces together." She placed her glass down on the bar top and eyed me. "You're gonna keep looking into it, aren't you?"

I nodded, avoiding her gaze. "I have to."

Erin nodded. "Then use this time wisely. The big cases will come. In the meantime, don't waste the breathing room."

I let out a slow breath, some of the weight on my chest loosening. Erin was right. It wasn't the role I wanted, but I could still make it work for me.

She changed the subject smoothly. "Still living at your dad's place?"

"Yeah," I said, finishing off the last of my scotch. "The commute's not bad, since I managed to get a spot here in the Houston office. So, for now, it works."

"Good. Speaking of Houston, I've been meaning to tell you—I officially transferred back a few months ago. The office needed another senior AUSA for their organized crime unit."

I raised an eyebrow. "So that's why you've been so persistent about getting me to join. You needed a familiar face around here."

"Maybe," she admitted with a half-smile. "Or maybe I just knew you belonged here all along."

I smiled. "Looks like we're both settling in."

She chuckled. "Something like that."

We fell quiet for a moment, sitting comfortably in the gentle lull of the conversation, the clinking of glasses and low hum of voices around us.

Erin glanced at the time on her phone. "I should head out before I start regretting tomorrow morning."

"Same," I said, stretching my arms. "First full day of government work really takes it out of you."

"Yeah, yeah. You'll adjust. And when you do? You're buying the next round."

"Deal."

Outside the bar, Erin headed off in the direction of her place while I made my way toward my car. The night air was crisp, carrying the distant hum of the city. I exhaled, my mind turning over everything we'd talked about.

Erin was right about one thing. For the first time in my life, I had time.

CHAPTER
THREE

STALE COFFEE COOLED in my mug as fluorescent lights buzzed overhead, casting harsh shadows across the stack of manila folders littering my desk. I glanced at the clock in the corner of my monitor. It crept toward noon, and I had already knocked out four reply briefs this morning—four cookie-cutter responses explaining why yet another federal inmate wasn't entitled to relief.

I stretched my arms, rolling out the tightness in my shoulders, then leaned back in my chair. The box of petitions still loomed at the side of my desk like an accusation—a cardboard monument to futility. Each folder mirrored the next. Same formatting, same desperate handwriting scrawled in margins, same pleas for justice that would almost certainly fall on deaf ears.

My eyes burned as I stared at the endless parade of human misery. Each petition represented someone's last hope, yet digging through them hollowed me out, leaving nothing but cynicism in its wake.

A few caught my attention momentarily—claims about ineffective assistance, prosecutorial misconduct, newly discovered evidence—but my brief time at the USAO had already taught me a harsh lesson. The system rarely admitted its mistakes. The bar for actual relief towered so high that most petitions amounted to little more than desperation on paper.

I flipped past one claiming an inmate's lawyer was "asleep" during trial. Another argued the judge was *secretly colluding* with the prosecution. One had the ever-popular sovereign citizen rambling, which I tossed aside without another glance.

I had already moved to the next file when two words jumped out at me. *Brady violation.*

My pulse quickened.

I spread the file open and devoured the pages. Gabriel Ortega, serving life without parole for felony murder. Twelve years into his sentence. According to his petition, the prosecution had deliberately buried a key witness statement—one that could have undermined the state's entire case against him.

The more I read, the tighter my jaw clenched. This wasn't a simple oversight. The prosecution had actively suppressed the witness's statement, keeping potentially exonerating evidence from the defense.

A Brady violation, in its simplest form, meant the prosecution failed to turn over exculpatory evidence to the defense. The term came from *Brady v. Maryland*, a 1963 Supreme Court case establishing a fundamental rule of fairness: if the government possessed evidence that might help prove a defendant's innocence or weaken the prosecution's case, they had to disclose it. No exceptions. Prosecutors couldn't play keep-away.

But prosecutors didn't always play by the rules.

I scanned Ortega's petition again. Unlike most inmates who filed vague, hopeful claims, Ortega provided specifics. He didn't merely suggest evidence might exist somewhere—he identified a particular witness statement that prosecutors had intentionally concealed. Even more striking, a retiring prosecutor had come forward, attaching his own name to the admission of misconduct. That detail froze me in place.

Anonymous tips in habeas petitions appeared regularly. But a former prosecutor voluntarily confessing to misconduct? Putting his professional reputation and possibly his license on the line? That raised this petition from routine to extraordinary.

I flipped to the court order attached to the petition. The judge had already demanded a preliminary response—they believed this claim carried enough weight to warrant an explanation from the government.

I pulled up Ortega's trial records on my screen, the details unfolding before me.

The case centered on a botched robbery. The feds played the interstate commerce card and rang it up federally. The prosecution had argued that Ortega participated in a crew that held up a liquor store in Houston. When the store owner pulled a gun, bullets flew, and someone died. Under the felony murder rule, even if Ortega hadn't pulled the trigger, his involvement in the robbery made him culpable for any resulting death.

But Ortega had always maintained his innocence, insisting he wasn't even at the scene.

One of Ortega's former associates had testified against him in exchange for a reduced sentence. That testimony formed the cornerstone of the prosecution's case.

And now I held in my hands a claim that another witness—someone the jury never heard from—had directly contradicted the prosecution's narrative. A witness the state knew about but deliberately kept silent.

My fingers tapped against the edge of the desk as I re-read portions of the petition. If true, this case represented everything wrong with the system—the power of prosecutors to shape narratives by controlling what evidence a jury sees.

A person might have spent twelve years in prison for a crime he didn't commit because someone decided winning mattered more than justice.

The calendar notification on my screen pulled me from my thoughts.

Meeting with AUSA Daniel Wexler — Habeas Unit Chief.

Damn. I was supposed to be in his office in five minutes. Ortega would have to wait.

I grabbed my notepad, straightened my blazer, and made my way through the maze of hallways to Wexler's office. As chief of the Habeas Unit for the Southern District of Texas, he reviewed all petitions filed against federal convictions in our jurisdiction—the ultimate arbiter of which claims deserved serious consideration.

When I got to his door, I knocked lightly.

"Come in."

The man behind the deep voice sat at his desk, sleeves rolled up, head bowed over a file. Wexler, mid-fifties, carried a thick head of salt-and-pepper hair and the kind of rounded shoulders that came from decades hunched over case files. Shelves of federal law books and case binders surrounded him like a fortress, each spine perfectly aligned with military precision. Not a paper clip out of place.

He glanced up as I entered and offered a small, practiced smile.

"Hayes. Take a seat." He gestured to the chair across from him. "How are you settling in?"

I slid into the seat, setting my notepad on my lap. "It's been good so far. Still getting my bearings, but I think I'm finding the rhythm."

He nodded. "Glad to hear it. First few weeks are always an adjustment. Government work moves at its own pace. Sometimes it feels like a slow crawl, sometimes it's like drinking water from a firehose."

That sounded about right.

"I appreciate you making time," I said. "I know you're busy."

"Of course." Wexler laced his fingers together, resting them on his desk. "Let's talk about your caseload. You've been moving through the petitions quickly—walk me through what you've handled so far."

I flipped open my notepad and ran down the list.

Jerome L. Barlow. Claimed ineffective assistance of counsel. Argued his lawyer should have objected to testimony about a cooperating witness's plea deal. No merit—the judge even asked Barlow if he was satisfied with his attorney on the record.

Tyrone Mitchell. Claimed actual innocence based on a "mystery witness" who conveniently never came forward at trial. No merit—no affidavits, no supporting evidence, just a rehash of trial arguments.

Leonard Torres. Fourth habeas petition. This time arguing the jury instructions were unconstitutional. No merit—he had already litigated this on direct appeal and lost.

Samuel Ross. DNA claim. No merit—the "new evidence" he cited had been available at trial, and his own lawyer had decided not to test it because it was more damaging than helpful.

Wexler listened without interrupting, nodding occasionally. When I finished, he leaned back in his chair.

"Sounds like you're doing great work," he said.

Wexler shifted, reaching for the file on his desk as if to silently end the conversation.

But I wasn't done yet. "There's one more I'm looking into now. Gabriel Ortega?"

Wexler's hand froze mid-reach.

He lifted his gaze to mine, studying me for the first time since I'd entered the room. His brows knit together, his expression shifting from neutral to something that resembled concern.

"Ortega?" Wexler repeated, shaking his head. "That conviction was twelve years ago."

I nodded. "That's right."

He leaned forward, resting his elbows on the desk. "You know the statute of limitations for habeas petitions, don't you?"

"The standard deadline is one year from when a conviction becomes final," I said. "After that, it's barred unless there's an exception—like newly discovered evidence or government interference."

Wexler nodded, his brows still furrowed.

Twelve years was way past the statute. By all accounts, Ortega's petition should have been summarily denied as untimely. Which made it curious that Wexler recognized the name instantly, without even checking his files.

I didn't press. Not yet.

"Yes," I said, my voice even, "but the court has ordered a response, so we're past the point of dismissal on timeliness. And if the claim is a Brady violation, that's a recognized exception."

Wexler's jaw tightened. "A Brady claim?"

I nodded. "A retired prosecutor came forward about burying a witness statement."

For a moment, he said nothing. Then he straightened and exhaled through his nose. "Why don't you hand that case over to me?" he said casually. "I'll take a look at it."

My stomach dropped, but I kept my expression neutral.

"Respectfully," I said, "I'd like to see it through."

Wexler smiled, but it was just a little too tight. "I understand, but these more complicated petitions—ones that go beyond standard reply briefs—are usually better handled by senior attorneys."

I hesitated, tilting my head. "Is there some reason you don't want me working on it?"

There was a beat of silence.

His expression smoothed out, his tone lighter. "No, of course not," he said with an easy chuckle. "Just didn't want you getting too buried in the weeds your first few weeks."

I narrowed my gaze but gave a short nod. "I appreciate that. I'll still take a look at the files and let you know what I find."

Wexler smiled tightly again. "Sounds good. You can talk to my assistant Cynthia if you need any additional case files. She can pull anything not in the system."

I stood, smoothing out my blazer. "I'll do that."

Wexler nodded, already looking back at his notes.

I left the office, closing the door behind me, and walked down the hall with suspicion coiling in my gut like a snake. Something about Ortega's case had triggered Wexler's alarm bells—and now mine were ringing too.

CHAPTER
FOUR

CYNTHIA'S DESK was a perfect study in controlled chaos.

Stacks of case files were piled high, arranged in a way that made sense only to her. A half-empty coffee cup sat precariously near the edge, next to a ceramic pen holder shaped like a gavel. The air smelled faintly of peppermint, and a calendar covered in colorful sticky notes hung on the wall behind her.

If Janice—my old gatekeeper at the DA's office—had run this desk, it would have been a fortress of post-it notes and sharp glares, a firm "no" at the ready for anyone who dared interrupt her day. Cynthia, though? She projected an aura of methodical competence beneath the apparent disorder, a little friendlier, a little less battle-hardened, but still the type who knew everything happening in this office before anyone else did.

She looked up as I approached. "Alex, right?"

"That's me."

Cynthia smiled. "What can I do for you?"

"I need the case files on Gabriel Ortega—everything we have."

"That's an old one." Her fingers flew across her keyboard, and she let out a low *hmm* as she scanned the screen.

"I know," I said. "I've got the habeas petition."

Nodding, she clicked a few more times. "Let me pull what we have from storage and send them to your office shortly. Shouldn't take too long."

"Appreciate it."

"Of course. Anything else?"

I hesitated. Wanting to ask if she knew anything about the case—if she had any idea why Wexler seemed so concerned about it—but I held back. No need to tip my hand just yet.

"Nope, just that," I said, giving her a nod before heading back to my office.

I had barely sat down when my phone rang. Lisa Cooper. My former colleague at the DA's office. A small part of me wanted to ignore it—not because I didn't want to talk to her, but because I didn't want to admit how little I had to say. Still, I answered, getting up to close my office door before sitting back down.

"Lisa," I said, leaning back in my chair. "To what do I owe the pleasure?"

"You act like I don't check in on you at least weekly. How's it going over there in *big fancy federal land*?"

I let out a dry chuckle. "About as exciting as you'd expect."

"So, still in bureaucratic paradise?"

"Oh yeah. I'm practically an expert at rejecting meritless appeals at this point."

Lisa's eyes would be rolling if I could see her. "Sounds thrilling. Have you figured anything out about the trafficking ring? Or about your mom?"

I hesitated, my fingers tightening around the phone. There was nothing I wanted more than to tell her I had a lead. That I was closing in on something big. That I had finally found the missing piece that could explain why my mother had been killed. But I hadn't.

Buried in habeas petitions, I was stuck writing legal responses no one would ever read, and the only case that had even remotely caught my attention had just been flagged by my boss as something I shouldn't be looking into.

I swallowed down the frustration. "Not yet."

Lisa was quiet for a moment, like she knew there was more I wasn't saying.

"Well," she said, her voice gentler now. "That's why you took this job, right? You'll get there."

"Yeah. Eventually." I forced a smile, even though she couldn't see it.

Lisa pivoted, her tone turning playful. "I better get an invite to your first *big* federal trial. I'm picturing you grilling some Wall Street fraudster in front of a jury, giving your best *'I am the government'* speech."

I forced a chuckle, but inside, the thought just made my stomach twist. Because I didn't have a big trial. Wasn't working a case that mattered. I was wasting time—time I had thought would get me closer to the truth. But I couldn't say that.

"Don't worry. I'll send you VIP tickets when the time comes."

"I'll hold you to that."

I needed to change the subject before the bitterness creeping into my voice became too obvious. "Enough about me. What about you? What are you working on?"

"You know," Lisa said, stretching the words out. "Same old stuff—homicides, gang cases, the occasional insurance fraud."

My lip quirked upward. "Sounds riveting."

"Actually," she said, "I do have one case that's interesting. I'll tell you over dinner."

That caught my attention. "Dinner?"

"Yeah. Let's catch up. Tomorrow?"

I hesitated—not because I didn't want to see her, but because the thought of hearing about her meaningful caseload while I shuffled papers felt like salt in a wound.

But then I remembered the case files I was about to get my hands on. Maybe by tomorrow night, I'd have something real to talk about.

"Sounds good," I said. "Dinner tomorrow."

"I'll text you the details."

We said our goodbyes, and I set my phone down. I busied myself organizing some of the scattered files on my desk, trying to shake the feeling that had settled in my chest since my meeting with Wexler.

I stacked my completed reply briefs in neat piles, labeling them with sticky notes to indicate which ones were ready to be filed. The monotony helped clear my head, at least a little.

I had just started drafting an outline for the Ortega reply brief when a soft knock at my door made me glance up.

Cynthia stepped in, a thin binder clutched against her chest.

She walked over and set it down on my desk with a thud.

"There you go," she said, brushing her hands off like she had just finished a workout. "The Ortega files you asked for."

I stared at the binder, then up at her. "Okay ... when will the rest get here?"

Cynthia blinked at me. "That's it."

I frowned. "What?"

"That's all we have on Ortega."

I let out a short laugh, expecting her to be joking. But she didn't laugh with me.

"This can't be it," I said, flipping open the binder. The pages inside were neatly hole-punched, the whole thing barely an inch thick. "This was a major case—multiple defendants, felony murder charges, a full trial. There should be boxes of records. Transcripts, investigative files, motions."

Cynthia gave a small, apologetic shrug. "Records retention policy."

I exhaled through my nose. "Right. The *policy*."

I knew the spiel. After a certain number of years, case files—especially closed cases—were purged from the system unless they were flagged for retention due to pending litigation or special circumstances.

But this wasn't just some forgotten case. Ortega had been filing appeals and habeas petitions for years. His case had never *really* gone cold.

"Let me guess," I said, keeping my voice neutral. "The rest was *disposed of*?"

Cynthia offered another noncommittal shrug, clearly not interested in being dragged into whatever bureaucratic mess this was. "That's what the system shows."

There was no point in arguing with her. It wasn't Cynthia's fault that these files had gone magically missing.

"Thanks anyway. I appreciate it."

She gave me a knowing look, like she could tell I wasn't buying it, but she didn't comment. "Let me know if you need anything else."

I nodded and she walked out, leaving me alone with what little remained of Ortega's case. I leaned back in my chair, staring at the wafer-thin binder in front of me.

Retention policy, my ass.

CHAPTER FIVE

THE HARSH FLUORESCENT lights buzzed overhead, casting an unnatural pallor across the stacks of papers littering my desk. The muted hum of printers and hushed conversations seeped through my closed office door, creating a constant backdrop of government efficiency. I stared at the Ortega binder, untouched since morning, as a paper cup of coffee grew cold beside my keyboard.

The entire day had been a waste. All I had wanted to do was dig into the Ortega files—what little of them I had—but instead, I'd been dragged through a never-ending loop of administrative meetings.

Apparently, *the* US Attorney for the Southern District of Texas, James Beckett, was visiting the office today. And for some reason, that meant that instead of doing actual work, everything ground to a halt. Meetings. Briefings. Some kind of roundtable discussion that felt more like a ceremonial bowing of heads to the top brass. I sat through them all, nodding when appropriate, pretending to take notes as I mentally cataloged all the time I was losing.

Before the last conference of the day wrapped up, I slipped out as quietly as I could, weaving through the now empty corridors, trying to make it back to my office before someone called me into another pointless discussion.

I was so close. Then I turned a corner. And walked right into James Beckett himself.

Fantastic.

I recognized him instantly—late fifties, tall, with the kind of presence that filled a room before he even spoke. His silver hair was still thick, combed back, and he wore a tailored navy suit that somehow made him look both relaxed and authoritative.

His reputation preceded him—former trial attorney turned government watchdog, the kind of prosecutor who actually believed in the law, not just in winning cases. He had spent decades walking the line between bureaucracy and principle and, unlike most, he hadn't lost himself in the system.

He had also just caught me sneaking out of a conference.

"And you are ...?"

I straightened. "Alex Hayes, sir."

"Hayes," he repeated, like he was committing it to memory. His gaze was sharp but not unkind, studying me rather than reprimanding me. "And why, exactly, are you not in the conference room with the rest of your colleagues?"

I could have lied. Could have said I had another meeting, or that I wasn't feeling well. But lying to my boss's boss in my first week seemed like a bad career move.

I cleared my throat. "I had an important case I wanted to get back to."

Beckett's lips quirked, like he wasn't expecting that answer. "Is that so?"

"Yes, sir."

"And what case is so important that it trumps today's meetings?"

For a second, I hesitated. I doubted a man of his rank cared much about habeas petitions. But there was something about him—the way he was actually listening, not just waiting for me to talk—that made me answer honestly.

"It's a habeas petition, sir."

Beckett nodded, his expression unreadable.

Most attorneys, let alone AUSAs I had met so far would have scoffed. Made some joke about how habeas petitions were just inmate Hail Marys, how I shouldn't waste too much time on them. But Beckett? His eyes lit with genuine interest.

"Everyone acts like habeas cases don't matter. But the truth is, they matter more than almost anything else we do."

I raised my eyebrows. "Really?"

Beckett tilted his head. "Do you know why we have habeas corpus in the first place, Hayes?"

"It's a safeguard against wrongful detention. A way to ensure that people aren't being held illegally."

"That's the technical answer. But it's more than that."

I stayed quiet, letting him continue.

"Habeas corpus is one of the few things that sets our legal system apart from others. It's not about bureaucracy. It's about accountability. It's about making sure our government—which has the power to take away someone's freedom—isn't doing so unjustly."

He gave me a long look. "You ever read about dictatorships? About how they keep power?"

I nodded. "By silencing dissenters."

"Exactly," Beckett said. "They lock people up. No charges. No trials. No chance to challenge their detention. That's what makes our system different. Habeas corpus is the last line of defense against government overreach. Against wrongful convictions. Against corruption."

The words resonated with the unease I'd felt since discovering the Ortega case—especially after Wexler's strange reaction earlier.

Beckett smiled again, a little softer this time. "Keep that in mind while you're writing your reply briefs, Hayes. Don't just follow bureaucratic routine—follow the spirit of the Constitution."

I nodded, absorbing his words. "Yes, sir."

Beckett winked. "I'll let you get back to it, then."

With that, he turned and walked back toward the conference room, hands in his pockets like he had all the time in the world.

I stood there for a second, my nerves buzzing with energy. For all the bullshit I had to wade through in this job, maybe there was still something real underneath it all. I turned back toward my office, ready to finally dig into Ortega's case.

Then I glanced at the clock. And groaned internally. It was past five. If I didn't leave now, I was going to be late meeting Lisa for dinner.

Grabbing my blazer, I stuffed the Ortega binder into my bag. I'd skim through it at home.

I stepped out of the U.S. Attorney's Office into the warm evening air, the Houston humidity still lingering despite the sun beginning to set. My car was parked in a nearby garage, but I opted to walk the few blocks to the restaurant.

Guard & Grace was one of those modern steakhouse-meets-upscale-lounges, just a short distance from the office. It wasn't the usual hole-in-the-wall bar where Lisa and I used to grab drinks after work. Since she had suggested it, I figured she wanted a real dinner instead of whiskey with a side of fries.

As I approached, the sleek glass exterior reflected the deep blues and oranges of the Texas sunset. The warm lighting inside cast a soft glow through the windows, and the place was already filling up with the post-work crowd—lawyers, finance guys in tailored suits, a few scattered dates tucked into booths.

Stepping through the glass doors, I was hit with the scent of charred steak, butter, and smoke. The kind of smell that reminded me of how little I'd eaten all day.

A hostess greeted me with a practiced smile.

"Good evening. Do you have a reservation?"

"I'm meeting someone," I said, scanning the room. "Lisa Cooper."

She nodded and glanced at the seating chart. "Right this way."

I followed her through the dining area, where low chatter and the occasional clinking of glasses filled the space. The restaurant was modern but warm—exposed wood beams, leather seating, an open kitchen where chefs moved with practiced precision behind the counter.

Lisa waved when she spotted me, already nursing a glass of red wine.

Shrugging off my blazer, I slid into the seat across from her. "Look at you, getting the fancy wine instead of a beer."

She tapped her glass with a manicured nail. "I felt like classing it up."

The waiter came by almost immediately. "Would you like to start with something to drink?"

After I glanced at Lisa's glass, then at the extensive wine list, Lisa raised her glass. "Red blend. "

"I'll take one of those," I told the waiter, handing back the wine list.

He nodded and disappeared, and I finally settled in, letting the tension from the day slowly ease out of my shoulders.

"You seem different." Lisa gave me a look, tilting her head slightly. "Less stressed than I expected."

I rubbed the tension from my neck. "Don't worry, still plenty of stress. I just had an unexpected conversation that shifted my perspective a bit."

"Good perspective or bad?"

"Jury's still out."

Lisa drummed her fingers against the stem of her wineglass and took a sip. "Let me tell you about the hell I've inherited since you left."

"Oh?"

She leaned back. "Turns out, when you bailed on us for the feds, I got half your caseload dumped onto me."

That hit me harder than I expected. I knew leaving meant shifting my cases to someone else, but hearing Lisa say it out loud made it more real. I had been moving up fast at the DA's office, building a reputation, getting assigned bigger cases. Leaving all of that behind had been a sacrifice, one I had willingly made—but I couldn't pretend it was easy to walk away from the momentum I'd built.

Still, I forced the feeling down and smiled. "At least it's good for you, right? More work means they trust you."

Lisa gave a dramatic sigh. "Yeah, yeah, I know. Doesn't make it suck less."

The waiter returned, setting my wine down and rattling off the specials. Lisa and I both glanced at the menu but barely absorbed it, too caught up in conversation.

When he left us to look at the menu, Lisa took another sip of wine and leaned forward. "One of the cases I picked up actually has me intrigued. Thought you'd find it interesting."

I raised an eyebrow. "Alright, hit me."

She set her glass down. "Guy got arrested for gun trafficking. We thought it was just a standard straw-purchasing case—you know, people buying guns legally and selling them to people who can't legally own them. But then we started seeing weird overlaps in wiretaps from some of our trafficking cases."

"Human trafficking?"

Lisa nodded. "Different rings, but some of the same contacts were showing up in both cases. Like, the same shell companies moving money, the same dummy accounts funneling cash."

That caught my attention. Because that sounded awfully familiar.

"Do you think they're connected?" I asked.

"Could be. Could also just be a coincidence. But I'm keeping my eye on it."

My mind started connecting invisible dots, storing this information away for later analysis. Something about those connections nagged at me.

The waiter came back, and we finally ordered, Lisa getting a ribeye while I opted for a filet. The conversation drifted into small talk—how some of our old colleagues were doing, which judges had been particularly insufferable lately.

Then Lisa tilted her head, giving me that look again.

"Alright, enough about me. What are *you* working on?"

I swirled my wine glass, watching as the liquid moved against the sides. "I actually might have a habeas petition worth looking at."

Lisa let out a short laugh. "Figures."

I looked up from my glass. "Figures?"

She leaned forward, resting her elbows on the table. "Come on, Alex. You think the universe isn't going to hand you the *one* habeas petition that might actually have merit?" She shook her head. "That's just your luck."

I tapped my fingers against the stem of my wine glass, considering her words. "We'll see."

We ate, the conversation shifting back and forth, and by the time the plates were cleared and the check arrived, the weight on my shoulders had eased slightly.

As we got up to leave, Lisa stretched. "Alright, so we're still good for next week?"

I nodded. "Same day, same time?"

"Sounds good." She pointed a finger at me. "Maybe by then, you'll have cracked your habeas case wide open."

"Let's not get ahead of ourselves."

We walked out onto the street, the Houston skyline glowing in the distance.

"See you next week," Lisa said, giving me a small wave before heading toward her car. I watched her go for a second before exhaling and heading toward my own.

The Ortega binder was still in my bag. And something told me that I wasn't going to be able to ignore it for much longer.

CHAPTER SIX

THE HOUSE WAS quiet when I got home, the familiar creaks and sighs of the old structure welcoming me back. My dad was still up, leaning against the kitchen counter with a beer in his hand, flipping absently through the mail.

"Late dinner?" he asked as I set my bag down.

I nodded, the tension in my shoulders easing slightly now that I was home. "I met Lisa to reminisce."

He gave me a knowing look, then tilted his chin toward my bag. "And now you're bringing the office home with you like always?"

I pulled out the Ortega binder and set it on the table. "You know me. Can't resist some good light reading before bed."

"You really need a home office, kid. This kitchen isn't big enough for all your case files."

"Nah. I like working in here." I shrugged off my blazer and draped it over the back of the chair before settling in. "Helps me feel like I'm not at work twenty-four-seven."

"Fair enough." Dad lingered for a second, like he was debating saying something else, but then just patted my shoulder. "Don't stay up all night with that thing."

"No promises."

He rolled his eyes and headed toward the stairs. "Goodnight, kid."

"Night, Dad."

Once I heard his bedroom door click shut, I exhaled, rolling my shoulders before opening the thin binder. The facts of Ortega's case, at least those on record, were straightforward.

Twelve years ago, Gabriel Ortega had been convicted of felony murder in connection with a botched liquor store robbery in Houston. Between Ruiz's testimony and cell phone tower records placing Ortega's phone somewhere near the liquor store that night, the jury had been convinced of Ortega's involvement.

The verdict had come back guilty, and the judge handed down a life sentence without the possibility of parole.

Ortega's appeals had gone nowhere.

David Peña had been a bystander, a customer who had been inside the liquor store during the shooting. His original statement said he'd only seen two men inside during the robbery. Not three. And neither was Ortega.

That testimony would have torpedoed the prosecution's entire case. A neutral eyewitness contradicting the state's star witness might have been enough to sway the jury toward reasonable doubt.

The kitchen's fluorescent light hummed overhead as I thumbed through the petition, the smell of my dad's coffee still lingering in the air. My fingers traced the edge of the paper, the tactile connection to a case that might have robbed a man of twelve years of his life.

In a criminal trial, the burden is on the prosecution to prove guilt beyond a reasonable doubt. If the jury had known that a neutral bystander's account failed to put Ortega at the scene, that alone could have created reasonable doubt.

And if the prosecution had intentionally withheld that information? That would have been a Brady violation—one of the most serious forms of prosecutorial misconduct.

Suppressing exculpatory evidence—especially evidence that contradicts a key witness's testimony—undermines the entire foundation of due process. It strips the defendant of their ability to challenge the government's case and denies the jury access to critical facts that could impact their verdict.

Now, years later, a former prosecutor with nothing to lose had apparently decided to clear their conscience. I flipped to the attachment at the back of the petition, the paper cool under my fingertips—a formatted affidavit. Official, but its brevity sent ice through my veins.

I, Samuel Grayson, being duly sworn, state the following:

The kitchen seemed to grow quieter as I read, the weight of the words on the page pressing down on me.

During my time as an Assistant U.S. Attorney in the Southern District of Texas, I handled numerous felony cases, including capital murder and felony murder trials. I have always conducted my work with the belief that justice must be served, regardless of outcome. However, I have recently come to terms with certain ethical concerns that I had failed to address at the time of trial.

In 2011, I was involved in the prosecution of United States v. Gabriel Ortega. At the time, I was made aware of a statement given by David Peña, a witness who had been present at the crime scene. The contents of this statement did not support the prosecution's theory of the case, and after discussion with senior members of the trial team, it was decided that this statement would not be disclosed to the defense.

This decision was wrong.

Had this statement been provided, it is my belief that the defense could have used it to challenge the credibility of the state's key witness and to undermine the conviction itself. By withholding it, the trial proceeded on an incomplete factual record.

I submit this statement freely and voluntarily, without coercion, in the interest of justice. I take full responsibility for my actions and regret not coming forward sooner.

I urge the court to review this matter carefully and ensure that justice is served, regardless of the outcome.

Signed, Samuel Grayson.

I leaned back in the wooden chair, its joints creaking in protest as my mind raced. The refrigerator hummed in the background, the sound filling the stunned silence.

Grabbing my laptop, I typed "Samuel Grayson prosecutor" into the search bar. His official profile from the AUSA's office was still available in archived news releases.

Grayson had been a lead prosecutor for the Southern Texas U.S. Attorney's Office for nearly twenty years. He had built a reputation as a ruthless trial lawyer who thrived in the courtroom. By all accounts, he had been on his way up the ladder—a strong candidate for Chief of Special Prosecutions, a unit that handled complex organized crime and homicide cases.

The website had once touted him as one of their top trial attorneys, an expert in homicide prosecutions and gang-related offenses. His win record was exceptional, nearly flawless.

And then?He retired.

A Houston Chronicle article from 2012 covered his unexpected departure, calling it a "personal decision" but offering little explanation. No scandal. No accusations. Just a sudden departure from public service, just a few months after Ortega's conviction.

I scanned through a few more mentions—his name popped up in old legal panels, continuing education seminars. Then radio silence. No post-retirement law firm announcements. No shift to private practice. No consulting work. Nothing.

My coffee had grown cold, but I barely noticed as I took a sip, my eyes fixed on the screen before me.

Why had he waited twelve years to come forward?

As I flipped through the sparse documents, another name jumped out at me. Ortega's defense attorney. I read it again, brows furrowing. Eric Hargrave.

That made me pause.

Hargrave was not some public defender. He was a high-profile federal defense attorney, the kind of guy who took big cases and charged even bigger fees. What the hell was he doing representing Gabriel Ortega? By all accounts, Ortega had no resources or connections. His record showed petty crimes and misdemeanors. He didn't fit the profile of Hargrave's typical clientele.

Continually flipping through page after page, I scanned the few court filings and administrative paperwork before reaching the end of the binder. They'd completely excluded trial transcripts, evidence lists, and investigatory reports.

The anemic stack of papers mocked me. I pressed my fingers against my temples, feeling the throb of a headache starting to form. I had seen basic traffic violations with more documentation than this.

They really wanted this case to disappear.

A pressure bloomed in the front of my head and I checked the time. 12:17 AM.

Snapping the binder shut, I pushed it away, the sound sharp in the quiet kitchen.

Someone had gone to great lengths to bury this case. And now I knew why.

CHAPTER SEVEN

THE MORNING SUN glinted off my windshield as I navigated through Houston traffic, mind racing faster than the cars around me. After a night of tossing and turning, I'd made my decision at dawn—I needed to speak directly with Samuel Grayson.

Finding his address hadn't been difficult. Public records and a courthouse database search had given me his current residence, a property purchased shortly after his retirement from the U.S. Attorney's Office. A quick check confirmed he hadn't moved since then.

I'd mapped the route, rehearsed what I'd say, and considered all the reasons he might refuse to speak with me. My position at the USAO meant I wasn't just some random person showing up at his door—I represented the very office he'd left under questionable circumstances. But I had to try. If Grayson had been willing to submit an affidavit that could destroy his professional reputation, maybe he'd be willing to tell me more.

What I hadn't fully processed was why this case mattered so much to me already. Maybe it was the thinness of that binder, or Wexler's obvious discomfort, or the way files that should have existed had mysteriously disappeared. Whatever it was, I couldn't let it go.

It wasn't far—a forty-minute drive from Houston out into the quiet suburbs, where the houses were spaced wider apart, the roads lined with mature oak trees, and the city noise faded into the background.

Samuel Grayson had traded his high-profile legal career for this peaceful anonymity, disappearing from Houston's legal circles almost overnight.

The house was modest but well-kept, a brick one-story with dark shutters, the kind of home owned by someone who had once made good money but wasn't looking to draw attention. A trimmed lawn, a shiny black sedan in the driveway, and wind chimes swaying softly from the porch. It didn't look like the home of someone with skeletons in their closet.

I parked along the curb, killed the engine, and took a moment to breathe. There was no guarantee he'd talk to me. No guarantee he'd even open the door. But he'd already taken the extraordinary step of submitting an affidavit admitting to prosecutorial misconduct. That meant something in him still cared about getting this right.

That meant I had a shot.

I got out, walked up the short pathway to the porch, and rang the doorbell. After a few moments, I shifted my weight, glancing toward the window on the side. No movement inside.

Maybe he wasn't home.

Or maybe he saw me coming and decided he didn't want to talk. I considered leaving—this was technically outside my normal duties, and if anyone at the office found out I was here, I'd have some explaining to do. But the thin binder nagged at me, along with Wexler's strange reaction and the missing files. I needed answers.

So I rang the doorbell again. This time, I heard movement inside. A few footsteps, the sound of something being set down, and then the door cracked open.

A woman stood there, somewhere in her early fifties, with graying blonde hair pulled back in a loose ponytail. Reading glasses perched on top of her head, and she wore a soft, well-worn sweater that spoke more of quiet afternoons with books than surprise visitors disrupting her morning.

She narrowed her eyes, cautious. "Yes?"

I offered my most non-threatening smile. "Hi. My name is Alex Hayes. I was wondering if Samuel Grayson is home?"

She hesitated, her fingers tightening on the edge of the door. "What is this regarding?"

There was something in her expression—apprehension, like she was already weighing whether she should tell me to leave. I wasn't about to launch into a legal discussion on her doorstep, so I kept my voice even.

"I'm an Assistant U.S. Attorney, and I'm working on a case he was involved in a while back."

Her eyes darkened with recognition.

"I just wanted to ask him a few questions," I added quickly. "If he's willing."

Hesitating again, she glanced over her shoulder. I heard another set of footsteps approach, and then a deep voice.

"It's alright, Jan."

The door swung open a little wider, and Samuel Grayson stepped into view.

Even after twelve years away from the courtroom, he still had the presence of a prosecutor—tall, sharp features, graying hair at the temples, and a posture that suggested he still sized people up the moment he met them. But there was something else about him now—a weariness that seemed to have settled into the lines around his eyes, the kind that comes from years of carrying regrets.

"What can I do for you, Ms. Hayes?" he asked, his tone polite but guarded.

I met his gaze. "I'm working on the Gabriel Ortega habeas petition."

For the briefest second, his jaw tensed. He asked, "And whose side are you on?"

"The side of justice."

His lips twitched, like he almost smiled at that. Then he nodded once, stepping back.

"Come in."

The house opened into a living room that felt both comfortable and slightly frozen in time. Bookshelves lined one wall, filled with legal texts collecting a thin layer of dust. A well-worn leather chair sat in the corner, a folded newspaper resting on the arm. Family photos decorated the mantle—Grayson and the woman who'd answered the door, along with what looked like grown children, all smiling in various vacation spots.

Grayson led me into the living room, gesturing toward the couch. "Can I get you something to drink?"

I shook my head. "No, thanks."

He walked over to a side table, where a decanter of dark amber liquid sat next to two short glasses. He poured himself a drink, and I glanced at the clock on the wall. Not even 10:00 AM.

Grayson caught my look and let out a dry chuckle. "You never really know what time it is when you're retired."

I kept my expression neutral as he took a slow sip and settled into the armchair across from me, assessing me with calculated patience.

"What brings a brand-new Assistant U.S. Attorney to my doorstep?"

"I got assigned the Ortega petition," I said, leaning forward. "And I want to get to the bottom of what actually happened. I was hoping you'd be willing to talk to me about it."

Grayson scratched the back of his neck, his gaze flickering toward the window. "Bit of a gray area here." He took a sip of whiskey. "Technically, I submitted an affidavit in support of the petitioner. Not exactly something I've done before."

I nodded, waiting.

He swirled his drink. "I suppose I don't need to notify Ortega's counsel that you came to visit. Neither of us is bound by attorney-client privilege in this situation."

"You should do whatever you feel is within the ethical bounds of the law. I'd never encourage anything outside of that."

Grayson studied me for a beat, his eyes crinkling at the corners. "I like you."

He took another drink, exhaling through his nose.

I took the chance to press forward.

"I read the petition and your affidavit. Can you tell me more about what happened with the Ortega case?"

He set his glass down on the table between us and straightened, his expression growing more solemn.

"You want the real story?" he asked.

I nodded.

Grayson rubbed a hand over his face, like he was mentally stepping back twelve years to a time he didn't particularly want to revisit.

"I was on the prosecution team for the Ortega case, but I wasn't the lead prosecutor. That was Vincent Delacroix—hotshot trial lawyer, ruthless in court, the kind of guy who saw every case as a win-or-lose game, not a pursuit of justice."

The name rang a bell. Delacroix had been a well-known name in Houston before he left the AUSA's office. One of those high-conviction-rate prosecutors who'd built his career on big cases and bigger sentences.

Grayson took another sip of his drink and leaned forward.

"When we were building the case, we interviewed everyone at the scene that night. The liquor store owner, employees, customers. That's when we got David Peña's statement."

I sat up straighter.

"Peña had been inside the store. He saw everything—the robbery unfold, the shooting, who was actually inside. And his statement?" Grayson shook his head. "It didn't fit the prosecution's case. He told us he only saw two men—not three."

"And that contradicted your star witness, Ruiz."

"Exactly. Ruiz had flipped on Ortega and told us that there were three of them in the store that night. That Ortega had been one of them. But Peña—who had no stake in this—said otherwise."

"So you knew his statement didn't fit," I said carefully. "What did you do with it?"

"I did what I was supposed to do—I brought it up to Delacroix. Told him Peña's statement needed to go into discovery."

My jaw tightened. "And?"

"He told me he'd take care of it." Grayson swirled his drink, staring into the glass for a moment before looking back at me. "I took that to mean he was turning it over to the defense—because that's what we're required to do."

"But he didn't?"

Grayson shook his head. "I didn't realize until trial."

"How?"

Grayson exhaled heavily, his frustration with himself evident. "Peña wasn't on the witness list. At first, I thought maybe the defense would call him—because a witness like that? If the defense had his statement, they absolutely would have used it."

I nodded. If Peña's statement had been disclosed to the defense, he would have been a critical witness.

"So when the trial started and the defense never mentioned Peña, that's when I knew something was wrong."

"You knew at trial that it hadn't been disclosed?"

"I suspected. Tried to bring it up to Delacroix, but it was too late. We were already in the middle of trial, and I was working off the assumption that if the defense didn't call Peña, maybe they had decided not to use him."

"But you didn't ask the defense directly?"

Grayson gave me a tight smile. "You don't walk into a courtroom and ask opposing counsel if they got your discovery disclosures. That's a one-way ticket to a mistrial."

I frowned, tapping my fingers against my knee. "Did you confront Delacroix after the trial?"

"I did." Grayson's shoulders slumped, as though the memory itself had physical weight. "And he brushed me off, gave me some line about doing what was right for the case, that Peña's testimony wasn't credible enough to matter anyway." His fingers tightened around his glass. "Said it wasn't his fault if the defense wasn't smart enough to follow up."

I narrowed my eyes, a cold knot forming in my stomach. "He made a strategic decision to bury a witness that didn't fit his narrative."

"I had a choice to make at that point, Hayes. I could have reported it. Could have gone to the judge, to the State Bar." Grayson's expression hardened, bitterness flickering across his face. "But by then, the case was over. Ortega had been convicted, and no one wanted to revisit a 'win.'"

The silence stretched between us. Outside, wind chimes gently clinked in the morning breeze. Somewhere in the house, water ran through pipes, and a clock ticked steadily on the mantle. I studied the family photos again—happy moments preserved in time, while Grayson carried the weight of this secret.

"And that's why you left," I said finally.

Grayson stared at me for a long moment before nodding. "It wasn't just Ortega's case. There were other cases, other moments I saw Delacroix pull some strings that weren't exactly illegal, but they sure as hell weren't ethical. And I had to ask myself if I wanted to be part of a system that valued winning over justice."

Exhaling, the implications hit me like a physical blow. This wasn't just about one case or one man's wrongful conviction. This was about the integrity of the entire system I'd just joined.

"And now?" I asked. "Now that Ortega is filing for post-conviction relief?"

Grayson looked down at his drink, then back at me. "Now, I guess I'm finally trying to do what I should have done twelve years ago."

CHAPTER EIGHT

THE MORNING LIGHT fell across Grayson's living room, casting patterns on the carpet as I sat back, turning his words over in my head.

"What happened to Delacroix?" I asked.

Grayson gave me a look, like he was waiting for me to connect the dots myself. When I didn't, he let out a short laugh and took another sip of his drink.

"He's a district court judge now. Lifetime tenure and everything."

Of course he was.

Grayson's eyes gleamed with bitter amusement at my expression. "Yeah. He's done very well for himself."

I sat forward again, placing my hands on my knees. "So let me get this straight—you're telling me the guy who suppressed evidence in a murder trial is now presiding over federal cases?"

"That's one way to look at it."

"It's the only way to look at it."

Grayson swirled his drink. "You'd think so. But talk to the man, and he'll have an answer for everything."

"You're saying he'd justify what he did?"

"Absolutely. And you know what? He'd sound convincing, too." Grayson rubbed a hand over his jaw. "That's the thing about people like Delacroix. They don't think they're corrupt. They think they're efficient. Smart. That they see the law for what it is—a game of strategy, rather than a moral compass."

A slow burn settled in my chest. "So, does that make him corrupt? Or—"

"Or does he just live by a different moral code than us?"

Grayson held my gaze, like he wanted me to sit with that thought.

So I did. And I didn't have an answer for him.

"Okay," I said, "but—at his confirmation hearing—didn't anybody bring this up?" My fingers curled into the fabric of my pants. "It sounds like this wasn't just a one-time thing. You said he skirted the rules for multiple cases. Surely someone would have flagged his record during the judicial nomination process."

"You seem to have a very glowing opinion of how our system actually works," Grayson said over the rim of his glass.

Huffing up, I crossed my arms. "You're telling me nobody dug into his trial history? Nobody raised a red flag about him bending the law?"

Grayson set his drink down. "Do you want to know what his confirmation hearing looked like?"

I nodded.

He leaned back, shifting his voice into a mock-serious tone.

"Mr. Delacroix, tell us about your experience in the courtroom!" He switched back to his normal voice. "And he did. He talked about his high conviction rate, his years of public service, and how he's dedicated his life to 'justice and upholding the rule of law.'"

Grayson snorted.

"They ate it up. He said all the right things. Wore the right suit. Had old colleagues draft glowing testimonials about his 'integrity' and 'dedication.'" He gestured loosely. "And boom. Rubber stamp confirmation."

My throat tightened as the reality sank in.

"Are you telling me they never even looked into his trial record?"

"They looked. And you know what they found?"

I tilted my head, waiting.

"They found a successful prosecutor. Someone who got big convictions, took on violent offenders, and played the game."

"Even if that meant burying exculpatory evidence?"

"Like I said, he has an answer for everything. Ask him about his trial tactics, and he'll justify every move he's ever made. The jury convicted the defendant, didn't they? The defense had a chance to make their case, didn't they?"

He lifted his glass again, but this time, he paused, studying the amber liquid before continuing.

"Did you ever hear the quote, 'If men were angels, we wouldn't need laws'?"

"James Madison. *The Federalist Papers*."

Grayson's mouth quirked upward, then took a slow sip. "There it is."

I stared at him, waiting for him to elaborate.

"We have laws because we need them. Because people in power can't be trusted to regulate themselves. But the system has cracks, and things—people—slip through. Including ones who end up on the bench."

The family photos on the wall seemed to watch us now, witnesses to a conversation that had veered into dangerous territory. A clock ticked somewhere in the house, marking time as the implications of his words settled around me like dust.

"So you're saying our entire judicial confirmation process is just a glorified theater act?"

Grayson gave me a pointed look, his lips curling slightly. "I'm saying that people believe what they want to believe. They saw a seasoned prosecutor with a tough-on-crime record and figured, why question it?"

I stared down at my hands. This man—this judge—had built a career from bending the rules, and now he had a lifetime seat on the federal bench. I pressed my palms together as if the pressure might contain the fury building inside me.

My words came out measured, deliberate. "This just became bigger than Ortega's conviction. This isn't just about getting one man out of prison. It's about exposing a federal judge who abused his power as a prosecutor."

Grayson held up his hands, palms outward. "Hold on there, Hayes."

My eyebrows shot up. "What?"

"That's not anything I'm willing to get involved with. I came forward because I was in the wrong. Because a man who doesn't deserve to be in prison for the rest of his life is still rotting in there, and I had something to do with it." His eyes locked onto mine. "That's where my involvement ends."

I clenched my jaw. "So I should just ignore a sitting federal judge who deliberately suppressed evidence and continues to pass judgment on others?"

Grayson exhaled through his nose, shoulders slumping slightly. "What I'm saying is that whatever you decide to do after that, is on you."

I narrowed my eyes. "What do you mean by that?"

He leaned back, studying me, and for the first time since I walked into his house, I saw something else in his expression.

Not just regret. Caution.

"There are people who put him on the bench," he said.

I held his gaze. "And there are people who don't want him to come off it."

There it was.

This *wasn't* just about one corrupt prosecutor turned judge—it was about who put him there.

Grayson let the silence hang between us for a moment longer before checking his watch.

He stood. "It's lunchtime, and I don't have much more to say. You best be on your way."

For a moment, the urge to press further tempted me—to ask if he was warning me or just trying to wash his hands of it all. But the set of his jaw told me I wouldn't get anything more out of him.

Rising from the couch, my hands automatically smoothed the wrinkles from my blazer. Grayson gave me one last look, his voice lighter now, but his words still carrying weight.

"Good luck with the petition."

With a nod, I turned and walked toward the door. As I stepped outside, the warm Houston air hit me, but I felt a chill creep up my spine.

I had come here to talk about Gabriel Ortega. And now I walked away with a whole new problem.

CHAPTER
NINE

THE OVERHEAD FLUORESCENTS flickered as I hunched over my keyboard, the Ortega binder taunting me from the edge of my desk. Its slender spine seemed to mock me with everything it didn't contain.

If the physical files had mysteriously disappeared, there had to be digital records somewhere. The federal government never truly deleted anything—even when they claimed to "purge" files for retention policies.

Opening the case management system, I navigated through screens of court records, searching for any trace of Ortega's trial. Most entries were mundane—docket numbers, scheduling orders, the original indictment, standard motions. But as I scrolled deeper, something useful emerged.

A complete list of all parties present during the trial.

Attorneys. Witnesses. Jury members. And—most importantly—the court reporter.

I scribbled down the name: Theresa Klein.

Court reporters were the unsung archivists of the legal system. Even if transcripts weren't in the official file, Klein might have her own copies tucked away. People in her position didn't just erase history—they preserved it, often for decades.

I pushed back from my desk, grabbing my notepad and the Ortega

binder, ready to track down Klein's office at the courthouse when—
Knock, knock.

Wexler materialized in my doorway before I could even look up, a tight smile fixed on his face and a thick stack of folders tucked under his arm.

"Busy?" he asked, eyes sweeping across my desk like he was conducting an inventory.

I forced my features into neutral territory. "Just looking through some files. What's up?"

Wexler stepped into my office and dropped the folders on my desk with a deliberate thud.

He tapped the top of the stack. "I need you to reprioritize some of your habeas petitions."

I flipped open the first one, scanning the heading. "These cases don't require a reply for at least two months," I said, glancing up at him. "Why the sudden rush?"

Wexler's lips curved upward, but the smile never reached his eyes.

"No reason," he said smoothly. "We're just prioritizing certain cases."

I sat back, drumming my fingers against the desk. "The Ortega petition requires a reply within the next week."

"And I expect these petitions to be completed before that."

Our eyes locked in silent combat, the subtext hanging between us like a live wire.

"Of course." I forced a tight smile. "I'll get right on it."

Wexler gave me an approving nod. "Glad to hear it." He lingered a second longer, his presence casting a shadow over my desk, then finally turned and walked out.

As soon as the door clicked shut, I let out a slow breath.

My eyes drifted back to the Ortega binder. The thin folder contained a man's life—twelve years stolen, possibly by corruption at the highest levels of our justice system. And now Wexler had just handed me a pile of busy work, conveniently timed to pull me away from it.

This wasn't coincidence. After my meeting with Grayson and the revelation about Judge Delacroix, suddenly Wexler needed urgent work on cases that weren't due for months? The timing was too perfect. Someone wanted to keep me away from Ortega's case.

The question was: how high did this go?

I stared at Wexler's stack of petitions, calculating how long it would take to clear them. Then, reluctantly, I pulled the first one toward me and got to work.

The stack of reply briefs grew smaller by the hour. I tore through one petition after another, citing precedent, rejecting claims, and filing responses that no judge would likely read past the first page.

The work drained my energy and numbed my mind. Each petition represented someone grasping at freedom, and here I sat, mechanically shooting them down without even the time to consider their merits properly.

All the while, the Ortega binder lurked at the edge of my desk, a constant reminder that I was wasting precious hours on busy work while a potentially innocent man remained behind bars.

I didn't even look up when Erin walked in.

"Whoa."

I kept typing, barely registering the sound of the door closing behind her.

"You're typing like those keys personally offended you. What gives?"

"Trying to get through these as fast as I can," I muttered over the clacking of my keyboard. "So I can get back to Ortega's petition."

"Okay." Erin pulled up a chair, eyeing the ridiculous stack of habeas petitions next to me. "Then why aren't you just working on Ortega?"

I hesitated. The walls in this building were notoriously thin, and I wasn't about to discuss Wexler's obvious interference or what I'd learned about Judge Delacroix where anyone might overhear. Especially not when I still didn't know who else might be involved.

Instead, I told her, "Things are moving fast."

Erin's eyebrows shot upward in disbelief. "Yeah, I gathered that much. You're gonna need to fill me in."

I stopped typing, flexing my cramped fingers as I considered how much to say.

"Why don't we grab a drink after work?" I suggested, keeping my voice neutral. "I'll tell you all about it then."

Erin studied me for a second, clearly debating whether to push. Then she nodded.

"Alright," she said, standing. "But I'm holding you to that."

"Deal."

With that, she left, and I returned to the petitions, my fingertips striking each key with renewed determination.

The rest of the day disappeared into a blur of legal motions and bureaucratic responses.

I plowed through every habeas petition Wexler had dumped on me, mechanically rejecting ineffective assistance claims, denying requests for additional DNA testing, and filing responses so routine they required almost no thought.

By the time I closed the last file, my suspicions had hardened into certainty. Wexler's "reprioritization" was a tactic—a deliberate move to keep me away from Ortega's case. First the missing files, then his attempt to take over the case entirely, and now this avalanche of unnecessary work.

The real question wasn't whether Wexler was interfering—it was why, and who else might be involved. Was he protecting Delacroix? Protecting himself? Or was there something even larger at stake?

I glanced at the clock on my computer screen and cursed under my breath. Wexler's last-minute workload had consumed my entire day, and I no longer had time to visit the Court Reporting Division before they closed.

I exhaled, massaging the base of my neck where tension had settled, and pulled up my email.

Subject: Morning Appointment

Wexler,

I have an appointment in the morning and may be a few minutes after 9:00. Just wanted to give you a heads-up.

— A. Hayes

I read the message twice, weighing how much information to provide, then hit send.

He didn't need to know that my "appointment" was with the Court Reporting Division at the federal courthouse. Let him believe it was something personal or medical—after all, he hadn't asked permission before burying me in pointless work all day.

Satisfied, I shut down my computer, gathered my bag, and made my way down to the lobby.

Erin waited by the entrance, phone in hand, her expression brightening when she spotted me.

"You look like someone who just survived a twelve-hour deposition."

"Close enough. Let's get that drink."

She pushed away from the wall, and we headed out into the early evening air. The streets were still busy with government workers heading home, briefcases in hand, ties loosened after long days. We walked three blocks to The Federal Bar, a dimly lit establishment where lawyers, agents, and reporters congregated for stiff drinks and discreet conversations.

The familiar scent of polished wood and whiskey greeted us as we claimed two stools at the corner of the bar. Brass fixtures gleamed under low lighting, and the murmur of conversation provided just enough cover for private discussions.

The bartender nodded at us in recognition.

Before he could even ask, I told him, "Scotch."

"Same," Erin added.

The bartender's mouth quirked as he reached for the bottle. "Long day?"

"Something like that."

He poured two generous glasses and slid them toward us before moving on to the next customer.

Erin turned toward me, taking a slow sip before setting her glass back down. "What the hell is going on?"

CHAPTER
TEN

THE SOFT CLINK of ice against glass and the low hum of conversations filled the dimly lit bar. Ambient light reflected off the polished surface of the bar top as I took a long sip of my scotch, letting the burn settle before exhaling.

"One of the petitions I'm working on—Ortega's—has merit."

Erin swirled her drink and narrowed her gaze at me. "A habeas petition has merit?"

I nodded and gave her the rundown on Ortega's case—the felony murder conviction, the cooperating witness who'd testified against him, and the recently discovered Brady violation.

Erin's forehead creased with concern. "What's the issue, then?"

I exhaled. "A former prosecutor submitted an affidavit, claiming they withheld a witness statement that could have changed the outcome of the trial. A statement that contradicted their star witness and might have proven Ortega wasn't even at the scene."

Erin's brow furrowed. "How do you know they didn't just ... lose the statement? I mean, a Brady violation is a huge accusation, Alex. What proof do you have?"

I glanced around the bar, lowering my voice. "There was an affidavit attached to the petition."

Erin leaned in. "From who?"

"Samuel Grayson."

"As in, former prosecutor Samuel Grayson?"

"The same." I took a sip of my drink, the amber liquid catching the warm light from the hanging fixtures above the bar.

Erin set her glass down hard enough that the ice clinked against the sides. "And you believe him?"

"I do." I locked eyes with Erin and told her, "I went to speak with him. And, yes, I believe what he has to say."

Erin's expression shifted to alarm. "Does Wexler know about this? That you went to meet with him?"

"No, but why is that such a big deal?"

"Alex, you went to speak to someone who provided an affidavit for the other side."

I blinked at her, my chest beginning to pound. "And?"

She blinked back at me. "And that's not something most AUSAs do."

I set my drink on the bar top. "He's not affiliated with Ortega, and it's not like I was meeting with defense counsel or some convicted felon behind bars."

Erin's nostrils flared. "Grayson had problems when he was at the U.S. Attorney's Office." Her fingertips drummed against the bar top.

"What do you mean?"

"I don't know all the details," she said, "but he didn't just leave because of some case he thought was handled wrong."

My stomach tightened in a hard ball. "That's not what he told me."

"I'm just saying, be careful with how much stock you put in his story."

I stared down at my glass, the scotch gleaming copper under the bar lights, a flicker of doubt creeping in. Grayson had seemed honest in our conversation. Guilt-ridden, even. But Erin wouldn't have warned me against him without reason.

Erin took another sip of her scotch and met my eyes. "Just make sure you know what you're walking into."

I nodded, but the thought lingered, settling like a weight in the back of my mind. Had Grayson held something back? I took another slow sip of my drink, choosing my next words carefully.

"I'm trying to dig into the case, but things are—" I paused, shaking my head, "—missing."

Erin furrowed her brow. "Missing how?"

"When I got assigned the Ortega petition, I expected to get a full case record—trial transcripts, motions, investigative reports, actual outlines of the case." I leaned forward, resting my forearms on the bar. "Instead, I got a single, barely filled binder."

"No trial record?"

"Nothing."

She drew back, eyebrows shooting upward. "Okay, yeah, that's weird."

"Right?" I gestured toward my drink. "I mean, this was a felony murder trial. Multiple defendants. A man got life without parole. There should be boxes of records on this case."

Erin rubbed her jaw. "Look, it's definitely odd. But to be fair, this case is from over a decade ago. Back when everything was still mostly paper files. Records get lost, especially when nobody's looking for them."

"Maybe," I said.

But I didn't believe that. Not really. And I wasn't sure how much more I wanted to tell Erin.

Her tone carried a hint of skepticism—not dismissing my concerns outright, but not fully embracing them either. She was searching for rational explanations while my gut screamed that someone had deliberately removed those files.

I sat back, pressing my lips together, the weight of my suspicions heavy against my chest.

Erin studied me for a moment before taking another sip of her drink. "So what's next?"

I forced a small half-smile. "First thing in the morning, I'm tracking down the court reporter."

She arched an eyebrow. "You really think they'll still have the transcripts?"

"Don't know," I admitted. "But I have to try."

Because if I was right—if they really did bury it on purpose—then the court reporter's transcripts might be the only complete account left of what actually happened in that courtroom.

I finished off the last sip of my scotch, relishing in the warmth against my throat. The conversation had veered into territory that made me uncomfortable—the last thing I needed was for Erin to see how deep my suspicions ran.

Setting my empty glass down with a *clink*, I tapped my fingers against the bar top. "What's going on with you? What big new thing are you working on?"

Erin tilted her head, her smile mirroring mine, but she hesitated. "You know I can't really talk about my cases, Alex."

"Come on." I nudged her lightly. "Like I haven't been on the other side of this before. I know how this works. You can give me a *little* something."

She sighed, glancing around the bar like she was checking for eavesdroppers, then leaned in slightly.

"Alright, but this doesn't leave this bar."

"Wouldn't dream of it."

She hesitated for a beat longer. "We're tracking some money laundering into the city."

That made me sit up a little straighter.

"Tracing prison calls, following cash movements, trying to find who's involved."

"And what are they laundering money for?"

"That's the thing," Erin said, stirring her drink with the edge of her straw. "We don't know yet. But there's a lot of movement, and it's happening through some key people in the system. People who shouldn't have access to that kind of cash flow."

"Like prison officials?"

Erin gave me a knowing look but didn't confirm or deny.

"We think it could be a bigger operation," she said, "a network for funneling money through the city. But for what purpose?" She shook her head. "That's what we're trying to figure out."

My mind raced with the implications. Money laundering through prison calls. A larger network that wasn't just stashing cash but moving it somewhere for a specific purpose.

And from Erin's tone, she wasn't chasing some small-time smuggling scheme. This was big.

"Damn," I said. "I almost miss working on cases like that."

"Oh, don't start," Erin said with a wave of her hand. "You'll get your big federal case soon enough."

CHAPTER ELEVEN

THE FEDERAL DISTRICT courthouse loomed before me, its stark granite facade casting long shadows across the plaza. Inside, polished marble floors reflected the morning light filtering through tall windows, giving the entire space an austere, authoritative air that demanded reverence.

Unlike the state courthouse—where I'd navigated the corridors with the ease of someone who belonged—the federal building still felt like foreign territory. At the DA's office, I'd known every shortcut, every judge's temperament, and which clerks could expedite paperwork when needed. The rhythms and unwritten rules were second nature.

But here, I was still an outsider learning the terrain.

I made my way through the security checkpoint, tossing my bag onto the conveyor belt, stepping through the scanner, and waiting for the inevitable second glance from the guards when they saw my badge.

One of them, a guy with graying hair and a tired expression, glanced at my ID and nodded. "Assistant U.S. Attorney?"

"That's me."

"You're good to go."

I grabbed my bag and stepped forward, following the directions I had written down earlier.

The court reporters' office occupied a windowless section down a corridor I might have missed if I hadn't been looking for it. The hallways echoed with that particular government building silence—the kind that amplified the sound of my heels against the marble floor and made even breathing feel conspicuous.

Pulling out my notes, I double-checked the name of the court reporter from the Ortega trial, Theresa Klein. The chances she still worked here after twelve years seemed slim.

I approached the front desk where a middle-aged woman with a nameplate reading "Sandra" looked up from her computer with mild curiosity.

"Can I help you?"

I slipped into my professional-but-friendly tone. "I'm looking for Theresa Klein. I know it's a long shot, but I'm hoping to track down a transcript from an old trial she reported on, over a decade ago."

Sandra's eyes widened slightly before her mouth curved into what looked like amusement. "Sure, she just came in."

I couldn't hide my surprise. "She still works here?"

Sandra nodded, a knowing look crossing her face. "Says she doesn't have any plans to retire any time soon."

I had been fully prepared to get redirected; to be told I'd have to track her down through some archive or that she had moved to another state.

"I can let her know you'd like to meet her?" she asked, standing.

I nodded. "That'd be great."

"Of course. Just wait here a minute."

I stepped back as she disappeared into the back office. A minute later, she returned, gesturing for me to follow her. My pulse quickened as I followed Sandra further inside, down a hallway lined with rows of labeled shelves undoubtedly filled with years of transcripts and case records.

She gestured toward an open office door, where a woman in her early sixties sat behind a cluttered desk, fingers moving across pages with the efficiency of someone who'd turned thousands of transcripts.

She had short, silver-streaked brown hair, reading glasses that hung on a brightly colored lanyard, and the expression of someone who had witnessed decades of courtroom drama without being fazed by any of it.

Sandra knocked on the doorframe. "Theresa, this is AUSA Alex Hayes—she's here about one of your old transcripts."

Theresa looked up, giving me a once-over before her mouth quirked upward. "I know who you are."

My eyebrows shot up. "You do?"

Theresa rested her elbows on her desk, eyes twinkling with decades of accumulated courthouse knowledge. "Honey, I've been around here since I was a teenager. There's not much that goes on in this courthouse that I don't know about."

"That sounds both impressive and a little ominous."

She waved a hand. "Relax. Just means I'm a wealth of information."

Sandra gave me an "I told you so" look before excusing herself, leaving me alone with Theresa.

I stepped further inside and took a seat across from her. "How long exactly have you been working as a court reporter?"

Theresa nodded. "Started off part time while doing closed captioning for TV—back before all this fancy speech recognition stuff. Wasn't long before I realized court reporting was my true calling."

I tilted my head. "How so?"

"I loved being around the action of a courtroom," she said, almost wistfully. "It was a heck of a lot more entertaining than typing up dialogue from late night TV shows, too. Made me feel like I was doing something important."

I nodded, understanding that pull toward meaningful work. It was the same drive that had pushed me through law school and into prosecution.

"Your hands must have amazing endurance, capturing everything in real-time like that."

She tapped a sleek machine on her desk. "This thing here? Stenograph machine. Works differently from a normal keyboard—it's got fewer keys, and we use a type of phonetic shorthand to capture every word as it's spoken.

"Most people think we're just typing really fast, but that's not it. The machine lets us press multiple keys at the same time, kind of like playing a piano chord. That way, we're recording whole syllables or words at once, instead of one letter at a time."

"So instead of typing sentences," I said, "you're basically writing in code?"

"Exactly. And we have our own dictionaries—customized to translate our shorthand into readable text. It's an art, really. That's why they can't replace us with AI—even though I know they're gonna try."

She gave me a pointed look, shaking her head. "They keep talking about using voice recognition software to replace court reporters but let me tell you—computers can't do what we do."

"I don't doubt that. I wouldn't trust a computer to pick up half the things that get mumbled in court."

Theresa laughed. "Not to mention, computers don't know when a lawyer is talking over someone, or when a judge cuts someone off mid-sentence. A seasoned court reporter can tell when someone is misquoting their own argument from earlier and knows how to keep track of it all in real time."

I tapped my fingers against the armrest. "And I'm guessing you've heard some stories in your time."

"You have no idea."

My gaze drifted to the shelves behind her—years of courtroom history neatly stored away, witness to countless legal battles, personal dramas, and life-altering decisions.

"I'm here about one of those old stories, actually."

Theresa leaned forward, her eyes lighting with interest. "Which one?"

"Gabriel Ortega."

Theresa's brows lifted. "Ortega," she mused, tilting her head in thought. "Felony murder, right? Liquor store shooting?"

I nodded, impressed by her memory. "That's the one. I've been assigned the reply brief on his habeas petition, and I was hoping to pull the trial record."

"You don't have a copy of it already?"

"For whatever reason, the prosecutor's office doesn't have a copy—at least, not one I can find." I leaned forward, not bothering to hide my desperation. "I was wondering if you still had the trial transcript."

Theresa pushed her glasses up on her nose, a hint of pride crossing her features. "I have a copy of every single trial I've ever transcribed."

My heart leaped, adrenaline surging through my veins.

She turned toward the filing cabinets behind her, scanning the labels with her pointer finger before pulling open a drawer. As she flipped through the physical records, she muttered, "Give me a second—should be right ... here ..."

After a moment, she pulled out a USB drive and plugged it into her computer. I watched as she clicked through a database, eyes scanning the screen.

A few beats later, she nodded. "Here it is."

I let out a small breath of relief. "That's amazing. Does it have everything?"

Theresa kept clicking through the files, squinting behind her glasses. "Looks like I have a series of pre-trial hearings—motions, evidentiary rulings, suppression hearings. You want those?"

"I want everything you have."

"Figured you'd say that."

She inserted a blank USB drive into another port and began transferring the files.

As I waited, I drummed my fingers against my knee, anticipation building. Soon I'd have what I needed—the unfiltered record of what happened in that courtroom twelve years ago. The truth, untouched by whoever had "lost" the official files.

A minute later, Theresa removed the newly loaded drive and handed it to me. "Here you go."

I held the small device in my palm, its weight nothing compared to its potential value.

"I cannot thank you enough," I said. "Having access to the full record changes everything."

Her gaze locked onto mine, and something in her expression suggested she understood more than she let on. "You should be able to review this in order to do your job."

I studied her for a moment. "You were there for that trial. Do you remember anything unusual about it?"

Theresa tilted her head, choosing her words carefully. "I remember

Delacroix—he was always a showman in court. Very aggressive, very sure of himself."

"And the trial itself?"

She tapped her fingers against her desk. "It was tight. The defense made some good points about the cooperating witness's credibility, but without another witness to contradict him ... " She shrugged. "Jury didn't need long to decide."

"Did you ever get the sense that something was ... off about the case?"

Theresa gave me a measured look. "I've been in this courthouse long enough to know that sometimes things happen in trials that don't make it into the record." She paused. "And I've been around long enough to know when to keep my opinions to myself."

The subtext was clear. She wasn't going to speculate, but she wasn't dismissing my concerns either.

I stood and tucked the USB drive carefully into my bag.

"Thanks again, Theresa."

She nodded, her expression softening slightly. "Good luck with your case."

The drive felt like it radiated energy as I made my way out of the office. For the first time since being assigned Ortega's petition, I had something solid to work with—something no one could take away or bury. Now I just needed to find out what was in it.

CHAPTER
TWELVE

THE OVERHEAD LIGHTS of the USAO office flickered as I hunched over yet another filing, my desk buried under stacks of habeas petitions that hadn't existed yesterday. The scent of burnt coffee lingered in the air, mingling with the dusty smell of old paper files.

Work had become a carefully orchestrated obstacle course.

Every time I carved out a moment to work on Ortega's case, another petition materialized on my desk, marked urgent by Wexler. Cases with deadlines weeks away suddenly required immediate attention. Minor procedural issues transformed into emergencies overnight.

Wexler was testing me, piling on work to see how much pressure it would take before I abandoned Ortega's petition altogether.

My jaw ached from grinding my teeth all day. There was no subtlety to his tactics—just brute force bureaucracy designed to bury me in paperwork.

I refused to let that happen. But by the time I dragged myself home, fatigue had settled deep in my bones. My mind felt numb from writing the same boilerplate rejections over and over.

Yet the deadline for Ortega's reply brief loomed closer, and I needed time to analyze the trial transcript if I stood any chance of crafting a meaningful response. Wexler had manufactured the perfect trap—keep me too busy to do the work that mattered, then watch the deadline pass.

The kitchen light cast a yellow glow over the table where I'd spread my notes and files. The USB drive from Theresa Klein had become my lifeline, the trial transcript filling my laptop screen as I picked at a now-cold dinner.

Sitting across from me, my dad pretended to read his newspaper while stealing glances at my screen. The paper rustled with each page turn, punctuating the quiet of the room.

I looked up from my screen and caught him watching. "Dad, if you have something to say, just say it."

He cleared his throat. "I just—I don't want to pry, you know? Attorney-client privilege and all that. I'm sure you can't share anything."

Pushing my chair back slightly, I stretched my cramped shoulders. "That's not how this one works."

He blinked and set the newspaper down next to his plate. "It's not?"

"Nope." I stretched out my arms. "This is an appeal. Everything in this case is open and on the record. Any member of the public could request these transcripts and read them."

"So, I can ask about it?"

"Ask away. Might actually be a good break for me."

Dad leaned forward, looking entirely too pleased to talk shop with me. "Alright then," he said. "Tell me—what is the case?"

"It's a habeas petition." I gave him the basics of Ortega's case—the felony murder conviction, the alleged missing witness statement, and the Brady violation claim.

Dad listened intently, his fork paused mid-air as I explained the legal implications. When I finished, he set his utensils down with deliberate precision.

"And you think there's a problem with his conviction?" Dad asked.

I took a sip of water. "The evidence suggests the prosecution buried witness testimony that could have changed everything."

"And the defense never knew about Peña's statement?"

"That's what the petition alleges."

Dad frowned, rubbing his chin. "That's pretty damning."

"I thought so too."

He gestured at my laptop. "So what are you looking for now?"

I glanced at the trial transcript on my screen. "Evidence showing whether the defense knew about Peña or his statement. I need to confirm how the prosecution built their case and what they might have deliberately hidden."

Dad nodded, then took a bite of his food, chewing slowly as he considered. Swallowing, he gave me a pointed look.

"And what happens if you prove they buried it?"

I stared down at the table, my jaw tight. "If the court deems this a Brady violation, the petition will be granted. Ortega's conviction will be overturned, and he'll be released."

"And then what?"

"Double jeopardy would probably bar retrying him," I said, "given the misconduct. I'm sure the office would review the case carefully to see if there was an exception we could argue—maybe some new charge or evidence unrelated to the original conviction—but after twelve years? Odds are slim."

"So, he'd just walk."

"Pretty much."

Hands resting flat on the table, eyes narrowed in thought, he finally asked, "What about the people who buried the evidence? What happens to them?"

There it was. The question I'd been trying not to think too hard about. I tightened my grip around the water glass. "Sanctions against them, at the very least. Possible disbarment."

Dad nodded, but I could tell he was expecting something bigger.

Hesitant, the rim of my water glass pressed against my lower lip.

"I don't know how this works, actually."

"What do you mean?"

I looked up and met his gaze. "The guy who allegedly buried this evidence?" The kitchen suddenly felt too warm, the familiar space constricting around me. "He's a federal judge now."

Dad stilled, his expression freezing in place. The distant hum of the refrigerator filled the silence that stretched between us. When he set his fork down, the metal clinked sharply against the plate.

His voice low and even, he said, "That's a hell of a problem."

I barked out a humorless laugh, the sound sharp in the quiet kitchen. "It is."

He picked up his fork again, but tapped it against the table. "Federal judge means lifetime tenure, right?"

I nodded.

Dad let out a slow exhale. "So, even if you prove this, he keeps his seat?"

"Unless Congress impeaches him. Which, let's be honest, would never happen."

Dad leaned back, his chair creaking under the shift in weight. "So this wasn't just a dirty conviction—it was a stepping stone to a lifetime position on the federal bench."

I rested my chin on my hands. "That's what it looks like."

Dad took a long sip of water, his expression unreadable. "Are you ready for what happens if you really push this?"

The question hit me like a physical blow. I stared at the grain pattern in the wooden table, the implications cascading through my mind. My future, my career, the promises I'd made to myself about my mother's case—all of it potentially sacrificed for a stranger's freedom.

Dad studied me, his expression serious. "Because this might mean your career, Alex."

I met his gaze directly, the decision crystallizing as I spoke. "I've considered that. But how could I look at myself in the mirror if I let an innocent man spend his life in prison just to protect my career?"

My father watched me, his expression softening with what looked like a mixture of pride and concern.

"How could I live with myself if I just let this go?"

His lips curved into a small, knowing smile. "That's the Alex I know."

I let out a breath, shaking my head with a soft laugh. "Yeah, well, I'm just trying to do the right thing."

Dad raised an eyebrow. "Trying to?"

I ran a hand through my hair. "It's not just this case," I said. "Ever since my supervisor found out about the Ortega petition, suddenly every other habeas petition has become urgent. It's like Wexler is burying me in busy work, making sure I have no time to focus on Ortega."

Dad leaned forward slightly, his brows furrowing. "You think they're trying to bury this?"

I exhaled slowly. "I don't know," I admitted. "They might be. But I can't say for sure."

Dad nodded, rubbing his chin. "It's suspicious behavior."

"Exactly. But I'm trying not to read into things too much until I have solid proof. Right now, all I have is a bad feeling and a lot of coincidences."

Dad nodded again, but his jaw tightened slightly, like he wasn't entirely convinced that I should be waiting for solid proof before trusting my instincts.

After a beat, he leaned back in his chair. "Well, keep pushing."

I smiled faintly. "Wouldn't know how to do anything else."

Dad stood, grabbing his empty plate and taking it to the sink. As he started cleaning up the kitchen, I glanced back at my laptop screen, the trial transcript still open, waiting for me.

He finished wiping down the counter, then looked at me before heading upstairs.

"Don't stay up all night."

I tapped my pen against the notepad. "No promises."

He shook his head with a quiet laugh, then disappeared up the stairs, leaving me alone with the record. I rolled my shoulders, took another sip of water, and turned my full focus back to the screen. It was time to find out what really happened in that courtroom.

CHAPTER
THIRTEEN

THE HOUSE SETTLED into nighttime silence, broken only by the soft hum of my laptop fan and the occasional rustle of paper as I flipped through my notes. A half-empty mug of cold coffee sat beside my elbow, forgotten hours ago.

I had the Ortega trial transcripts open but decided to start from the beginning rather than jumping straight to the trial itself. If Peña's statement had been deliberately concealed, the manipulation might have begun long before the trial—in the preliminary hearings and motions that shaped the case.

Maybe it all started with the foundation.

I scrolled to the first major pre-trial hearing and found a motion that caught my eye.

Motion to Suppress Defendant's Statement.

I skimmed the first page of the transcript, landing on the date and courtroom details before moving to the actual proceedings.

IN THE DISTRICT COURT FOR THE SOUTHERN DISTRICT OF TEXAS

BEFORE THE HONORABLE JUDGE EVERETT LELAND

THE COURT: *We are here today on the defense's motion to suppress statements made by the defendant, Gabriel Ortega, during his initial interrogation. Mr. Bard, let's hear it.*

I double-checked the names at the top of the transcript.

Defense Counsel: Gregory Bard, Public Defender.

Bard handled countless cases for the Public Defender's Office—overworked, underpaid, and perpetually racing against impossible deadlines. Not a bad attorney by any means, but someone fighting with one hand tied behind his back against prosecutors with unlimited resources.

I kept reading.

MR. BARD: *Your Honor, the statement made by my client should be suppressed on the grounds that it was obtained in violation of his Miranda rights. My client was in custody, subjected to hours of interrogation, and repeatedly requested an attorney, which he was denied. Any statements made under these circumstances are inherently coercive and should not be admissible at trial.*

THE COURT: *Mr. Delacroix?*

MR. DELACROIX: *Your Honor, the government maintains that the defendant was not in custody at the time of the interview. Mr. Ortega came in voluntarily and was free to leave at any time. The agents advised him that he was not under arrest and that he was simply there to answer questions regarding an ongoing investigation.*

I gritted my teeth. Delacroix employed the oldest trick in the prosecutor's playbook.

Officers had detained Ortega, questioned him for hours, and only released him after extracting what they needed—but Delacroix argued that since they hadn't officially arrested him, Miranda warnings weren't required.

MR. BARD: *Your Honor, my client was handcuffed the moment he arrived at the station—*

MR. DELACROIX: *For safety reasons.*

MR. BARD: *—and placed in an interrogation room for over five hours before he made a statement.*

THE COURT: *Was he told he could leave?*

MR. DELACROIX: *He was advised that he was not under arrest.*

MR. BARD: *That's not the same thing, Your Honor.*

THE COURT: *I understand the argument, Mr. Bard. However, the record reflects that the defendant was not explicitly placed under arrest, and therefore, Miranda does not apply. The motion to suppress is denied.*

My fingers tightened around my pen, knuckles whitening with pressure against the plastic.

It followed the familiar pattern—Ortega's statement strengthened the prosecution's case, so Delacroix fought to keep it in evidence, regardless of how it was obtained.

But that wasn't what I was searching for.

Scanning the rest of the transcript for Peña's name yielded nothing—not even a passing reference.

The next hearing transcript might offer more clues. If they had buried Peña's statement, perhaps there had been a fight over discovery.

Navigating to the next pre-trial hearing, the title caught my attention:

Motion to Exclude Prior Bad Acts

IN THE DISTRICT COURT FOR THE SOUTHERN DISTRICT OF TEXAS

BEFORE THE HONORABLE JUDGE EVERETT LELAND

THE COURT: *We are here on the defense's motion to exclude evidence of prior alleged criminal activity. Mr. Bard, go ahead.*

MR. BARD: *Your Honor, the prosecution is attempting to introduce uncharged allegations against my client—incidents that have nothing to do with this case. They want to bring in an alleged unlawful firearm possession from three years ago, even though my client was never charged for that incident. There is no conviction. There is no case file. The only thing they have is a vague police report that never resulted in charges.*

My stomach tightened. This was a classic dirty tactic.

Prosecutors often tried this move when their evidence wasn't strong enough on its own. If the jury heard that Ortega had previously been suspected of carrying an illegal firearm, they'd be more inclined to believe he was armed during the robbery, even without solid proof.

THE COURT: *Mr. Delacroix, why does the government believe this evidence is relevant?*

MR. DELACROIX: *Your Honor, the defendant's prior history of unlawful firearm possession is highly probative in this case. The United States' theory is that the defendant was armed at the time of the robbery. The fact that he was known to carry weapons illegally in the past supports that theory.*

MR. BARD: *Your Honor, that is a massive leap. My colleague is attempting to introduce pure character evidence—which is not admissible. Just because someone allegedly possessed a firearm in the past does not mean they had one on them the night of this crime.*

THE COURT: *Mr. Delacroix, was the defendant ever convicted for this alleged prior possession?*

MR. DELACROIX: *No, Your Honor, but—*

THE COURT: *Was he ever charged?*

MR. DELACROIX: *No, but—*

THE COURT: *Then explain to me why you think a jury should hear about it.*

A small, satisfied smile crossed my face. At least the judge had some backbone.

MR. DELACROIX: *Your Honor, the probative value outweighs the prejudicial effect—*

THE COURT: *I disagree. Motion granted. The prior firearm possession is excluded.*

These maneuvers were exactly what I'd expect from a prosecutor who might resort to hiding evidence. Delacroix built his case on implications rather than facts—cell phone tower data that only proved Ortega's phone was in the area, not Ortega himself, and the testimony of a cooperating witness with every reason to lie.

As I continued scrolling through the list of transcripts, one caught my attention:

Defense Motion to Compel Complete Witness List

The kitchen clock ticked loudly in the background as my pulse quickened. Maybe Peña hadn't been completely hidden. Maybe the defense had simply failed to follow up properly. Maybe they'd had the information but didn't recognize its significance.

The leather of my chair creaked as I leaned forward, my eyes straining in the dim light.

IN THE DISTRICT COURT FOR THE SOUTHERN DISTRICT OF TEXAS

BEFORE THE HONORABLE JUDGE EVERETT LELAND

THE COURT: *We are here on the defense's motion to compel the complete list of witnesses the state intends to call at trial. Mr. Bard, you may proceed.*

MR. BARD: *Your Honor, we have repeatedly requested a full and final witness list from the prosecution. My colleague has been slow to disclose who they intend to call, and we are now at a point where we are days away from trial and still do not have a complete list. This puts the defense at a significant disadvantage in preparing our case.*

My heart pounded against my ribs, each word on the screen potentially revealing the truth I was searching for.

THE COURT: *Mr. Delacroix, why has the witness list not been provided in full?*

MR. DELACROIX: *Your Honor, the government has already turned over its primary witness list in accordance with discovery obligations. However, there are some witnesses we may call for rebuttal, depending on how the defense presents its case.*

MR. BARD: *Your Honor, this is precisely the problem. The prosecution is attempting to hold back names to use as a surprise tactic. We need to know who will be testifying—not just a vague promise that they 'may' call people later. That is not how fair trials work.*

Adrenaline coursed through me. This could be it—Peña might have been on that withheld list, a potential rebuttal witness that Bard never knew existed.

THE COURT: *Mr. Delacroix, does the United States intend to call any new fact witnesses who were not included in the previously disclosed materials?*

MR. DELACROIX: *No, Your Honor. The witnesses in question are primarily investigators and experts who may be called based on the arguments presented at trial. All fact witnesses have been disclosed in accordance with the rules.*

My breath caught in my throat.

No.

No, no, no.

I skimmed down the page, searching frantically for Peña's name, for any hint that his testimony had been disclosed to the defense.

Nothing. Not a single mention.

The defense wasn't fighting about Peña because they didn't even know he existed. This wasn't evidence that got misplaced or overlooked—Peña had been deliberately concealed. And no one—not the judge, not the defense—had any clue.

I closed my eyes, pinching the bridge of my nose as the truth crystallized. If Peña was never disclosed before trial …

Then Delacroix hadn't just manipulated the case.

He had rigged it from the start.

CHAPTER FOURTEEN

THE KITCHEN WAS quiet except for the soft hum of the refrigerator and the occasional click of my mouse. The screen's blue glow illuminated my face as shadows gathered in the corners of the room. My coffee had gone cold hours ago, but I barely noticed.

I exhaled slowly, bracing myself as I clicked into the trial transcript.

This was it—the core of the case, the unfiltered account of how Delacroix built his argument, and how Ortega's defense tried to fight back. If David Peña had been deliberately hidden from the proceedings, this would be where the truth became impossible to ignore.

I scrolled to the beginning, and the trial unfolded before me.

THE GOVERNMENT'S OPENING STATEMENT

MR. DELACROIX: *Ladies and gentlemen, what you will see over the course of this trial is clear and overwhelming evidence that the defendant, Gabriel Ortega, took part in a crime that resulted in a man's death. This is not about intent—this is about responsibility. When you commit a violent felony, when you participate in an armed robbery, you are responsible for what happens. Gabriel Ortega made a choice. And that choice led to the death of Luis Robles. And by the end of this trial, we will ask you to hold him accountable.*

This was a classic prosecution tactic, framing the case in black-and-white terms. Ignore the details. Ignore the contradictions. Just focus on one thing—someone died, and Ortega was there.

My shoulders tensed as I read further, the familiar rhythm of a criminal trial playing out on my screen. I'd stood in courtrooms like this dozens of times but seeing it from this perspective—hunting for deliberate misconduct—made my stomach twist.

THE DEFENSE'S OPENING STATEMENT

MR. BARD: *This case is not as simple as the government wants you to believe. My client, Gabriel Ortega, was not inside that liquor store. He was not armed, and he did not participate in a robbery. The United States will rely on the testimony of a single cooperating witness—Hector Ruiz—a man who has every reason to lie to save himself. You will not hear physical evidence tying my client to this crime. You will not see surveillance footage of him inside the store. The state's case rests on words. And words, as we know, can be manipulated.*

I underlined that last sentence, feeling a slow burn in my chest. Bard had been right about that much—the government's case was built entirely on testimony. Ruiz, the flipped witness, formed the foundation of everything.

I scrolled ahead, past procedural matters, past the swearing-in of witnesses. My breath hitched as I reached Ruiz's direct examination.

THE UNITED STATES CALLS HECTOR RUIZ

MR. DELACROIX: *Mr. Ruiz, you were involved in the armed robbery of Mendez Liquors on the night of August 14, correct?*

MR. RUIZ: Yes, sir.

MR. DELACROIX: *And who was with you that night?"*

MR. RUIZ: *Luis Robles and Gabriel Ortega.*

MR. DELACROIX: *You saw Mr. Ortega inside the store?*

MR. RUIZ: *Yes. He was there. He was the one who was supposed to grab the cash while I kept an eye on the door.*

MR. DELACROIX: *And what happened when the store owner, Rafael Mendez, pulled his gun?*

MR. RUIZ: *Everything got crazy. Mendez started shooting, Robles fired back, and people were screaming. I just ran. Ortega ran too.*

I pressed my lips together, a sharp pang of frustration filling my chest—and something else. I'd stood on that side of the courtroom before. I'd relied on cooperating witnesses, too, pushing them to say what we needed to hear. But there was always a line—one that separated zealous prosecution from crossing into misconduct. I'd never stepped over it.

Delacroix had.

CROSS-EXAMINATION

MR. BARD: *Mr. Ruiz, when you were first interviewed by the police, did you immediately tell them Gabriel Ortega was involved?*

MR. RUIZ: *... No.*

MR. BARD: *In fact, you originally told them Ortega had nothing to do with it, correct?*

MR. RUIZ: *Yeah, but that was before—*

MR. BARD: *Before you were offered a plea deal.*

MR. RUIZ: *... Yes.*

I rolled my neck, trying to release the tension building there. Bard had done his best to undermine Ruiz's credibility. But without another witness to counter him, it wasn't enough.

I flipped forward in the transcript, past procedural arguments, past objections, to the jury instructions and closing arguments. Peña's name never came up.

Delacroix had been confident—so confident that his final words before the jury deliberated were practically dripping with arrogance.

THE GOVERNMENT'S CLOSING ARGUMENT

MR. DELACROIX: *There is no reasonable doubt here. The defense wants you to believe that Gabriel Ortega was uninvolved. That he was wrongly accused. But we have a witness—Hector Ruiz—who was there. Who saw Ortega with his own eyes. If Ortega wasn't involved, why did he run? Why did he lie? Why didn't he come forward and say he had nothing to do with it? Ladies and gentlemen, the truth is simple. Gabriel Ortega made his choices. And now, you must hold him accountable for them.*

I skimmed the defense's closing, Bard doing his best to highlight the lack of physical evidence, but I already knew what was coming.

JURY VERDICT

THE COURT: *Madam Foreperson, have you reached a verdict?*

THE JURY FOREPERSON: *We have, Your Honor.*

THE COURT: *Please hand the verdict form to the bailiff.*

(The bailiff hands the form to the judge, who reads it silently before returning it.)

THE COURT: *In the matter of the United States v. Gabriel Ortega, on the charge of felony murder, how does the jury find?*

THE JURY FOREPERSON: *We find the defendant guilty.*

I scrolled through the rest of the files, opening every remaining transcript on the USB drive, searching for anything I might have missed.

But it was all the same.

Pre-trial motions. Jury selection. Trial proceedings. Closing arguments. Verdict. Sentencing.

Nowhere—nowhere—was David Peña's name mentioned.

I checked the hearing records again, thinking maybe I had overlooked something. Maybe there had been an off-the-record discussion. A reference buried in footnotes or side remarks.

Nothing.

This was everything. Theresa said she had given me all the files she had.

I closed the last document, my laptop screen dimming as I leaned back in my chair, my fingers still resting against the keys. The silence of the kitchen felt thicker now, heavier than before. Because there was no doubt anymore. The petition was valid. The defense had never received Peña's statement because the prosecution had never turned it over. And that meant the government—my own office—was on the wrong side of a constitutional violation.

I pressed my palms against my eyes, the weight of what I'd discovered settling into my bones. This wasn't about being a good lawyer anymore. This was about basic human decency.

If I filed the government's reply brief arguing against Ortega's petition, I'd be knowingly defending a case built on a lie. I'd be complicit in keeping an innocent man in prison.

I exhaled slowly, pushing back from the table, the chair legs scraping against the kitchen floor.

I needed sleep. I needed to think.

Because now I had to figure out which side of justice I wanted to be on.

CHAPTER
FIFTEEN

THE HUMMING WHITE noise of the office faded as I stretched my arms over my head, feeling the tightness in my shoulders from the hours spent hunched over my desk. It was past lunchtime. I needed a break—needed to step away from my growing sense of unease. I grabbed my bag and was just stepping out of my office when I heard my name.

"Hayes."

I turned.

Wexler.

He was standing just outside his office, arms crossed, his expression calm, unreadable.

"You don't need to worry about the Ortega petition anymore."

"What do you mean?"

He gave me one of those tight, measured smiles. "We had someone take another look at it, given what we discussed in our last meeting—that it wasn't just a run-of-the-mill habeas."

Maybe he had actually recognized that something was wrong. Maybe someone had done the right thing.

"And?"

"They drafted the reply brief already, so it's all taken care of."

The words didn't register at first.

"They what?"

Wexler's smile didn't change. "It's already been filed."

I froze, my grip tightening around my bag strap.

"I'm the AUSA assigned to this case," I told him. "Why wasn't I the one to draft it?"

"Given that it wasn't just a standard case, we had someone else step in."

With my heart pounding in my ears, I forced my voice to stay level. "What did it say?"

"We argued that the defense should have found Peña's statement in discovery," Wexler said. "Not sure how they're really going to get around that. Sloppy lawyering on the part of the defense attorney. They should have caught it before trial."

My stomach dropped and my throat constricted when I asked, "What discovery are you talking about?"

Wexler tilted his head, like he was amused by the question.

"I don't think you need to worry about it," he said, giving me that same patronizing tone. Then he gave me a mock-friendly nod. "Enjoy your lunch."

I couldn't even think about food anymore. Not even remotely.

As soon as Wexler walked off, I turned right back around to my office, slamming the door behind me

Grabbing my phone, I dialed Theresa Klein's number.

She picked up on the second ring.

"Court reporters' office, this is Theresa."

"Theresa, it's Alex Hayes."

"Ah, Ms. Hayes," she said, her voice pleasant. "I take it you've been going through the transcript?"

"Yes, I have," I said, pacing the length of my office. "And I need to ask you something."

"Go on, dear."

I stopped pacing, resting my free hand on the desk. "Are you absolutely sure you gave me everything you had on the Ortega case?"

"Yes, I did. I copied every file I had onto that drive. You have the full trial record, all pre-trial hearings, and anything officially transcribed under that case number."

"Okay, but is there any chance that another court reporter handled any of the evidentiary hearings? Or even another judge?"

There had to be a missing hearing where Peña's statement was discussed. No defense attorney would ignore exculpatory evidence if they knew about it.

Silence filled the other end for a beat.

"No," Theresa said, and I could hear the certainty in her voice. "This case was overseen by the Chief Judge at the time. And I was his dedicated reporter for years. I handled every single proceeding tied to that case. Leland wasn't the sort of judge to hand things off to a magistrate. He liked to handle things from start to finish."

Then there had to be no evidentiary hearing transcript involving Peña.

"You're absolutely certain no one else handled even a single evidentiary hearing? Maybe you were out sick, or—"

"Alex, I told you. Judge Leland never used substitutes. Not once. If I was out sick, he canceled or rescheduled. Always."

I pressed my fingertips against my temple, processing what this meant. "Okay. Thank you, Theresa."

She hesitated for a moment, concern creeping into her voice. "Is something wrong, dear?"

I pinched the bridge of my nose. "I'm not sure yet."

Theresa didn't press, but even over a phone call I could tell she wanted to.

"Alright," she said gently. "You let me know if you need anything else, alright?"

"I will," I promised, and then hung up.

The fluorescent office lights seemed suddenly too harsh as I turned to my computer and typed Judge Everett Leland into the federal judicial archives.

He had retired from the bench five years ago. Perfect.

A quick property records search gave me his current address. I grabbed my bag and made my way toward the elevators when I nearly collided with Erin.

Startled, she looked me over. "Where are you going?"

"I need to go talk to someone."

Erin narrowed her eyes, then grabbed my arm and pulled me toward a quiet corner in the hallway.

"Alex," she said, her voice low and tense, "I vouched for you to take this job, and I feel like you're about to get yourself into a world of trouble. You're only a week in."

A pang of guilt hit my chest. Erin had put herself on the line for me. But this?

I met her gaze. "This isn't something I can just ignore, Erin."

She clenched her jaw, eyes flashing with frustration. "Alex—"

"I mean it. This case is not adding up. I have to follow it through."

Erin closed her eyes for a second, then let out a slow, resigned sigh. "Fine. I'm going with you."

I blinked. "What?"

"If you're about to go digging up more trouble, at least let me come along so I can try to keep you out of a complete disaster."

I stepped back, irritation flaring. "I don't need a babysitter, Erin."

"No, but you do need someone who isn't running headfirst into a career-ending mess a week into the job."

"So what? I'm supposed to just turn a blind eye because it's inconvenient?"

"I'm coming along," Erin said. "End of story."

I huffed but knew there was no use in arguing. We made our way down the elevators.

"Complete disaster," Erin muttered as we speed-walked to the parking garage. "That's what this feels like already."

I ignored her and unlocked my car, sliding in and throwing my bag into the back seat. Erin climbed into the passenger side and buckled up. As I pulled out of the garage and onto the street, she turned to me, arms crossed. "Where are we going?"

"Judge Everett Leland's house."

Erin blinked. "As in former Chief Judge Everett Leland?"

"Yep."

She let out a disbelieving huff. "And why are we paying a retired judge a house call?"

I tightened my grip on the steering wheel as we hit the main road, the city buildings giving way to quieter, tree-lined streets.

"I read through every single transcript Theresa gave me. Went through all the pre-trial hearings, motions, trial records. Peña's name isn't anywhere. There's no mention of his statement, no reference to him at all."

"And?"

"And now Wexler claims there's supposedly some discovery disclosure that the defense somehow missed. And before I could even review Ortega's case fully, someone else drafted and filed the reply."

Erin's forehead creased with concern, shifting in her seat. "So you're saying there's a missing transcript?"

"There has to be, right? For the defense to just decide not to use this witness doesn't make sense. I just confirmed with Theresa that she was the only court reporter for Judge Leland at the time. If there had been a hearing about Peña, she would have transcribed it."

Erin's gaze bored into me, but she didn't say anything right away.

She finally asked, "You really think Wexler is lying?"

"At best, he's covering his ass. At worst?" I glanced over at her. "He's hiding something."

Erin stared out the windshield, her shoulders tense. "Alex, this is more than a serious accusation. These are people I've worked with. They might be bureaucratic as hell, but I'm just not seeing some grand conspiracy like you are."

"I hope you're right."

"Do you? Because it seems like you want to be right about this."

"What I want," I said through gritted teeth, "is to not stand by while a man rots in prison when he didn't get a fair trial."

"Alex—"

"And you know who the prosecutor on the case was?" I glanced at her briefly before turning my focus back to the road.

"Who?"

"The Honorable Vincent Delacroix, United States District Judge."

The name landed like a lead weight in the car. Erin jerked her head toward me. "What are you—

"Delacroix prosecuted Ortega's case. The same Delacroix who

buried Peña's statement. The same Delacroix who built a conviction off a co-defendant's testimony and a missing witness. The same Delacroix who is now a federal judge."

Erin remained stock still in her seat. "Alex, do you hear yourself? You're talking about accusing a sitting federal judge—a man with lifetime tenure—of hiding exculpatory evidence. Do you have any idea how big this is?"

My pulse hammered against my chest. "I don't care how big it is. I care that he sent a man to prison for life on a trial that wasn't fair."

"Jesus, Alex." Erin dragged a hand through her hair. "This isn't just about some missing file or shady behavior from Wexler. This man holds a lifetime appointment from the President. You think you can just, what? Expose him? Take him down?"

I didn't answer right away. Because I didn't know the answer. But I couldn't ignore it.

I gripped the wheel tighter, my stomach twisting. "I can't pretend it's nothing."

Erin was quiet for a long moment, staring out the window. "We're in it now."

"I took an oath to the Constitution," I said firmly, flicking my turn signal and merging onto a quieter suburban street. "That oath was not to my supervisor, and not to the convenience of the office. If I ignore this, if I let it go because it's *easier*—what the hell does that make me?"

Erin was quiet for a long moment.

"You're not wrong. But there's a right way and a wrong way to do this. And storming up to a retired federal judge's house unannounced is dangerously close to the wrong way."

"Then maybe he shouldn't have signed off on a trial where exculpatory evidence disappeared."

Erin muttered something under her breath before saying, "Fine. But if this blows up in your face, I'm going to say I told you so."

Ignoring her, I pulled onto a quiet residential street lined with large, well-maintained houses. The tension between us filled the car as I focused on navigating the tree-lined streets.

I checked my phone for the address, then slowed the car in front of a modest brick home with a manicured lawn and an American flag hanging near the porch.

"Let's go see if this guy is even home," Erin muttered.

I took a deep breath, pushed open the door, and stepped out onto the curb.

It was time to get some answers.

CHAPTER
SIXTEEN

THE WALK up to Judge Everett Leland's house felt surreal, with only the occasional rustling of oak tree branches swaying in the breeze, breaking the silence. A rocking chair sat on the front porch next to a neat pile of firewood. The brass doorbell on the wall looked well worn from years of use.

I hesitated at the threshold, suddenly aware of what I was about to do—confront a retired federal judge at his home about a possible cover-up. Taking a steadying breath, I pressed the doorbell.

For a second, nothing happened.

Then a deep, frantic barking exploded from inside the house. I jerked back as Erin flinched beside me, my heart pounding against my ribcage.

Erin clutched her chest, eyes wide. "Jesus Christ."

The barking continued, relentless and sharp, accompanied by the scrambling of paws against hardwood floors. Then came a gruff voice shouting over the chaos.

"Duke! Knock it off! Go lay down—now!"

The barking didn't stop immediately, but after a few more sharp commands, it finally faded into grumbling whines and the click of nails retreating across the floor.

My racing pulse began to slow just as the front door swung open.

The man who appeared could have been the dictionary definition of "retired federal judge." Mid-seventies, silver-white hair that was still mostly thick, dressed in a simple sweater and dark jeans, a pair of reading glasses perched on his nose. His posture remained as straight as if he were still on the bench, upright and composed, even in retirement.

But his expression suggested exasperation, aimed somewhere behind him.

"Sorry about that," he said, rubbing a hand down his face. "Duke's friendly, just scared of the damn doorbell."

I gave a small, polite smile. Before I could introduce myself, though, his eyes landed on Erin and lit up with recognition.

"Well, well, Erin Mitchell." A bright grin spread across his face. "Come in, come in! What are you doing here?"

I shot a questioning glance at Erin, who looked equally surprised by the judge's warm greeting. She stepped forward, smoothly taking the lead.

"Judge," Erin greeted, smiling as she walked in. "It's been a while."

"That it has," Leland agreed, closing the door behind us. "Last time I saw you, you were still handling major crimes. I hear you're with Organized Crime now."

"That's right," Erin said, clearly caught off guard by how much he still kept up with things. "Still wrangling fraudsters and money launderers."

Leland chuckled. "Good for you. Always knew you were headed places."

I followed them further inside, trying to process this unexpected connection between Erin and the judge.

Erin finally turned to me. "Judge, this is AUSA Alex Hayes. We have some questions about an old case."

Leland's expression shifted, the warmth in his eyes dimming just a fraction as he turned toward me. His voice now carried the measured tone of a man who had spent decades reading between the lines. "That so?"

I straightened my posture. "Yes, sir. If you have a moment, we'd love to talk."

He studied me for a beat, then gave a short nod. "Let's talk."

Leland led us into a comfortable living room that spoke of decades of use. Every piece of furniture had history—a large wooden coffee table in the center, its surface polished but worn with age, stacked with neatly arranged books and a few scattered legal journals. A brick fireplace, unused but still commanding attention, stood against one wall, and a cabinet of old case files and framed photos filled the space near the window.

Leland motioned for us to sit on a worn leather couch, while he settled into a plush armchair, crossing one leg over the other. Duke, the infamous doorbell-hating dog, was curled up in the corner, watching us with lazy suspicion.

I leaned forward slightly, keeping my expression professional. "Judge, I'm working on a habeas petition for Gabriel Ortega. He was convicted of felony murder twelve years ago in connection with a liquor store robbery."

Leland hummed, nodding.

"It's been alleged that there was a Brady violation in the case," I continued. "A witness statement was deliberately withheld from the defense."

"Isn't that what they all allege?" He settled back in his chair, giving me a pointed look. "You must be new on the job if you're chasing one down personally."

I ignored the jab. "I spoke with Theresa Klein, the court reporter who worked with you during that time. The only reporter who's ever transcribed for you."

Leland nodded, folding his hands over his stomach. He glanced toward the hallway, where the faint sound of a grandfather clock ticking filled the silence. "I had a core staff. I didn't like to change anyone out."

"What if she called in sick?"

Leland fixed me with a look that suggested the question itself was absurd. "If Theresa was unavailable, we didn't proceed."

His expression tightened, his eyes narrowing. "What are you searching for here?"

I took a measured breath, choosing my words carefully. "There's an allegation in Ortega's petition that a witness statement was suppressed

—a man named David Peña gave a statement that contradicted the prosecution's key witness. The defense is claiming the government buried it."

Leland gave a small nod, following along, but his expression remained skeptical.

"I went to Theresa Klein," I continued. "She gave me everything she had on the case—the full trial transcript, pre-trial hearings, everything."

"And?"

"And now, my supervisor claims Peña's statement was properly disclosed to the defense. In fact, they've already filed a response to the petition, claiming the defense simply missed it." I held the former judge's gaze. "I'm trying to understand how that statement and Theresa's complete records can be true at the same time."

For the first time since seeing Erin outside his door, Leland smiled.

Not a warm smile. Not a reassuring smile.

A knowing, tired smile.

"They're not," he said.

My fingers dug into the leather cushion. "What?"

"They're not both true. You have your answer."

I stared at him, waiting for more.

When it didn't come, my frustration spiked.

"Okay," I said, my voice firmer now, "but if that's true, then someone is actively trying to cover up a Brady violation and deprive a man of a fair trial."

Leland watched me with calm detachment.

I pressed on. "Why Ortega? He's a low-level criminal. What makes his case so important that someone would risk their career to keep him locked up?"

"Who knows?" he said, his voice easy, unbothered. "Does it matter?"

I straightened, my jaw tightening. "Of course it matters."

Leland sighed, watching me with the thin patience of a man who had long since stopped fighting these battles himself.

"Let me ask you something," he said, leaning forward and resting his elbows on his knees. "What would you do in my position?"

I hesitated, caught off guard by the shift in conversation. "What do you mean?"

"The response brief is already filed," Leland pointed out. "The argument's been made. The court will review it. In your position, what do you do now?"

I set my jaw. "I don't know yet."

Leland smirked like he already knew my answer before I did.

"You sit tight," he said. "You don't do anything. You wait. You see what happens next."

I leaned forward, my voice hardening with conviction. "With all due respect, Judge, I can't just do nothing while an innocent man remains in prison."

"Yes, you can. And in this case, you should."

"That's not who I am," I countered, hands clenched into fists on my knees.

Leland sighed, rubbing his jaw. "Alex, habeas cases are usually reviewed by the same judge who oversaw the trial—but in this instance?" He gave me a pointed look. "That would be my successor."

I opened my mouth but—

"Thank you so much, Judge," Erin interrupted, plastering on a polite smile as she grabbed my arm.

"Wait—"

"Really appreciate your time!" Erin continued loudly, already dragging me toward the door. "We'll let you get back to your afternoon."

She gave a quick wave over her shoulder as she hauled me out of the house, leaving my questions hanging in the air.

CHAPTER SEVENTEEN

BEFORE I COULD GET another word in, Erin shoved me off the front porch, slamming the door behind us.

I turned to her, fighting against her hand clasped around my arm. Rage filled my chest, almost ready to boil over. "Erin, what the hell?"

Erin kept her grip iron-tight on my arm and shoved me toward the car.

I barely had time to process before she yanked open the driver's side door—apparently, she was driving now—and threw herself into the seat. I hesitated before climbing into the passenger seat, slamming the door behind me.

"Are you—"

Erin threw the car into reverse and sped out of the driveway.

We hit the curb with a hard jolt, the car bouncing as Erin yanked the wheel.

"Jesus, Erin!" I gripped the door handle until my knuckles turned white.

She didn't answer, the engine roaring a little too loudly for a residential neighborhood. Blowing through a stop sign earned an angry honk from a minivan. Picket fences and manicured lawns blurred past us as Erin navigated the streets with reckless determination.

"Are you mad at me or just at the entire concept of smooth driving?"

"Both."

I folded my arms. "You do realize that was a retired federal judge, right? A judge we probably shouldn't have just fled the scene of like criminals?"

Erin let out a sharp laugh, one hand gripping the top of the wheel a little too tightly.

"Alex ... you need to get better at reading between the lines."

I turned to face her fully. "What?"

Erin glanced at me before turning onto the main road. "Leland wasn't just telling you to sit tight for the hell of it. He was telling you *he's* going to do something."

"That's what you got from that?"

"Yes!" Erin huffed, speeding up. "He was trying to give you an out! To make sure you weren't the one who had to torpedo your entire career over this. People like him? They don't just come out and say things. They work in subtle ways."

I let that sink in for a second, my fingers tapping against my knee. "But what if he doesn't actually do anything?"

"Then you'll know. But for right now, you do need to sit tight, stop acting like the entire government is corrupt, and just see what happens."

Letting out a slow, frustrated breath, I crossed my arms and turned to look out the window. "This is not going to be easy for me."

Erin's hands stayed firm on the wheel, her eyes locked on the road. "I honestly do not care."

The car roared down the highway, Houston's skyline glinting under the late afternoon sun. The tension in the air hung between us, electric and unresolved.

Frustration simmered beneath my skin. "You know," I muttered, "this is a pattern with you."

Erin flicked on her turn signal. "Here we go."

Turning to face her, my jaw clenched tight with indignation. "I'm serious. You tell me I need to trust you, but the last time I did, I ended up with a bullet in my shoulder."

Erin's grip on the wheel tightened. She didn't look at me as she replied, "I told you I was sorry for that."

I scoffed, shaking my head. "One half-hearted 'sorry' doesn't change the fact that you used me to take down Andrews. You didn't tell me half of what you knew. And when it all went to hell, I was the one bleeding out on the floor while you were playing damage control."

Erin let out a slow exhale, her jaw muscles working. "I get it. But what was I supposed to do? Just let him keep operating? Let him keep killing people? Do you think I *wanted* you to get shot?"

We sped through a yellow light just as it turned red, horns blaring behind us as Erin cut across two lanes to make the highway entrance.

"I think you wanted results."

"Jesus Christ. You're not the only one who got hurt in all of that. Do you think it was easy for me? Watching you get caught in the middle of that? Knowing I could have stopped it if I'd just—

She cut herself off, her jaw tight with frustration.

My own pulse hammered inside my chest. Years of pent-up emotion roiled inside of me and threatened to spill over. The highway stretched before us, endless concrete cutting through the Texas landscape, as endless as the rift between us.

"Sometimes I think about it. And it makes me so damn angry." My voice came out quieter, raw with emotion. "Because I don't know how or whether I *can* trust you again."

Erin was silent for a moment, her hands white-knuckling the steering wheel as her nostrils flared. "I think that's a little uncalled for."

I slammed my palm against the dashboard. "Is it?"

"I did what I had to do." She glanced at me before looking back at the road. "You think I don't live with that? You think I don't replay it in my head? You think I don't see you getting shot every time I close my eyes?"

I forced myself to stay quiet even though I so badly wanted to scream and yell at the woman next to me.

"I didn't set you up, Alex," she said, her voice raw. "I made a call. A bad one, maybe, but I wasn't trying to use you. I was trying to get to the truth. Just like you."

I looked out the window again, my pulse still too high.

The tires rumbled as Erin pulled into the parking garage of the U.S. Attorney's Office, the moment settling thick between us.

Erin slowed the car to a stop in a space near the elevator, but she didn't move to turn it off right away.

"I don't know how or when you'll trust me again," she said, voice quieter now. "But I'd never let something like that happen again. Not to you."

I swallowed hard, battling the conflicting emotions raging through me. I wanted to believe her. I just didn't know if I could.

CHAPTER EIGHTEEN

FOR THE FIRST time in maybe my entire life, I did exactly what I was told. I waited.

I forced myself to sit on my hands, to keep my head down, to pretend that I wasn't thinking about the Ortega case every single minute of the day. Each morning I'd arrive at the office, do my assigned tasks, and go home without raising any alarms. But that didn't mean I wasn't watching.

I had managed to get my hands on a copy of the reply brief. The moment it landed on my desk, I locked my office door and read through it three times.

And sure enough, it referenced some magical discovery disclosure that absolved the prosecution of all wrongdoing. No Brady violation. No misconduct. No need for post-conviction relief.

As I scanned to the exhibits section, looking for this mystical piece of evidence, I found …

Nothing.

The discovery itself wasn't attached.

I clenched my jaw, my fingers tightening around the edge of the printed copy.

Was this someone's attempt at lying to the court, thinking no one would dig deeper?

I glanced at the signature line of the brief, expecting to see Wexler's name. Instead, an unfamiliar signature caught my eye. AUSA Michael Langford? Who the hell was he?

I pulled up the office directory, quickly typing in the name.

No results appeared in the Houston office. I expanded my search to include all Southern District branches, scrolling through several pages of results before finding him. Michael Langford, senior counsel at the Galveston division—twenty years with the office, highly respected, senior-level. Why would someone from another branch be brought in? And why assign someone with his credentials to quietly file a reply brief on what should have been a routine habeas case?

The reality was, I didn't know. And nobody wanted me to know. These questions haunted me as I followed Leland's advice, waited, and watched.

Three weeks passed.

Three weeks of me burying myself in busy work, even as the Ortega case weighed on my conscience like an anchor dragging me down. Three weeks of Wexler acting like nothing had happened, business as usual.

Until, on a Friday afternoon, an order came down from Judge Warren Pritchard—Judge Leland's successor.

The second it hit the docket, I locked my office door and pulled up the document. My pulse spiked as I scanned each word.

ORDER FROM THE UNITED STATES DISTRICT COURT

SOUTHERN DISTRICT OF TEXAS

IN THE MATTER OF GABRIEL ORTEGA, PETITIONER CASE NO. 24-HC-3192

Having reviewed the petition, the response brief, and the underlying trial record, the Court finds that the allegations raised in the petitioner's claim warrant further inquiry.

Among his claims, the petitioner has alleged a Brady violation, resulting in the suppression of exculpatory evidence that may have impacted the outcome of his trial.

Upon review of the Government's reply brief, the Court notes that reference is made to a critical discovery disclosure which does not appear in the record and has not been provided to the Court. Given the serious nature of this omission and the gravity of the allegations levied against the prosecution, this Court hereby orders the following:

1. *A full evidentiary hearing shall be held to determine the veracity of the Brady claim and whether relief should be granted to the petitioner.*
2. *Due to the allegations of prosecutorial misconduct, the Court finds it inappropriate for the Government to continue handling this matter.*
3. *Therefore, the Court hereby appoints a Special Prosecutor to oversee the evidentiary hearing and to conduct an independent investigation into the handling of the original prosecution.*

The Special Prosecutor shall have full authority to investigate the claims made in the petition, including, but not limited to:

- *Whether exculpatory evidence was knowingly withheld from the defense.*
- *Whether the prosecution engaged in misconduct in violation of ethical and constitutional obligations.*
- *Whether any current or former officials engaged in an attempt to conceal misconduct in the post-conviction proceedings.*

The hearing date shall be scheduled within thirty (30) days of this Order.

Signed: WARREN PRITCHARD UNITED STATES DISTRICT JUDGE

My hands trembled as I gripped the edge of my desk. This wasn't just a hearing anymore. This was an investigation.

A Special Prosecutor works independently of regular prosecutorial offices, appointed only in cases where the government itself faces serious allegations of misconduct.

They don't appear often. But when they do, it signals a seismic shift.

A judge had determined—in no uncertain terms—that the U.S. Attorney's Office couldn't be trusted to handle the Ortega petition.

My pulse roared through my ears as I reread the order.

Wexler had tried to sweep this under the rug, bury it where no one would ever find it.

Someone had falsified information in a court filing, lying directly to a federal judge.

And now, a Special Prosecutor would arrive to ask all the questions I'd been asking from the beginning. If I had pushed harder, spoken louder, maybe this extreme measure wouldn't have been necessary. But I'd played by the rules, waited as instructed, and now the consequences were about to rain down on everyone.

I had waited. I had sat on my hands. And now?

The dam was about to break.

By the next morning, the USAO's normally controlled atmosphere had transformed. Tense whispers traveled from cubicle to cubicle. Coffee cups sat abandoned as attorneys huddled near windows, speaking in hushed tones. Support staff exchanged meaningful glances as they passed in hallways.

The Special Prosecutor had arrived. James Holloway. Not just any prosecutor, but a former Department of Justice Public Integrity Section attorney with a reputation for methodically dissecting corruption cases—the kind of attorney they only deployed when the situation was dire.

I hadn't seen him yet, but his presence electrified the office. Through the glass walls of Nathan Callahan's office, I could see he and Wexler locked in intense conversation, neither looking pleased. Other AUSAs circled nervously, stealing glances toward the closed door, speculating about who would be questioned first.

I tried to focus on my caseload, typing responses to emails while my mind raced. It was only a matter of time before they called me in—the AUSA who had been assigned the petition that started this avalanche.

Around noon, Cynthia appeared at my door, her usual brisk, no-nonsense demeanor fully intact.

"Hayes. You're wanted in the conference room."

I froze, my stomach twisting into a solid knot of dread.

"Now?" I asked, keeping my voice neutral, even as my heart pounded in my chest.

"No, next Tuesday." Cynthia didn't fight to hide her exasperation. "Yes, now. Let's go."

I shut my laptop and grabbed a legal pad—not that I expected to take notes. I just needed something to clench between my fists.

The walk to the conference room passed in a blur. My mind tried to anchor itself with sensory details—the bitter smell of stale coffee from an abandoned mug, the rhythmic tapping of someone's keyboard, the slight squeak of my shoes against the polished floor—anything to distract from the thundering anxiety pulsing through my veins.

Was this how I lost my job? A week into a career I'd worked years to build? God, why did I always feel like I was going to get fired? I probably needed to talk to a therapist about that. But honestly—what lawyer doesn't need therapy?

I walked into the conference room, expecting to find Wexler and Callahan waiting with stern expressions, ready to make me the scapegoat for this entire mess.

But they weren't there.

James Holloway sat alone at the head of the long table, flipping through a file. The man was probably in his mid-forties, with dark hair touched lightly at the temples with gray. His sharp, intelligent blue eyes scanned the pages before him with methodical precision. Everything about him radiated competence and authority.

He glanced up as I entered, offering a polite nod.

"Ms. Hayes."

I hesitated only a moment before stepping inside and pulling the door shut behind me. "Mr. Holloway."

He gestured to the general area in front of him. "Have a seat."

I slid into one of the chairs and set the legal pad on the table in front of me.

He set his file down, folding his hands over it before speaking.

"I'll make this easy for you," he said. "I want you to join this investigation as my second chair."

My mouth fell open. Of all the scenarios I'd imagined walking into this room, this wasn't even on the list.

"Excuse me?"

"You heard me." His matter-of-fact tone suggested this wasn't an insane thing to say to someone who had only learned about this investigation yesterday.

I stared at him, waiting for him to elaborate on this unexpected proposition. When he didn't, I cleared my throat. "May I ask why?"

He gave me a knowing look. "Do I really need to answer that?"

No, he didn't.

I was the only one in this office who had been asking the right questions—any questions—about this case. The only one who had refused to look the other way when evidence of misconduct appeared.

He studied me for a beat, then leaned forward. "Tell me everything you know about this case so far."

I tapped my pen against the legal pad. "Before I do, what did Wexler and Callahan have to say about all this?"

"That it's been handled."

"Handled how?"

"You don't need to worry about it."

I let out a dry laugh. "With all due respect, Mr. Holloway, when someone tells me I don't need to worry about something, it's precisely what I should be worried about."

The corner of his mouth twitched upward, but the expression vanished instantly. "Your job is safe, Ms. Hayes. That's all you need to know."

"And what guarantees do I have of that?"

"Does that really matter to you?"

"Of course it does."

"Does it?" he asked again, his voice steady, measured. "Or are you the kind of person who's going to do what's right regardless?"

I stared at him for a long moment, his words striking at the core of who I wanted to be as an attorney. My career had barely begun, yet here I was, facing a choice that could define it. Would I risk everything—my job, my future, the goals I'd worked toward for years—for the sake of justice? For a man I'd never even met?

I nodded once, the decision crystallizing with surprising clarity.

Holloway's expression softened slightly, approval flickering in his eyes. "Then let's begin."

CHAPTER
NINETEEN

I FINISHED LAYING everything out for Holloway—the full timeline of what I'd uncovered, the missing transcript, the conversation with Judge Leland, and Wexler's suspicious pattern of keeping me busy with other work.

Holloway listened patiently, occasionally jotting down notes but mostly watching me with a calm intensity, his eyes tracking my every expression as I spoke.

When I finished, he slid a document across the table. I didn't need to look at it to know it was the reply brief.

"I've seen this," I said, flipping through the pages anyway. "But I've never met the attorney who signed it. Do you know him? Langford?"

Holloway rested his chin atop steepled fingers. "No, I don't."

"What did Wexler have to say about it?"

"Claims he never assigned the reply to anyone else," Holloway replied. "He said it was 'handled' above his pay grade—at the executive level. And he says that has happened occasionally on sensitive cases."

I scanned the open pages. Langford was Wexler's superior and based in a different office entirely. Why would someone at that level quietly file a reply brief on a twelve-year-old habeas case without telling anyone?

"Did you talk to Callahan?" I asked, wondering if the Criminal Division head had been involved.

Holloway nodded. "Claims complete ignorance. Said he had no idea Langford was even involved."

I set the brief down slowly. "That all sounds convenient."

Holloway smiled. "I agree."

"Okay," I said, "so what's next?"

"We have a meeting with Judge Pritchard tomorrow morning."

I straightened in my chair. "I don't know much about him."

"He's tough but fair," Holloway said simply. "Old-school, but he doesn't like games. If there's a problem, he'll deal with it head-on."

"That's good," I said, more to myself than to him. The last thing I wanted was a judge who'd sweep this under the rug.

Holloway gave a small nod. "The meeting's at nine sharp. Head to his chambers when you arrive."

"What can I do to prepare?"

Holloway tilted his head. "Nothing. Not at the moment."

My pen stopped mid-tap against the notepad. "Nothing? Really?"

"There may be questions the judge asks you directly," Holloway said. "And when he does, I want you to speak freely during the meeting."

I stared at him, certain I'd misheard. In my experience, junior attorneys were expected to stay silent unless specifically addressed, and even then to speak only from carefully prepared talking points.

"Something wrong with that?" he asked.

I tucked my hair behind my ear, buying a moment to collect my thoughts. "No, it's just—" I let out a breath, choosing my words carefully. "I've never been told that before. Usually, it's quite the opposite."

"Ah. You're used to people telling you to stay in your lane. 'Stick to the script.'"

"That's putting it mildly."

Holloway's smirk didn't fade. "Well, Ms. Hayes, welcome to the other side of the justice system."

The fluorescent lights hummed overhead as his words sank in. For the first time in my career, someone wanted my unfiltered opinion—not what I thought others wanted to hear.

The thought was as liberating as it was terrifying.

Holloway tapped his fingers against the table, studying me with quiet curiosity. "Ms. Hayes, if you had to guess—just based on everything you've seen so far—what's going on here?"

The question hung in the air between us. My heart raced as I considered how to answer. Saying my theory aloud would make it real—would transform speculation into something concrete and irreversible.

But Holloway wasn't the type to ask idle questions.

"I think Delacroix deliberately buried Peña's testimony. And then he used his flawless conviction record to catapult himself into a lifetime-tenured position, where he's now untouchable."

Holloway didn't blink.

I continued. "He had everything to gain from this. If this gets dug up, it tarnishes his entire career. And maybe... maybe this wasn't just a single occurrence."

Holloway's expression didn't change, but something flickered in his eyes.

"Grayson seemed to suggest as much."

The afternoon sun filtered through the blinds, casting sharp lines across Holloway's face as he gave a slow nod, his posture still perfectly relaxed.

"You're not saying much," I noted, eyes narrowing. "What's your take?"

Holloway smirked, but it wasn't a humored smirk. It was thoughtful, calculated.

He said, "I haven't had enough time with the information to decide."

"But you have thoughts."

"Of course I do." Holloway closed the file in front of him and gave me a long, measured look. "You should take the rest of the day off."

"What?" The abrupt change of subject caught me off guard.

"Seems like you've been working more than overtime lately. And I need you sharp for tomorrow's meeting with Pritchard."

"I should probably check out with Wexler and Callahan before—"

Holloway cut me off with a shake of his head. "No need."

My eyebrows shot up. "No?"

"You report to me now, Ms. Hayes. At least for the time being."

I leaned back in my chair, arms crossing defensively. "So, what? I'm supposed to ignore my actual supervisors now?"

"You limit your interaction with them," Holloway clarified, "and with anyone else in this office, actually."

The implication hit me like a cold wave.

"Anyone?" I repeated.

"Anyone."

Holloway wasn't just isolating me from Wexler and Callahan—he was cutting me off from the entire office. This wasn't about protecting the investigation; it was about protecting me. He wasn't certain who else might be involved in the cover-up or how deep it ran.

"Get some rest," Holloway said, standing. "I'll see you at nine tomorrow."

I remained frozen for a moment, fingers gripping the edge of my chair, before slowly gathering my things. The walk out of the office felt surreal, like moving through a building that had transformed into something unrecognizable. Yesterday, I was drowning in reply briefs, thinking Wexler was just a pain in my ass. Today, I was second chairing an investigation that involved a federal office and potentially a sitting federal judge.

I was three feet from the exit when Erin stepped out from her office and caught my arm.

Before I could react, she pulled me into her office and shut the door behind us. The familiar scent of her coffee and the faint trace of her perfume filled the small space, now claustrophobic with tension.

She let go of me and planted herself between me and the door, her chin tilted upward in challenge. "What is going on?"

I stepped back, creating distance between us. "I'm really not supposed to be talking to you."

Erin's jaw clenched. "What the hell is that supposed to mean?"

I glanced toward the door, then let out a breath and locked it. That was all Erin needed to see. Her expression shifted, her eyes sharper now.

"I'm second chairing Holloway," I admitted. "And I'm not supposed to talk to anyone in the office as much as I can help it."

"Is that supposed to include me or something?" she asked, arms crossing tightly over her chest, her face flushing with anger. "Are we all under investigation now?"

The diplomas and certificates on her wall seemed to mock the tension between us. I fought the urge to match her fury with my own.

"No, nothing like that. Holloway just wants to be careful about what's shared with who."

Erin scoffed as she ran a hand through her hair, her frustration palpable. "You really do seem to just attract this kind of trouble."

I let out a dry laugh, my own annoyance bubbling over.

"That's really rich, Erin, coming from you," I shot back. "You're the one who dragged me into it in the first place."

Her eyes flashed, but she didn't immediately bite back. Instead, she took a slow, measured breath, her jaw clenching. "I'm not going to argue with you about this. Not here. Not now."

I exhaled sharply, trying to ignore the sting in my chest.

Erin looked at me like she wasn't sure whether to be frustrated or disappointed. "Just go off and do your job. And keep me out of it."

I yanked open her door. "Gladly. That was my plan before you dragged me in here."

I stormed out, letting the door slam behind me. The sound echoed down the hallway as I left, my pulse hammering in my ears.

Erin was pissed.

I was pissed.

And for the first time in a long time, I wasn't sure if I was truly on my own—or if she'd come around when it really mattered.

CHAPTER TWENTY

THE BOB CASEY Federal Courthouse stood like a fortress of cement and glass, towering over downtown Houston, its reflective windows gleaming under the harsh Texas sun.

Even though I had been here before, something about walking inside today felt different. This wasn't just another status conference or routine hearing. This was a closed-door meeting with a federal judge about a case that could unravel a sitting member of the judiciary.

I stepped through the revolving doors, the blast of air conditioning hitting me as I made my way toward the security checkpoint.

The tile floors gleamed, polished to perfection, and the high ceilings made the space feel cavernous. It smelled like coffee and faint industrial cleaner, the usual scents of a building that ran on bureaucracy.

At the security line, I dropped my bag and phone into the X-ray tray and stepped through the metal detector. The marshal behind the desk barely looked up as he waved me through. Once I was cleared, I grabbed my things and made my way toward the elevators, pressing the button for one of the upper floors, where the judge's chambers were located.

The hallways were quiet, clinical, lined with dark wood paneling and portraits of stern-faced jurists who had presided over this courthouse through the decades. When I reached Judge Pritchard's chambers, I stopped in front of a plain, unmarked door with a buzzer system.

I pressed the intercom button and waited.

A voice crackled through. "Yes?"

I put on my professional voice and said, "AUSA Hayes, for the meeting with Judge Pritchard."

There was a brief pause, then the lock clicked open, and I stepped inside.

The chambers were expansive, but not ostentatious. I moved between the walls lined with towering bookshelves, filled with legal volumes, federal case law, and statutes—many collecting dust despite their continued importance in judicial decision-making.

A large mahogany desk dominated the space, neatly stacked with briefs, binders, and a few framed photographs of family and judicial ceremonies. Behind it sat a young woman, early thirties at most, with sleek brown hair pulled neatly back, highlighting a composed, intelligent face. Her sharp eyes scanned me, curiosity evident behind wire-rimmed glasses. A small brass nameplate on her desk read "Sarah Grimes, Law Clerk."

But before I could introduce myself, I spotted someone already sitting in one of the chairs opposite the judge's desk.

Eric Hargrave.

For a moment, I had imagined this as a private conversation between Holloway, the judge, and me. But that would have been entirely inappropriate. Ex parte communications—discussing a case without all relevant parties present—violated fundamental judicial ethics.

As Ortega's original attorney, Hargrave deserved his place at the table. And his presence confirmed that this meeting carried serious implications.

I kept my expression neutral, giving Hargrave a brief nod as I stepped inside. He said nothing as he watched me carefully.

I turned my attention back to Sarah. "Good morning."

She offered me a polite smile. "The judge isn't quite ready yet, but he will be shortly."

"Thank you," I replied quietly, returning her smile before glancing back at Hargrave.

Which meant we were about to have a few very interesting minutes of waiting.

The silence stretched between us, tense and heavy. Just when I thought the awkwardness might suffocate me, the door behind us opened and Holloway strode in like a breath of fresh air.

"Hargrave," Holloway said, his tone casual but respectful. "It's been a while."

Hargrave smirked, setting his legal pad down. "Didn't think I'd see you in Texas again. You get lost on your way back to D.C.?"

Holloway chuckled, adjusting the cuffs of his immaculate navy suit. "What can I say? The weather's better down here. Less swamp, more steak."

Hargrave shook his head. "You still drink that awful, overpriced bourbon?"

Holloway put a hand over his heart, mock-offended. "That's Kentucky's finest, thank you very much."

I watched the exchange with growing curiosity. They had clearly been on opposite sides of the courtroom before but held a mutual respect.

Before the conversation could go further, the door to the judge's private office swung open, and Judge Warren Pritchard stepped out. If Leland had been the kind of judge who radiated calm, calculated patience, then Pritchard was the exact opposite.

He had the broad frame of a former linebacker, thick shoulders that filled out his black judicial robe, and a short-cropped head of silver hair that made him look twenty years younger. But his eyes stood out the most—steel gray, sharp, and perpetually skeptical, like he could see any bullshit before it even left someone's mouth. He had been on the federal bench for nearly a decade, and his reputation preceded him. Tough, fair, and completely unforgiving of incompetence. He didn't tolerate games, nor excuses.

As he stepped into the room, his jaw set with determination, his gaze moved from one of us to the next, taking us in before he even spoke.

"Gentlemen." He nodded at Holloway and Hargrave before his gaze landed on me. "Ms. Hayes."

I straightened. "Your Honor."

Pritchard gave me a long, assessing look, then motioned toward the door to his chambers. "Let's get to it."

The judge's chambers were what I expected them to be—immaculate, no-frills, and ruthlessly efficient.

There were no unnecessary decorations, just walls lined with dense legal books, a few framed certificates, and a neat stack of paperwork atop his desk.

A single shelf held a few personal items—a framed photograph of what I assumed was his family, a military plaque, and a collection of well-worn books, mostly on constitutional law and ethics. Pritchard gestured for us to take the seats in front of the large wooden desk.

I took my place beside Holloway as Hargrave settled in across from us. The judge lowered himself into his own chair, folding his hands over his desk.

"Let's talk about Gabriel Ortega."

CHAPTER TWENTY-ONE

THE JUDGE WASTED NO TIME, his tone making it clear that this was not up for debate. "I'm authorizing discovery under Rule 6 of the Rules Governing Section 2254 Cases."

I started jotting down notes, reminding myself to revisit the text of Rule 6 later. Federal post-conviction proceedings were different from standard trials, but I'd never watched a judge invoke these special rules in real-time.

"I'll also be expanding the record under Rule 7," Pritchard continued, his steel-gray eyes sweeping over us. "Anything relevant to the resolution of this case—whether it favors the petitioner or the government—will be added to the record."

I underlined Rule 7 in my notes. I'd have to read up on how this worked on the federal side as well.

Holloway and Hargrave, meanwhile, seemed completely unfazed—like they had expected this exact decision. Which meant that I was the only one in the room who wasn't already familiar with this process.

Not an ideal position. But that was why I was taking notes like my career depended on it.

Pritchard leaned back slightly, folding his hands together. "Now, let's talk about the reply brief."

"I'm still looking into that myself," Holloway said, "but for the time being, I request that it be withdrawn."

Pritchard's eyes flicked over to Hargrave. "Any objection to that motion?"

Hargrave's expression quickly turned sharp. "No objection, Your Honor. But I'd like to note for the record that the government's response is exactly the sort of thing my client is fighting against in the first place—prosecutorial misconduct."

I glanced up from my notes, watching Pritchard's reaction.

He gave Hargrave a flat, unimpressed look. "Save your breath, Hargrave. There's no jury here."

Hargrave's smirk widened slightly, but he dipped his head in acknowledgment. "Understood, Your Honor."

I let out a slow, steadying breath, absorbing everything. The judge had just made it crystal clear—this wasn't about grandstanding. This wasn't about arguing philosophy or making speeches.

This was about getting to the truth. And from the way Pritchard was handling this? It was becoming very clear that he was just as curious as I was about what the hell was actually going on.

Pritchard flipped through a thin stack of notes on his desk. "Let's set a date for this hearing. Four weeks. That enough time for both sides to pull together everything you need?"

Holloway nodded. "That's sufficient, Your Honor."

Hargrave followed suit. "Agreed."

I jotted the date down, but before I could process what that meant in terms of the workload ahead, Pritchard had already moved on.

He closed the file in front of him and looked up. "Lastly, we need to discuss the media."

I glanced at Holloway, but his expression didn't change.

Holloway merely tilted his head. "Media? I wasn't aware this was attracting any attention."

Pritchard's gaze flicked over to Hargrave, as if the other man already knew where this was going. Hargrave offered a casual shrug, but I didn't miss the way his eyes gleamed.

"I'd expect there will be reporters involved," he said smoothly. "The court appointing a Special Prosecutor is a big deal. People tend to get interested when a case reaches this level."

I swallowed. Hargrave intended to make this a spectacle. This would be a major story—one he could capitalize on.

Pritchard exhaled through his nose, barely concealing his annoyance. "Which brings us to cameras in the courtroom."

Holloway remained unbothered, but Hargrave straightened, already preparing his stance.

"The default in federal courts is to prohibit cameras," Pritchard continued. "But given the public interest and the nature of the allegations, I'll take arguments from both sides before making a ruling. Preferences?"

"I'd prefer them, Your Honor," Hargrave said without hesitation.

Holloway, on the other hand, barely lifted an eyebrow before responding.

"No, Your Honor. I'd prefer to have them out of the courtroom." His tone was cool, even.

Pritchard sighed, like this was the most predictable exchange of his career.

"I'll issue a formal ruling on that shortly."

I tapped my pen against my legal pad, already dreading the inevitable media storm if Pritchard allowed cameras inside.

This wasn't just about Gabriel Ortega anymore. It wasn't even just about Delacroix. This was about to become a very public fight over the credibility of the justice system itself.

Judge Pritchard wrapped up the meeting with a pointed look between Holloway and Hargrave.

"I don't expect to hear from either of you until I see you at the hearing," he said, his tone chiding but firm. "Because you'll both play nice during discovery, won't you?"

Hargrave smirked. Holloway gave a noncommittal nod.

Pritchard clapped his hands together, clearly done with us. "You all have work to do. Get out of my chambers."

With that, we all rose from our seats. As we made our way out of chambers, down the hall, and out of the courthouse, I kept my thoughts to myself.

The sunlight was blinding after the dim, controlled atmosphere of the courthouse. The buzz of traffic and distant voices filled the humid Houston air.

Holloway and Hargrave paused on the courthouse steps, talking for a moment longer while I waited beside them.

Finally, Holloway gestured toward me.

"Hargrave, this is AUSA Alex Hayes," he said. "She'll be second chairing this case with me."

Hargrave turned his sharp eyes on me, assessing me with mild amusement before extending his hand. "I've heard of you."

I kept my expression neutral as I shook his hand. "I hope only good things."

Hargrave grinned. "Depends on who you ask." Then, casually, he added, "If you ever get tired of working for the government at discount rates, give me a call."

Before I could react, Holloway let out a low chuckle and shook his head, his voice teasing but edged with warning. "I'm not quite sure that's an appropriate offer to make right now."

"Stick to investigating the prosecutor's office, Holloway."

They both laughed, the kind of knowing laugh shared between two men who had probably clashed in court more times than they could count.

Hargrave gave me a final nod, then disappeared into the crowd, leaving Holloway and me standing on the courthouse steps.

Holloway turned to me, jerking his chin toward the street.

"Come on, Hayes."

I paused. "Where are we going?"

"Coffee."

CHAPTER
TWENTY-TWO

BOOMTOWN COFFEE HAD the kind of warm, industrial-chic atmosphere that made it feel casual but not sloppy—the kind of place where lawyers could blend in with journalists, and conversations about case law and politics drifted through the air over the sound of grinding espresso beans.

Holloway and I grabbed our coffee—he took his black, I opted for a latte—and found a quiet table in the back, away from the more crowded tables near the window.

He sat down first, loosening his tie, his posture relaxed but deliberate. I settled across from him, stirring my drink as I waited for him to start.

And he did. "We're turning over everything in discovery," Holloway said, stirring his own coffee idly. "Even things they don't ask for."

Pausing mid-stir, I frowned slightly. "Why go that far?"

Holloway took a slow sip of his coffee before answering.

"Because this case isn't about Ortega," he said. "Not really. It's about someone inside the prosecutor's office."

I nodded, already having suspected as much.

"Whether that was Delacroix or not," Holloway continued, "clearly someone else is still there. Someone who is still pulling strings."

"You think it's Wexler?" I asked.

Holloway exhaled through his nose, shaking his head. "Too early to tell."

"But you think it's someone still in the office?"

"Has to be. Nothing about how this case was handled happened by chance. Someone is still actively covering for this."

I tapped my fingers against my cup, my mind spinning. "What do you need me to do?"

Holloway scoffed faintly, like he'd expected that question.

"I'm going to start digging through discovery. See where everything magically disappeared. Find out who handled what, who had access to what files. There's a trail somewhere, and I intend to follow it."

I nodded, waiting for him to continue.

He locked eyes with me. "And while I'm doing that, I need you to be my shadow."

"Shadow?"

"Where I go, you go." He leaned forward. "And while I'm talking to people, you watch. You notice how they react, who looks nervous, who suddenly has an excuse to leave the room. You pick up on what I miss while I'm busy playing nice."

I blinked. "So, I'm your lie detector?"

"Essentially."

I let that sink in for a moment before nodding. It wasn't what I had expected when I first walked into work a few weeks ago, expecting just another case assignment. But now?

Now, I was sitting across from a Special Prosecutor, investigating something that was clearly bigger than a single buried statement. And if Holloway was right—if someone inside the U.S. Attorney's Office was still orchestrating a cover-up—then we were about to stir up a hornet's nest.

I picked up my latte and took a slow sip, locking eyes with him.

"Alright," I said. "I'm in."

Leaning back in my chair, my fingers idly traced the rim of my coffee cup, letting the weight of everything settle.

"What about Ortega?" I asked finally. "What do you think happens to him?"

Holloway took a slow sip of his black coffee, the steam curling up between us.

"Ultimately, it'll be up to Judge Pritchard to decide whether Peña's absence was *prejudicial* to the defendant."

I huffed. "We both know it was."

Holloway gave a careful shrug, his expression unreadable.

"Maybe," he said. "But that's not our call."

"Come on, Holloway." I narrowed my eyes. "A missing exculpatory witness? A statement that directly contradicts the prosecution's star witness? That's *textbook* Brady material."

"Sure," he said, unfazed. "But we're not the ones who get to decide that."

I tilted my head, expecting more.

Holloway scowled slightly, leaning back. "That's the best part about being a lawyer, Hayes. *You* don't have to decide the outcome. *You* just have to make the argument."

"That's a very convenient philosophy."

Holloway smiled over the rim of his cup. "It's a survival skill."

I took another sip of my coffee, letting Holloway's words linger for a moment before shifting gears.

"Enough about the case." I set my cup down. "Tell me about you."

Holloway raised an eyebrow. "What about me?"

I shrugged. "Who are you? Where are you from? How'd you land this gig?"

He chuckled, shaking his head slightly. "You asking because you're curious or because you're trying to size me up?"

"A little of both."

Holloway exhaled, tapping his fingers against his coffee cup. "Alright. James Holloway, originally from Boston, but don't hold that against me. DOJ alum, spent a decade in Public Integrity, mostly political corruption and law enforcement misconduct cases. Took down a sitting U.S. Senator once—still have the hate mail to prove it."

"Impressive."

"Depends who you ask." His eyes glinted with dry humor. "After that, I bounced around a bit—some special counsel work, a stint overseas consulting for anti-corruption task forces. Then I came back, did some time in Main Justice, and now here I am."

"And how did you land this particular gig?"

"Got a call. Someone up top figured this case was worth investigating, and I had the right background."

I eyed him. "So you were handpicked?"

"Most special prosecutors are."

"So this case is big enough that Main Justice wanted someone outside the normal chain of command."

"Looks that way."

Main Justice—the headquarters of the DOJ in Washington, D.C.—didn't get involved in everyday prosecutions. Their focus was on national priorities, high-profile investigations, and cases with broader implications beyond just one district. If someone at Main had stepped in, it meant they saw something bigger at play—something that might not stop at just one corrupt judge.

It wasn't just Pritchard who thought this case was worth digging into. Someone at the top did too.

I turned the conversation back on him. "And do you like it? Being the guy they recruit when things get ugly?"

"That's an interesting way to put it."

"Tell me I'm wrong."

"You're not." A small grin tugged at the corner of his mouth. "I do like it. Some people are built for corporate law or securities fraud. I like the fights that matter."

I nodded, recognizing in his words an echo of my own motivations.

Then he shifted the conversation. "And what about you, Hayes?"

I raised an eyebrow. "What about me?"

He took another sip of his coffee. "You're young for an AUSA. And I've read about the Martin trial. That was a hell of a case."

I inhaled sharply at the mention of it—the case that had nearly ended my career before it had even started.

"Yeah," I said after a beat. "It was."

Holloway studied me with measured intensity. "I read the transcripts. Hell of a case you put together. You were the one who pulled the threads that tied everything back to the mayor's conspiracy, weren't you?"

"Not exactly how I planned it."

"You motioned to drop the charges against your defendant after learning he wasn't the real killer. That's rare. Most prosecutors don't—"

"I wasn't about to let an innocent man take the fall. And besides, that's what led to the feds charging him with conspiracy. And when they dug into that, they found their way to the mayor. I just connected the dots."

"Connecting dots is what wins cases."

"It didn't feel like a win when I was sitting across from a dirty cop and he tried to kill me."

His expression darkened. "I read about that, too."

I met his gaze, a flicker of something unspoken between us.

"Part of the job," I muttered, looking away.

"Not a part you should have to get used to."

My fingers tightened around my cup as memories of that day surfaced—the cold sweat, the metallic smell of blood, the searing pain in my shoulder. The truth was, I hadn't gotten used to it. Wasn't sure I ever would.

I shrugged, not wanting to dwell on it. "Anyway, that's how I ended up here. My friend Erin Mitchell suggested I make the move to the feds. Thought it was a better fit."

"So you followed her lead?"

"Something like that. Though, given recent events, I'm not sure how much she appreciates that."

Holloway arched a brow. "Trouble in paradise?"

"Let's just say she doesn't love how deep I'm getting into this."

"That's usually the sign that you're onto something." I rolled my eyes, but before I could respond, he leaned forward.

"And what about before the Martin case? What got you into all this?"

My stomach tightened. The easy answer was law school, the desire to be a prosecutor, the usual drive for justice. But that wasn't what he was asking.

"It's a long story."

Holloway tilted his head. "I've got time."

I forced a tight smile, then shook my head. "I'm not ready to tell it just yet."

Holloway studied me for a moment, but he didn't push. "Fair enough."

I nodded, taking another sip of my coffee. Some wounds were still too raw to expose to the light. My career was one thing—my mother was something else entirely.

CHAPTER TWENTY-THREE

HOLLOWAY and I sat in the courthouse in a small, windowless room stacked with boxes of files.

Between us sat Hargrave's discovery requests, a neat, stapled stack of paperwork detailing everything he wanted from us. I flipped through the first few pages, scanning the requests carefully. He wasn't asking for anything surprising—prosecutorial files, communications, any and all evidence related to Peña's statement, internal memos from the DA's office at the time.

But it was broad, almost like he was casting a wide net, hoping something would float up.

Holloway leaned back in his chair, reading over his copy, his expression unreadable.

I continued flipping through the pages. "What do you think?"

"I think he's doing exactly what I'd do in his position," Holloway said, sipping his coffee. "He knows we're about to turn over everything, so he's making sure nothing gets overlooked."

I nodded, tapping my pen against the table. "I keep coming back to something, though."

Holloway raised an eyebrow. "What's that?"

"How did Ortega land someone like Hargrave in the first place?" I asked, frowning. "Guys like him don't just take random habeas cases for fun. Ortega isn't rich, he's not famous—so what's the angle?"

Holloway chuckled, shaking his head.

"Come on, Hayes. You know how this works." He set the papers down and folded his hands in front of him. "A lot of big-time defense attorneys will take cases like this pro bono because it's a slam dunk. Makes them look good. There's a reason Hargrave wants cameras in the courtroom."

"So this is just another chance for him to build his profile?" I asked.

"Not just publicity," Holloway said, smirking. "It's an investment. If Hargrave gets Ortega's conviction overturned, he's suddenly the guy who took on the government and won."

"So the next time some white-collar criminal gets charged with fraud he actually committed …"

"That guy is going to pay Hargrave a boatload of money to get him the same mandatory minimum he could've gotten with a public defender."

I let out a short laugh, shaking my head. "So this is just a stepping stone to bigger clients?"

"That's how the game is played, kid." Holloway laughed, then leaned forward, tilting his head slightly. "Why? You thinking about going to the other side?"

I blinked, caught off guard. "What?"

"I saw the way Hargrave was recruiting you outside the courthouse. Was half-expecting you to call him back already. Do I need to get jealous?"

"Yeah," I scoffed. "Because that would go over real well right now."

Holloway grinned. "Wouldn't be the first time someone flipped sides after seeing how the sausage gets made."

"I'm not going to defense work, Holloway."

"Good. I'd hate to have to beat you in court someday."

I let out a dry laugh, flipping to the next page of discovery requests. "Like that'd happen."

Holloway chuckled, but didn't argue.

"Besides," I said, "I don't want to spend my career protecting hedge fund criminals or finding loopholes for tax fraud."

Holloway nodded approvingly. "You're an asset to the side of justice."

My face heated, not expecting that kind of direct compliment from him. I cleared my throat. "Uh—thank you."

Holloway gave me a small nod before flipping through another page of discovery. "Alright, so this is all pretty standard—requests for memos, old emails, depositions, trial prep notes. Nothing unexpected."

I nodded, skimming over the details. "So, what's our next move?"

Holloway reached into his briefcase and pulled out another file, thicker than the discovery request.

"I have a list of names of people who worked on the case back then—investigators, clerks, junior AUSAs. I've scheduled interviews with each of them to see what they remember."

I sat up straighter. "Okay."

Holloway flipped to the first page and tapped his pen against it.

"First up: Richard Lawson, former federal investigator assigned to the Ortega case." He checked his watch.

"Let me guess," I said. "The interview is soon?"

Holloway nodded, standing up. "Five minutes."

"You're kidding."

"Nope," he said, already gathering his files. "Grab your notebook, Shadow."

Sighing, I snatched my legal pad and stood up to follow him.

We made our way down the hall toward a different conference room, my pulse picking up.

The conference room was as unremarkable as any other in the courthouse—sterile white walls, a heavy oak table, and a few chairs that were just comfortable enough to keep people from shifting too much.

Richard Lawson was waiting for us as we sat down, his posture relaxed, his fingers tapping idly on the table. We sat down across from him.

The interview itself? A complete dud.

Lawson remembered the case, vaguely. He had worked dozens of investigations back then, and the Ortega matter was just another file in his pile.

"Look," he said, scratching his chin. "It was twelve years ago. I don't recall anything unusual about it. Standard investigation—evidence came in, people got interviewed, the prosecution built their case. I don't remember any fireworks."

When I glanced at Holloway, he remained unbothered, nodding along as if this wasn't completely useless.

"Nothing stood out to you?" I pressed. "No missing witness statements, no suppressed evidence?"

Lawson let out a dry laugh. "If something shady was going on, they sure as hell weren't looping me in. I just followed orders, put my reports together, and moved on to the next case."

After a few more noncommittal answers, Holloway wrapped it up and stood. "Thanks for your time, Mr. Lawson."

Lawson shrugged, standing as well. "Wish I could've been more help."

With that, he left, and the room fell silent as I tapped my pen against my notebook.

I sighed, leaning back in my chair. "That was a whole lot of nothing."

Holloway frowned slightly, but didn't seem disappointed in the slightest.

"What are we even hoping to find here?" I asked. "These people were just doing their jobs, right? If Delacroix buried this evidence, he wasn't exactly telling his investigators."

Holloway tucked his legal pad under his arm and gave me a thoughtful look. "It's not always about what they remember. It's about inconsistencies between statements, patterns that don't quite line up."

"So we're just waiting for something to contradict itself?"

"I'll know it when I see it."

"Wasn't it Justice Potter Stewart who said that? 'I know it when I see it?'"

Holloway agreed. "You do know your case law."

I rolled my eyes but smiled despite myself.

"So I guess we're just digging until something hiding in plain sight reveals itself?"

"That's the idea," Holloway said. "If there's something to find, it'll show up. People misremember things, details start shifting—that's when we know where to push harder."

I sighed, rubbing my temple. "Who's next?"

Holloway glanced at his list and tapped a name with his finger.

"Nancy Cooper, former trial paralegal in the U.S. Attorney's Office. She handled case files and discovery records."

"So if anything went missing, she might've been the one to notice?"

Holloway gave a knowing nod. "Only one way to find out."

CHAPTER TWENTY-FOUR

A WEEK OF BACK-TO-BACK INTERVIEWS, countless hours of digging through old files, and still—nothing concrete.

We had spoken to paralegals, investigators, clerks, and even junior AUSAs who had worked around Ortega's case, but every interview had ended with the same shrug, the same vague recollection of nothing out of the ordinary.

And yet, as we headed into the next scheduled interview, Holloway looked almost excited.

Squinting, I followed him down the courthouse corridor, shifting the legal pad under my arm. "Why do you look like a kid on Christmas morning?"

Holloway grinned, but didn't answer immediately.

"Who is this guy?"

He glanced at me. "Delacroix's second chair at trial."

That made me pause.

"His co-counsel?"

"Yep."

That wasn't unusual. Big cases usually had more than one AUSA on the file. But something in Holloway's tone told me there was more to it.

"And why is that exciting?" I asked.

"Because," Holloway said, slowing as we neared the conference room, "Delacroix very much did not bring him along for the ride when he climbed the ladder."

"And you think that might loosen his tongue?" I asked, my pulse quickening.

"Maybe."

"But does that really make him reliable?"

"Depends. Sometimes a witness can be unreliable—too eager to tell you what you want to hear. But sometimes ..." He glanced at me, his gaze fading into something more thoughtful. "Sometimes it'll give you just enough of a lead to find the real story."

I nodded slowly, rolling my shoulders back. "Let's see what he has to say."

As we stepped into the conference room, I got my first look at the man who might have answers we desperately needed. He was in his mid-forties, dressed in a charcoal-gray suit, his tie loosened—like he'd made an effort to look professional but didn't actually care to be here.

"Daniel Kessler," he said as we walked in, extending his hand to Holloway before glancing at me.

"AUSA Alex Hayes," I offered, shaking his hand firmly before we all sat down.

Kessler leaned back in his chair, arms crossed over his chest, and let out a long, exasperated sigh.

"Let me guess," he said. "This is about Delacroix."

Holloway glanced up, opening his notebook. "That obvious?"

Kessler snorted. "Anytime someone drags me in for an 'old case review,' it's usually about that self-righteous bastard."

"Not a fan?" I asked, keeping my tone casual.

"You want my honest opinion? Vincent Delacroix is not as good as people think he is."

Holloway gave a slow, expectant nod, letting Kessler vent without interruption.

"Guy had a big personality, a big presence, sure," Kessler continued, shifting in his seat. "Knew how to work a jury, sell the case. But legally?" He let out a dry chuckle. "I've seen better first-year associates. He was all about flair—not about substance."

Keeping my face blank, I filed his words away in my mind.

Holloway, however, didn't let him spiral too far down the rabbit hole.

"That's good to know," Holloway interrupted, tapping his pen against his legal pad. "But I want to bring this back to Ortega's case."

Kessler let out a sigh, rubbing his temple. "Yeah, yeah, I figured."

"Tell me about Peña."

Kessler stilled, his expression tightening. "That was ... a mess."

"How so?" I asked.

Kessler exhaled sharply. "I remember asking Delacroix about that damn witness statement early on. I saw it. I read it. And I remember thinking, this is going to be a problem. So I went to him and asked, 'How are we handling this at trial?'"

"And what did he say?" Holloway asked.

"He brushed it off. Gave me that whole 'I'm the senior attorney, I'll handle it' routine."

I winced, a familiar sinking feeling settling in my stomach. The dismissive tone, the implication that a junior attorney's concerns weren't worthy of serious consideration—I'd been on the receiving end of that same treatment more times than I could count.

Kessler leaned forward now, his voice sharper, his frustration still lingering after all these years.

"It was just gone." He snapped his fingers for emphasis. "One minute, it was part of the case, something we were supposed to deal with—and the next? Nothing. No strategy meeting. No motions filed. No discussion. It never came up again."

My stomach tightened. I asked, "Delacroix never disclosed it to the defense?"

"No. And you know what's worse? I didn't even realize it until after the trial was over. I assumed we'd filed something, that Delacroix had dealt with it quietly—but there was nothing."

He ran a hand through his hair,shaking his head. "I should have pushed harder. But I wasn't going to go up against Delacroix—especially not back then, when I was a newbie and he was already building his perfect record."

The fluorescent lights hummed overhead as an electric tension filled the room. Here was what we'd been searching for—direct, firsthand confirmation that Peña's statement hadn't just been forgotten or misplaced. It had been deliberately kept from the defense by someone who knew exactly what he was doing.

I thought of Ortega, twelve years in prison, while Delacroix ascended to the federal bench. The injustice of it burned in my chest, a slow, smoldering anger that only grew as I watched Kessler's haunted expression. He'd known something was wrong but had lacked the power or courage to stop it—and had lived with that knowledge for years.

Holloway closed his notebook, gave Kessler a polite nod, and said, "Thanks for your time. We'll be in touch."

Kessler stood, adjusting the sleeves of his suit like he was ready to put this whole thing behind him. But just as he reached for the door, Holloway stopped him. "One last thing."

Kessler turned. "Yeah?"

"Would you be willing to testify at trial about this?"

Kessler blinked, clearly not expecting the question. He hesitated for a beat before answering.

"I mean, yeah. But why would I? You're with the prosecution. It's not like this helps your case."

Holloway shrugged, completely unfazed. "That's fine. I just wanted to know."

Kessler studied him for a second longer, then shook his head with a dry chuckle. "You really are a different breed, Holloway."

"That's what they tell me."

Kessler gave a final nod, then left, the door clicking shut behind him.

Turning to Holloway, I watched him carefully. "What was that about?"

Holloway leaned back in his chair, crossing his arms. "I wanted to see if he'd stand behind his statements," he said simply.

"And?"

"And he will," Holloway confirmed. "Which means this isn't just him being bitter about being left behind. He's not just trying to take Delacroix down out of resentment."

I exhaled slowly, tapping my pen against my legal pad.

"Where does that leave us?"

Holloway sighed, rubbing his temple. "It leaves us in not a great position."

I frowned. "Why?"

Holloway gestured vaguely. "Because what we've got is a sitting federal judge who, based on everything we've seen, committed prosecutorial misconduct when he was a prosecutor."

I nodded. "That's problematic, obviously—"

"It is bad. And it's a problem."

My mind raced ahead, connecting the pieces. "Wait—we've been looking for a conspiracy, for other people who helped cover this up. But you're thinking it might just be Delacroix who deliberately buried that statement?" I sat up straighter as realization dawned. "And now we have to go after a sitting federal judge."

Holloway nodded grimly. "Think about it, Hayes. Everyone we've talked to? They weren't complicit in what Delacroix did. They didn't bury the statement. They just didn't realize it never made it into evidence. And Wexler? As shady as he might be, there's nothing tying him to this yet. Same with Callahan."

I sat back in my chair, feeling the weight of that realization.

"So, what are you saying?" I asked carefully.

Holloway sighed.

"I'm saying that unless someone higher up decides to impeach Delacroix, this case is going to hit a dead end."

CHAPTER TWENTY-FIVE

I SAT FORWARD, tapping my fingers against the table. "What about Delacroix?"

Holloway raised an eyebrow. "What about him?"

I exhaled, frustrated. "Are we just not going to confront him about this?"

Holloway let out a short, humorless laugh. "And what exactly do you think is going to happen, Hayes? That we walk into his chambers, ask him if he knowingly buried exculpatory evidence, and he just confesses on the spot?"

"No, but—shouldn't we at least talk to him? If we're about to accuse him of prosecutorial misconduct, don't we have a duty to ask him directly?"

Holloway studied me for a moment, his expression unreadable.

Then he sighed. "You do have a point."

"Wouldn't be the first time."

He smiled slightly, then glanced at his watch. "If we hurry, we might still be able to catch one of his hearings before he leaves for the day."

I blinked. "Wait, you mean now?"

"Unless you'd rather schedule a polite sit-down meeting with him next week."

I grabbed my legal pad and stood. "This works."

"Good," he said, already heading toward the door.

I hurried after him, heart pounding, preparing for one hell of a conversation.

Usually, when I walked into a courtroom, it was to argue a motion, present evidence, or fight for a conviction. Today, I was here to watch.

Holloway and I slipped into the back row of Courtroom 4B, quietly taking our seats as we caught the tail end of a sentencing hearing. The air felt different on this side of the gallery—tense with the weight of lives being decided, yet oddly detached from the machinery of justice I normally operated.

Judge Vincent Delacroix sat at the bench, wearing the black robe that symbolized his authority, his expression serious but not unkind as he addressed the defendant before him.

The man at the podium—young, maybe late twenties, wearing an ill-fitted suit, his tired eyes suggesting he hadn't slept in days—stared at the judge with a mix of fear and resignation.

I barely glanced at the case docket before tuning into Delacroix.

"Mr. Johnson, your choices have led you here today. And the choices you make going forward will define the rest of your life."

"Yes, Your Honor."

"I'm sentencing you to eighty-four months in federal custody. That is not an insignificant amount of time. But it is not a lifetime. You will have opportunities in front of you. What you do with them will be up to you."

The defendant nodded, hands clenched in front of him.

Delacroix leaned forward, his voice even but not without weight.

"I don't take pleasure in sending people to prison. But the law exists for a reason. Justice exists for a reason. I hope you take this time to think about the kind of person you want to be when you walk out of those gates. This system isn't built to help you—it's built to hold you accountable. You have to be the one to decide if you'll make the most of it."

There was silence for a moment, then Delacroix sighed, nodding to the court clerk.

"Sentencing is complete. Mr. Johnson, you are remanded to the custody of the U.S. Marshals for transfer to federal prison. I wish you luck."

The sound of papers shuffling and murmurs from the gallery filled the room as the hearing wrapped up.

For a man I had spent the last several weeks investigating, he didn't come off as the kind of power-hungry, arrogant prosecutor-turned-judge I had built up in my head.

He came across as measured. Thoughtful. Like someone who cared about the job. Maybe he was just going through the motions—repeating lines he had told a thousand defendants before.

Delacroix stood, gave another quick nod to his clerk, and disappeared through the side door to his chambers. The defendant was escorted away by two marshals, his lawyer whispering something to him as they walked.

Holloway wasted no time.

He stood, straightened his tie, and made his way to the court clerk's desk. I followed closely, heart pounding slightly, but I forced my expression to remain neutral.

"Excuse me, ma'am," Holloway said, flashing a polite but firm smile. "James Holloway. Special Prosecutor. I was wondering if Judge Delacroix might have a moment to spare."

The clerk, a woman in her mid-fifties with short-cropped hair, gave him an appraising look. She glanced between him and me, clearly taking in the request carefully. "I can ask. Wait here."

With that, she turned and disappeared into chambers. I noticed the buzzing mechanism, the security card swipe, the multiple layers of clearance that separated Delacroix's world from ours.

I let out a slow breath, glancing around before muttering, "Why does it always seem like every clerk hates their job?"

"Because they work for judges." Holloway quipped, sliding his hands into his pockets.

"Besides, it's a thankless job—doing all the work, writing all the opinions, and watching some guy in a robe take all the credit."

"Sounds personal."

"Just an observation."

It wasn't long before she reappeared with Judge Delacroix. I tensed, bracing myself for what, I wasn't sure. But instead of the defensive, arrogant man I had built up in my head, Delacroix strode into the courtroom with a comfortable ease. His robe was unfastened, his expression calm and open. And when his eyes landed on Holloway, his face broke into something almost resembling a smile.

Delacroix stepped forward and offered his hand. "James Holloway."

Holloway shook it, matching the other man's tone. "Vincent. Been a while."

"It has. You keeping busy?"

"Always."

They both exchanged a knowing look, and I realized they knew each other. Not in the purely adversarial way that Hargrave and Holloway did. But in the "we've been in the same circles long enough to respect each other" way.

I wondered if there was anyone Holloway didn't know in the entire state of Texas.

Then Holloway, never one for unnecessary buildup, got straight to it.

"I've got something somewhat difficult to discuss with you," he said, his voice still measured but polite.

Delacroix raised an eyebrow, but didn't seem rattled at all. Instead, he gestured toward the now-empty defense table.

"By all means," he said. "Let's discuss it."

CHAPTER TWENTY-SIX

I TOOK A SEAT BESIDE HOLLOWAY, still watching Delacroix carefully.

He seemed unbothered. Not defensive. Not arrogant. Not how I expected him to be at all. He was almost supportive. Like he wasn't walking into an ambush, but rather an interesting conversation he was more than happy to entertain.

And that? That threw me even more.

Holloway leaned forward, resting his elbows on the table, his expression calm and measured.

"I've been appointed Special Prosecutor for a habeas petition involving a case you prosecuted during your time at the U.S. Attorney's Office."

Delacroix tilted his head, watching Holloway with mild curiosity. "That right?"

"The Ortega matter."

Delacroix furrowed his brows, thinking for a moment before nodding. "I vaguely remember that one. Felony murder case, correct? The liquor store shooting?"

"That's the one."

"I assume the petition is arguing ineffective assistance of counsel? Or newly discovered evidence?"

"Not quite," Holloway said, his tone still easy but deliberate. "The defense is claiming you committed a Brady violation."

Delacroix's expression didn't change, but I noticed his shoulders tense slightly, the rhythm of his breathing shifting for just a moment before he let out a low exhale.

Holloway continued, unfazed. "There's evidence at the U.S. Attorney's Office suggesting a witness statement was buried. Circumstantial, at the moment, but compelling enough that Judge Pritchard has authorized discovery and an evidentiary hearing."

For the first time, Delacroix's expression shifted—not into panic or even concern, but more like he was mildly annoyed by this conversation.

"And since you were lead prosecutor on the trial," Holloway continued, "we figured it would be best to speak with you about this directly."

Holloway leaned back, waiting.

Delacroix exhaled, his expression earnest. "I certainly would have turned anything over. That's not my style. Never has been. I believe cases should be tried on merit, not on the skill of their attorneys."

His voice carried the conviction of someone who meant it—not just someone reciting a well-crafted defense.

He gestured around the courtroom. "And I carry that forward in my own courtroom. I don't play games with evidence. I never have."

Studying him, I watched for any signs of falsehood, any cracks in his demeanor, But I didn't see any.

Holloway tilted his head. "Do you have any evidence that a statement from David Peña was turned over to the defense?"

Delacroix considered the question for a moment, then gave a slow nod.

"I can certainly search my case notes," he said. "I don't have my journals with me, but I can look through them tonight when I get home."

Holloway studied him for a moment, his expression unreadable. He gave a slow nod. "That would be helpful."

Delacroix nodded back, his face still calm, almost reassuring.

Holloway let a beat of silence pass before adding, "Kessler is willing to testify that you buried Peña's statement. Grayson submitted an affidavit swearing to it."

For the first time, something flickered across Delacroix's face—a brief shift, just enough to tell me he was processing that information carefully.

He exhaled, then leaned back slightly, tilting his head. "Kessler, I can understand."

Holloway raised an eyebrow.

Delacroix sighed, something resigned settling into his tone. "Kessler and I never saw eye to eye on how to litigate cases. He was young, ambitious, but too rigid in his thinking. He thought every case needed to be won in pre-trial motions, that the courtroom was just a formality. I disagreed." He gave a small, almost bitter chuckle. "And I wasn't exactly diplomatic about it. I was dismissive of him back then. Something I regret now, but I tried to reach out over the years, and he never wanted to speak with me."

I exchanged a quick glance with Holloway. Delacroix's words felt genuine—but that didn't mean they invalidated Kessler's accusations.

Delacroix shook his head. "I didn't involve him closely in my case strategy and preparations as a result. It's a shame to hear he thought I'd do something like that. I suppose I shouldn't be surprised."

Holloway nodded, then smoothly pivoted. "And Grayson?"

Delacroix hesitated this time.

"Grayson always had a strong moral compass. He was a good lawyer." Delacroix pressed his lips together for a moment, then finally sighed, rubbing his jaw. "But he liked his liquor."

Holloway's gaze sharpened. "You mean he had a drinking problem?"

"He had some issues, yes. He didn't leave because of a disagreement over a case. He left because, well—because he needed to." His voice softened. "I tried to help. We all did. But he was too proud to take it."

Holloway leaned back, exchanging another glance with me.

That was it.

That was the missing piece.

Grayson's departure wasn't about Peña's statement or a disagreement over ethics—not entirely. He'd been falling apart long before then.

Had Grayson actually remembered the case clearly when he'd signed that affidavit?

Or had he needed something to hold on to, a scapegoat for his own failures? And why, after twelve years of silence, would he suddenly come forward now?

I thought back to my meeting with him, the way he had poured a drink at 10 a.m. like it was nothing. The way his house had felt too still, too empty, like a place someone was simply existing in, not living.

At the time I had written it off—figured retirement had made him restless, that maybe a man like him needed an excuse to stay in the game.

But what if he had been rewriting history to suit his guilt?

Holloway didn't press Delacroix further, but I could tell he had the same thought I did.

Delacroix gave us both a measured look, his face calm once more. "I hope that helps clarify things."

Holloway nodded, slipping his notebook back into his briefcase. "We appreciate your time, Judge. We'll be in touch."

Delacroix nodded, looking as if he were about to turn back toward his chambers—but then he paused, his gaze shifting toward me.

His expression was thoughtful, almost curious.

"I know you," he said, his tone casual but certain. "You're the former ADA who left to go to the feds."

I blinked, caught off guard.

"Uh, yes, Your Honor."

"That was a high-profile exit. The Martin case, right?"

"Yes, sir."

Delacroix leaned slightly against the edge of his bench, arms crossed. "You remind me of myself when I was younger."

I stiffened slightly at that, not sure how to feel about it.

"I don't know if that's a good thing," I muttered before I could stop myself.

To my surprise, Delacroix chuckled. "That depends. If you let this job consume you, it'll eat you alive. If you control it instead of letting it control you, you'll do great things."

It was messing with me.

Holloway, standing beside me, clapped his briefcase shut. "Well, we won't take up more of your time, Judge."

Delacroix nodded. "Good luck with your case, Ms. Hayes. I think you'll do well."

I gave a tight smile. "Thank you, Your Honor."

With that, we turned and exited the courtroom, making our way down the long marble hallways and through the main doors of the courthouse. The moment we stepped onto the granite courthouse steps, Holloway let out a low chuckle.

I turned to him, narrowing my eyes. "What?"

"You're rattled."

"I am not rattled."

Holloway just smirked.

I crossed my arms, letting out a slow breath. "I just, wasn't expecting that."

"Expecting what?"

I gestured back toward the courthouse doors. "That. Him."

Holloway exhaled through his nose. "Yeah. He's good."

"Do you think he's faking?"

"I think he's a man who knows exactly what he's doing at all times."

That didn't make me feel any better. I stared out at the city skyline stretching beyond the courthouse plaza, my mind still spinning. Because the man we had just spoken to did not seem like the kind of man who would intentionally bury exculpatory evidence.

And that? That was a problem.

I turned to Holloway as we reached the bottom of the courthouse steps, shoving my hands into my coat pockets.

Holloway let out a slow exhale, rolling his shoulders like he was loosening tension that had built up. "I'll admit," he said, "I'm surprised he was as forthcoming as he was."

"But what he produces in the next day or so is really going to make up my mind. If he hands over detailed case notes, actual documentation proving that Peña's statement was turned over, then we're looking at an entirely different argument for the evidentiary hearing."

"And if he doesn't?"

"Then I won't be surprised."

I chewed on that for a second before Holloway asked, "What about you? What's your takeaway?"

I hesitated, then let out a breath. "He doesn't match what I expected after everything Kessler told us."

Holloway gave a short chuckle. "Perception is subjective."

I glanced at him, waiting for him to explain.

"People's views of their bosses, superiors, or competitors are shaped by their own experiences, their own resentments or biases. To some, Delacroix is a ruthless, self-serving prosecutor who bulldozed his way to a federal judgeship."

"Which is who Kessler sees."

Holloway nodded. "But to others? He's just a man who did his job well enough to climb the ladder. Success alone breeds resentment. People want to believe the worst about those who outrank them."

I mulled this over, unsettled by how easily Delacroix had undermined the certainty I'd been building about this case. After all our interviews and investigation, I'd been convinced of what happened. Now? I wasn't so sure.

Holloway checked his watch. "Go get some sleep. I'll reach out if we hear anything from Delacroix."

I nodded, adjusting my bag over my shoulder. "See you tomorrow."

With that, we parted for the evening, but my mind was still spinning. Despite Holloway's skepticism, I couldn't shake the unnerving feeling that there was more to this story than either Kessler or Grayson had told us—and that Vincent Delacroix might not be the villain I'd assumed he was.

CHAPTER
TWENTY-SEVEN

MY PHONE BUZZED as I was tossing my bag onto the passenger seat of my car.

Still on for dinner? Lisa texted.

I stared at the screen for a second, my brain taking a moment too long to process the message.

Shit. I had completely forgotten this was our monthly dinner date day.

I texted back quickly, *Yeah, I'll be a few minutes late, but I'm on my way.*

Lisa responded almost immediately. *Good. I was about to be offended.*

Chuckling to myself, I shook my head as I pulled out of the courthouse parking lot and headed toward the restaurant.

Lisa had picked Guard & Grace as our unofficial monthly spot. The moment I stepped inside, I was hit with the scent of grilled meat, truffle butter, and aged whiskey, the low hum of conversation blending with the clinking of glasses and silverware.

Dim lighting cast a warm golden glow over the space, and as always, the restaurant was packed. Well-dressed professionals filled the tables, some looking like they'd just wrapped up deals over drinks, others leaned in close, whispering about whatever courtroom drama had unfolded that day.

Lisa was already at the bar, swirling a glass of bourbon, her gaze flicking toward me as soon as I walked in.

"Finally," she teased. "I was starting to think you got pulled into another crime scene on the way over."

Smiling, I shook my head as I slid onto the stool next to her. "Give it time." I flagged down the bartender, ordering a whiskey neat. "In my defense, my day involved a federal judge, a missing witness statement, and potentially career-ending levels of misconduct."

"And that made you forget dinner?"

"Yes. That made me forget dinner."

She leaned forward on her elbows. "I'm intrigued. But first—let's eat."

I glanced around at the packed restaurant. "Do you think we can get a table?"

Lisa gave me a pointed look, then gestured toward the bar. "We're already at a table. Problem solved."

I let out a small chuckle, nodding.

As I reached for the menu, I finally allowed my shoulders to relax for the first time all day. Lisa was good at that—at making me slow down, even for just a meal. She swirled her bourbon in her glass, tilting her head as she studied me.

"I heard about the whole Special Prosecutor thing."

Glancing around to see if anyone was paying attention to our conversation, I sighed. "Of course you did."

Lisa laughed. "Come on, Alex. You know how things work. Word travels. Fast."

"Yeah, well. It's going."

"And how's Holloway?"

I frowned. "What do you mean?"

"I mean, I saw his picture in the newspaper." Lisa took a slow sip of her bourbon before arching an eyebrow. "He's not bad to look at."

I rolled my eyes. "Lisa."

"I'm just saying. Tall, dark, broody, lawyer-y. That's your type."

"I hadn't noticed."

Lisa gave me a flat look.

I huffed, shaking my head. "You're ridiculous."

"And you're avoiding the question."

I ignored her, focusing on the menu instead. After a few seconds, she relented, setting her glass down.

"Fine. Be boring." She said. "What's the latest on the case?"

I rubbed the bridge of my nose.

"The entire time, I thought we had it figured out. We were so sure that Delacroix had buried Peña's statement—that he was just another prosecutor cutting corners for a conviction, climbing the ladder off the backs of the cases he won."

Lisa nodded, waiting for me to continue.

"But we met with him today," I said. "And now I'm not so sure."

Lisa tilted her head. "What do you mean?"

"He just didn't act like a guy who was caught. He didn't get defensive, didn't deny anything outright, but he also didn't act like someone who had knowingly buried evidence and was about to have his entire career burned down."

Lisa let out a low whistle. "So now you think it wasn't him?"

"I don't know. Maybe it was, and he's just really good at playing it off. Or maybe it was a person working the case at the time—someone who had access to the evidence."

"And you'll know for sure in a day or so?"

"Yeah. He's supposed to go through his case notes and see what he finds. If he has records proving that Peña's statement was turned over, then we're dealing with something else entirely."

"Damn. So what's your gut telling you?"

My fingers drummed against the bar top as I considered the question. The face Delacroix had shown us today didn't match the villain I'd constructed in my head, but Holloway's skepticism lingered. Was I being manipulated by a master persuader, or had we been chasing the wrong target all along?

Then, finally, I admitted: "My gut is telling me this isn't over."

The bartender came back, and we both put in our orders—Lisa opting for a steak salad, while I ordered a burger. After the week I'd had, I needed the comfort food.

As the bartender walked away, I glanced at Lisa.

"Enough about me," I said, taking another sip of my drink. "How's your case going? The gun trafficking one, right?"

Lisa let out a long sigh, pushing her napkin to the side. "Yeah. And honestly? Not great."

I raised an eyebrow. "What's the holdup?"

She leaned forward, lowering her voice just enough to keep it from carrying. "We know someone's running illegal firearms through the city, but we can't track the shipments. The guns aren't moving through our usual intel sources, and anytime we get close to a seller, they go radio silent."

"No obvious distribution network?"

"Nothing that fits the typical mold. These aren't street gangs buying up weapons in bulk, and it's not a cartel pipeline either—at least, not the usual suspects. These weapons are showing up at crime scenes, but the trail leading to them keeps hitting dead ends."

I tapped my fingers against my glass, thinking. "What about the financials? You following the money?"

"Of course we are, Alex. I do know how to run an investigation."

Obviously frustrated, she sighed again. "The money laundering angle isn't helping. Shell companies are washing the cash clean before it hits any of our flagged accounts."

I sat back in my chair, letting the patterns come together in my mind. Lisa's description nagged at something in my memory—a conversation from weeks ago, something about money movement and connections that shouldn't exist.

The cold glass pressed against my palm as I lifted my drink, and suddenly it clicked.

I leaned forward. "Have you been able to track any of the people involved once they disappear? Where they end up?"

"That's the problem. We lose them completely. Some of them surface later, out of the country, but others? Gone without a trace. And then a few have ended up in jail, but we haven't been able to get anything out of them."

"What about prison calls?"

Lisa blinked. "Prison calls?"

"Yeah. If these guys are ending up inside, it's possible they're still coordinating. It's worth trying to listen in and see if you can get anything from them."

Lisa's brows furrowed. "That's actually not a bad angle."

I nodded, taking another sip of my drink. "Might be a long shot, but worth a try."

Lisa nodded, picking up her wine again. "See, this is why I keep you around, Alex. Your occasional moments of brilliance."

"Yeah, yeah. Just don't forget to buy me a drink when it pans out."

"Deal."

CHAPTER
TWENTY-EIGHT

HOLLOWAY SET down the discovery documents then reached for his phone.

"What now?" I asked, watching as he scrolled through his contacts.

"I'm going to let Hargrave know," he said, already hitting call. "If they're still planning to move forward with this petition, they need to know we've got an additional discovery item coming their way."

I nodded, crossing my arms as I listened to the line ring on speaker.

After a few moments, Hargrave picked up.

"Holloway. Wasn't expecting to hear from you this early in the morning. You calling to concede?" Hargrave's voice carried its usual smugness through the speaker.

Holloway's lips quirked upward, but he didn't take the bait.

"Not quite. We've got a new discovery item coming your way. Thought you'd want to know."

A pause filled the line—the silence almost tangible.

"What kind of discovery?" Hargrave finally asked, his tone sharpening.

Holloway glanced at me, then back at the phone.

"Prosecution's initial discovery disclosures. Including a Bates-stamped document identifying David Peña as a witness and turning over his statement to the defense. Looks like the evidence was provided, after all."

Another pause—longer this time.

I met Holloway's gaze, my stomach tensing as we waited for Hargrave's reaction.

When it came, it was surprisingly measured.

"Alright. Appreciate the heads-up."

Holloway's brow furrowed. "That's it? You're still moving forward with the hearing?"

"Yep."

Holloway shifted forward in his chair. "Hargrave, come on. You and I both know this changes everything. The entire foundation of your petition was that the statement was buried—that the prosecution suppressed it. This proves it was turned over. What's left to argue?"

"I guess we'll find out at the hearing, won't we?"

My pulse quickened. The response wasn't what either of us expected.

Hargrave wasn't just annoyed—he sounded genuinely unfazed.

Holloway pressed the issue. "Are you seriously telling me you still think you can win?"

A dry chuckle crackled through the speaker, but it lacked Hargrave's typical arrogance.

"See you in court, Holloway."

And with that, he disconnected.

For a few seconds, neither of us spoke. The air conditioning hummed softly in the background, punctuating the silence.

Holloway stared at his phone, his jaw tight, before placing it down on the desk. "What do you make of that?"

I ran my tongue over my teeth, taking a moment to consider. "You know him better than I do."

"And I can't make sense of it."

"Maybe he has something we don't."

"Meaning?"

"Meaning, Hargrave isn't stupid. He wouldn't keep pushing forward unless he had something up his sleeve. Something that clinches the case for them."

Holloway traced his fingers along his jawline, his eyes distant. "That's the only thing it could be."

I nodded, unease creeping up my spine like cold fingers. The confidence in Hargrave's voice—it didn't make sense unless he had an ace we couldn't see. Hargrave knew something we didn't. And if we didn't figure out what it was soon, it was going to blindside us at the hearing.

"Caffeine," I muttered, rising from my chair. The word hung in the air as a flimsy excuse for needing a moment to think.

I stepped into the hallway, the fluorescent lights harsh against my tired eyes. My mind raced, trying to piece together what Hargrave might know that we didn't. As I passed Erin's office, I noticed her door was open.

At her desk, she focused intensely on her laptop screen, fingers attacking the keyboard with purpose. I hesitated, then kept walking.

The breakroom was empty, the coffee pot already full. The rich scent filled my nostrils as I poured a cup, but my thoughts remained with Hargrave's puzzling reaction. And with Erin.

Our last conversation had ended poorly. The tension between us had been building for weeks, and I couldn't keep ignoring it. Not when it gnawed at me this way.

Cup in hand, I returned to the hallway. This time, I stopped at Erin's doorway and knocked lightly on the frame.

"Hey," I said, keeping my voice neutral. "Got a minute?"

Erin didn't look up. "I'm busy, Alex."

"I know. But I just—I don't want things to be like this between us."

At that, her typing paused, fingers hovering over the keyboard.

She finally glanced up, her expression guarded. "Like *what*, exactly?"

I took a breath, the coffee warming my palm. "Like this. Cold. Tense. We've been through too much for that."

Erin gave a short, humorless laugh. "Maybe if you didn't immediately assume that the entire office was corrupt, we wouldn't be here."

"I didn't assume anything, Erin. I followed the facts. And for weeks, those facts looked like something was being covered up by our own."

"Right," she countered, her eyes flashing. "And now that you've found the missing document, suddenly everything's fine?"

"That's not fair. I was doing my job."

"No, you were on a crusade. You came in here acting like you were the only one who cared about doing the right thing. Like the rest of us were just blind or complicit."

"That's not how I saw it."

"Of course it's not. Because you don't see how you bulldoze through things without thinking about the fallout. You think people like me don't give a damn about justice? You think Wexler is some cartoon villain, and that you're the only one who cares about the truth?"

The words stung, partly because I recognized the kernel of truth in them. I opened my mouth to respond, but before I could, a stern voice cut through the tension.

"That's enough."

We both turned as Callahan appeared in the doorway, his sharp eyes moving between us.

I lowered my gaze, my coffee suddenly interesting.

Callahan crossed his arms. "Mitchell, I need you in my office. Now."

Erin exhaled through her nose, but nodded, grabbing a notepad from her desk. Before leaving, she gave me one last look—not quite anger, not quite regret—and walked past me.

Callahan turned his attention to me. "Get back to work with Holloway. We need this case wrapped up."

I nodded, swallowing against the tightness in my throat.

Callahan departed, footsteps echoing down the hall. I stood there for a moment, feeling hollow. The distance between Erin and me had never felt so vast, and I wasn't sure how—or if—we could bridge it.

The coffee had cooled by the time I returned to Holloway's office. My steps dragged, weighted with the remnants of the confrontation.

Holloway glanced up as I entered.

He set down his pen. "What's wrong?"

I sank into the chair across from him. "Nothing."

Arching a brow, he pointedly eyed the coffee in my hands. "That took a while."

I stared into the dark liquid. "Yeah."

Holloway leaned back, giving me a knowing look. "Let's try again. What's wrong?"

I exhaled, drumming my fingers on the armrest. "Things aren't great with Erin."

Holloway didn't respond immediately. The silence stretched between us.

"She's the one who got me this job," I continued, my voice quieter than I intended. "She vouched for me, pulled strings, convinced me I'd be a good fit. But now …" I shook my head. "Now, she thinks I stormed in here accusing everyone of misconduct and betraying her trust."

"And do you think she's right?"

"No," I said carefully. "I think I've been doing my job. I think I had legitimate concerns, and I followed where the facts took me. But—" I paused, searching for the right words. "I think she's hurt. And I hate that."

Holloway observed me silently, his gaze thoughtful. The air conditioner kicked on again, filling the quiet with its soft hum before he finally spoke.

"You know, Hayes, I've been in this line of work for a long time. And if I've learned anything, it's that loyalty and truth don't always walk hand in hand."

I tilted my head, curious.

"You want to believe you can have both, that you can chase the truth while still keeping the people close to you happy. But the reality is, sometimes you can't. That doesn't mean you were wrong to chase the truth."

His words sank into me, resonating in places I didn't want them to. I studied Holloway as he returned to flipping through a file, seemingly at ease. Lisa's ridiculous comment from the other night flashed unbidden into my mind. *He's not bad to look at.*

Heat crept up my neck as I pushed the thought away. *Focus, Alex.*

I cleared my throat. "I guess we just need to focus on what's in front of us, right?"

Holloway nodded, glancing back up. "That's usually the best plan."

"Lawyers don't really have friends anyway, do they?"

Holloway considered this, his expression softening slightly. "I don't know," he said, meeting my eyes. "I'd like to think that you and I are friends."

The simple statement caught me off-guard, warmth spreading through my chest.

I expected him to follow it with something sardonic or dismissive. To make some cynical remark about how friendship and law don't mix. But he didn't.

"Yeah," I said, my voice softer than I intended. "I guess we are."

CHAPTER
TWENTY-NINE

THE FIRST DAY of the evidentiary hearing had arrived.

Holloway and I sat at the respondent's table, the government's side, ready to argue against the petition for habeas relief. The irony wasn't lost on me. Weeks ago, I'd been silently rooting for Ortega, convinced his case represented everything wrong with our justice system. Now, after digging through evidence, after finding the truth buried in those boxes, I wasn't sure what to believe about the man himself. His case had become a puzzle to solve rather than a crusade—and that shift unsettled me more than I cared to admit.

We had our strategy mapped out, our exhibits prepared, and after Delacroix's production of discovery, we felt confident in our position.

Still, as the courtroom filled, the familiar weight of anticipation settled in my chest. The wooden chair beneath me creaked as I shifted my weight, the sound lost in the quiet murmur of conversations around us.

This wasn't like a traditional trial. There was no jury.

This was akin to a bench trial, meaning Judge Pritchard alone would be deciding the outcome. But the reporters behind me—their pens poised, their gazes sharp—were a reminder that this was just as serious, if not more so, than a traditional trial.

In habeas petitions, the burden was on the petitioner—in this case, Gabriel Ortega, represented by Hargrave—to prove that his conviction had been unconstitutional, whether through a Brady violation, ineffective assistance of counsel, or some other legal defect.

The government's position—our position—was clear: defend the conviction, uphold the sentence. The mantle of that responsibility pressed down on my shoulders, heavier than I'd expected. Just weeks ago, I'd been advocating for cases like Ortega's. Now I was the one standing in opposition. Not because I thought Ortega was guilty, not because I had some vendetta, but because the law—and the evidence—said his conviction should stand.

The stakes were high, but without a jury, there wouldn't be emotional theatrics—only facts, law, and the judge's interpretation.

At precisely 9:00 a.m., the bailiff called the courtroom to order.

"All rise. The United States District Court for the Southern District of Texas is now in session, the Honorable Judge Warren Pritchard presiding."

The heavy double doors opened, and Judge Pritchard strode to the bench, his robe settling over his broad shoulders as he took his seat. His footsteps echoed against the polished floor, cutting through the tension in the room.

The moment he sat, the courtroom followed.

Pritchard wasted no time adjusting his glasses as he looked over the room.

"Good morning. This is the matter of Gabriel Ortega v. United States. Before we begin, let's establish some ground rules."

Holloway and I exchanged a brief glance as Pritchard continued, his voice carrying the quiet authority that came with years on the bench.

"There will be no jury in this hearing, as is standard for post-conviction relief proceedings. I will be ruling on the admissibility of evidence, the credibility of testimony, and the ultimate merits of the petition."

Pritchard's gaze swept the room, pale eyes missing nothing.

"Both parties will conduct themselves professionally and efficiently. I am not interested in grandstanding or delays. Understood?"

"Yes, Your Honor," I said alongside Holloway, my voice mingling with his.

From the petitioner's table, Hargrave nodded, his expression unreadable. Beside him, Gabriel Ortega sat stiffly, his posture tense, eyes flicking around the courtroom like he was cataloging every detail.

He looked different than I imagined. His dark hair was buzzed short, his jaw sharp, face lined with the kind of hardness that only came from surviving on the inside. But his eyes—calculating, assessing—held a sharpness that told me he hadn't been broken.

The man folded his hands in front of him as if restraining himself. But there was an undercurrent of something else, something coiled, waiting, beneath his stillness. Not the desperate innocence I'd projected onto him from those petitions, but something more complex. More dangerous.

I found myself wondering again about the night of the robbery. What had really happened? What had been his role? The shifting narrative left me uncertain where the truth lay.

"Very well," Pritchard said, setting down his pen. "Since the petitioner bears the burden of proof, I invite counsel for Mr. Ortega to proceed with their opening statement."

Before turning forward, I glanced over my shoulder. And froze. Erin was sitting in the audience. She was a few rows back, arms crossed, her expression unreadable. Our eyes met for a fraction of a second—long enough for my stomach to twist with guilt and regret. I turned back around before I could let her distract me, focusing instead as Hargrave approached the podium.

"Thank you, Your Honor," Hargrave said smoothly, his voice carrying through the silent courtroom.

He strode to the podium, adjusting his cuffs before placing his hands firmly on either side. He surveyed the courtroom, the faint scratch of pens against notepads filling the air as reporters in the back rows scribbled furiously, sketch artists already at work capturing the scene. No cameras, per Judge Pritchard's ruling, but the press was still here, watching, documenting.

I exhaled slowly, keeping my focus forward. The last thing I needed was to get distracted by the press. Their presence prickled at the back of my neck like an unwelcome touch.

Holloway had told me it was a foregone conclusion that the media would be here. He wasn't wrong.

I dragged my attention back to Hargrave as he squared his shoulders, looking every bit the polished, high-profile defense attorney. He was still pretending there was a jury. So much for no grandstanding.

"May it please the Court," Hargrave began, his voice steady, measured. "The petitioner, Gabriel Ortega, stands before you today as a man convicted of felony murder—a conviction that, we contend, was secured through constitutional error."

I clasped my hands together on the table, readying myself for him to launch into the Brady violation argument. The cool surface of the table grounded me, focusing my thoughts.

"The government would have you believe that this case was litigated fairly, that Mr. Ortega was given a full and zealous defense at trial," Hargrave continued. "But the evidence that has come to light through this Court's expansion of the record and additional discovery tells us otherwise."

I glanced at Holloway, whose jaw was set tight, his hands curling into fists on the table. The tension in his posture mirrored the knot forming in my own gut.

Hargrave continued, his gaze flicking to Judge Pritchard. "What we now know, Your Honor, is that the failure to introduce David Peña's exculpatory testimony—the single most crucial witness for the defense—was not a result of prosecutorial misconduct, as we initially believed."

I stiffened, alarm creeping up my spine. Something in Hargrave's tone warned me he was about to pivot.

"But rather," Hargrave went on, turning slightly to glance at Ortega at the petitioner's table, "a failure on the part of the defendant's court-appointed attorney."

My stomach dropped. The courtroom seemed to tilt slightly as the implications crashed through me.

Judge Pritchard's brow lifted slightly, and he leaned forward, the leather of his chair protesting softly.

"Counsel," the judge said, his voice laced with mild irritation, "are you trying to tell me that you're resting the claim of a Brady violation?"

A ripple of movement went through the reporters seated behind us, pens scratching faster against notebooks. The air in the courtroom felt suddenly charged, electric with the unexpected turn.

Hargrave gave a measured nod. "Yes, Your Honor."

Silence hung thick in the air before Hargrave continued.

"Through the Court's authorization of discovery, we now understand what actually happened in Mr. Ortega's case. And that rests on the ineffective assistance of counsel provided by his defense attorney, Gregory Bard, at trial. The government did, in fact, disclose David Peña as a witness. But Mr. Ortega's lawyer—the man assigned to protect his interests—ignored that evidence. He never called Peña. Never even investigated what he had to say."

I barely had time to react before I heard Holloway's chair scrape back, and he was on his feet.

"Your Honor," Holloway said, voice taut, "this is an ambush. This wasn't discussed or raised as the primary argument. We came in prepared to litigate a Brady claim."

Hargrave gave him an unbothered glance. "On the contrary, counselor, ineffective assistance of counsel was included as one of the claims for relief in the original petition."

Pritchard sighed, flipping through his notes before nodding. "That's true."

I tightened my grip on my pen, my mind racing to catch up with the sudden shift in terrain. The cool confidence in Hargrave's demeanor told me this wasn't improvisation—he'd planned this move.

We had anticipated Brady. We'd prepared for Brady. We'd developed arguments, gathered evidence, and crafted our defense around Brady. In my head, I could almost hear the sound of our carefully constructed case crumbling.

Ineffective assistance was something entirely different. It moved the spotlight from the prosecution to the defense. From systemic failures to individual incompetence. From our office to a man who was probably long retired by now, who might not even remember the details of a case from years ago.

My throat tightened as I flipped through my notes, searching for anything we had on Gregory Bard. There was nothing substantial—just mentions of his name, his role. We'd dismissed him as a peripheral figure, someone whose actions weren't central to our defense. Now Hargrave had made him the linchpin of their entire argument.

The Strickland standard flashed through my mind—the two-pronged test for ineffective assistance. First, prove the attorney's performance was deficient. Second, show that the deficiency prejudiced the defense.

If Bard had truly ignored a key exculpatory witness whose testimony could have changed the outcome of the trial, Hargrave might clear both hurdles.

We had talked about the claim, sure, but we hadn't actually dug into it. Hadn't interviewed Gregory Bard, Ortega's original defense attorney, or anyone from his team. We hadn't gone through his trial strategy, his case notes, or his decision-making process.

Mentally I kicked myself. Bard should have been our first stop after finding Delacroix's discovery document. He would have known why Peña was never called. He could have told us if there was a legitimate reason—if Peña had credibility issues, if his testimony conflicted with Ortega's account, if there was some strategic calculation behind the decision. That information would have been crucial.

But we'd been so focused on disproving the Brady claim that we'd never considered the ineffective assistance angle might become central. Now we were scrambling, outmaneuvered by Hargrave.

The threshold for overturning a conviction based on ineffective counsel was high, but if Hargrave had evidence of gross incompetence—especially if he had a witness to back it up—then we were in a very different fight than the one we'd prepared for.

Holloway exhaled sharply beside me, dragging a hand down his face before gesturing toward the judge.

"Your Honor, we request an adjournment. This is a major shift in the petitioner's argument, and we need time to properly prepare."

A few murmurs rippled through the courtroom like wind through tall grass.

Pritchard sighed, then shook his head.

"Request denied. We're already here. We might as well hear it."

CHAPTER THIRTY

"MR. HOLLOWAY, would the respondent like to make an opening statement?" Judge Pritchard asked.

I glanced at Holloway, but he was already looking at me. He paused in a silent exchange that I couldn't quite interpret before Holloway pushed back his chair and stood.

"Your Honor," Holloway said, buttoning his suit jacket. "At this time, if the Court is not inclined to grant a recess to allow us to better prepare for this unexpected shift in the petitioner's argument, then the government will not be in a position to present any sort of case."

My mouth went dry. I dug my fingernails into my palm to keep from visibly reacting. Was he serious? Holloway—confident, measured, always-ten-steps-ahead Holloway—was openly admitting defeat before we'd even begun? Part of me wanted to yank him back into his seat, to insist we could adapt, improvise. The other part recognized the strategy—showing the judge just how blindsided we'd been, planting the seed that Hargrave had deliberately ambushed us.

"That's a shame," Pritchard replied.

The courtroom went dead silent, except for the faint scratching of reporters' pens at the back of the room. Pritchard tapped a pen against his desk, the soft rhythm like a countdown. My heart kept pace with each tap as I waited for his ruling, the tension coiling tighter in my chest.

"I am not inclined to grant a recess at this time, Mr. Holloway. However, given the length of the petitioner's case, it is likely that the court will adjourn for the day before the respondent is required to present. Perhaps tomorrow you'll be ready."

A few murmurs rippled through the audience. I forced my breathing to remain even, though my mind was already calculating how much time that would give us—twelve hours? Maybe sixteen if we worked through the night?

Holloway didn't blink. "In that case, Your Honor, the government would like to defer its opening statement until such time as we present our case."

Pritchard gave him a measured look, then nodded. "Very well. Petitioner, call your first witness."

I exhaled as Holloway took his seat beside me. I leaned toward him, lowering my voice. "That was a bold move."

Holloway's lips quirked upward, his eyes still trained ahead. "Let's hope it pays off."

I settled back into my chair, the blood rushing in my ears. The hearing had barely begun, and already we were playing defense—a position I'd rarely found myself in and never enjoyed. I inhaled deeply, trying to center myself. This wasn't just about winning anymore. It was about salvaging what we could from Hargrave's surprise attack.

Hargrave stood, buttoning his jacket. "The petitioner calls Gregory Bard to the stand."

A brief stir moved through the courtroom as a man in his late fifties stood from the gallery, making his way toward the witness stand. Each step he took seemed deliberate, almost performative in its steadiness.

Gregory Bard. The former Federal Public Defender who had represented Ortega at trial. The man who, according to Hargrave, had single-handedly undermined his client's case. My eyes tracked his every movement, searching for tells, for cracks in his composure. His suit hung slightly loose at the shoulders, as if he'd recently lost weight. His tie sat a fraction off-center, a small imperfection in an otherwise meticulous appearance.

His hair was salt-and-pepper, combed neatly to the side. He didn't look nervous, exactly, but his eyes darted once toward Ortega before fixing straight ahead—a brief acknowledgment of their shared history, perhaps. Or guilt? I couldn't be sure. His face settled into careful neutrality, the kind of detached professionalism I'd seen from seasoned defense attorneys who had long since learned how to mask their real emotions.

But underneath that practiced calm, I sensed tension. The way his hand gripped the railing as he stepped into the witness box. The slight tightness around his eyes. This wasn't just another day of testimony for him. His reputation was on the line.

The clerk stepped forward. "Please raise your right hand. Do you swear to tell the truth, the whole truth, and nothing but the truth, under penalty of perjury?"

Bard raised his hand. "I do."

The clerk nodded, stepping back.

Judge Pritchard turned to Hargrave. "Proceed, Counselor."

Hargrave took his time, stepping up to the podium and adjusting his papers with practiced precision. The theatrical pause was calculated—building anticipation, making everyone in the courtroom lean forward slightly.

"Mr. Bard, let's start at the beginning," he said. "You were appointed as Gabriel Ortega's defense attorney for his trial, correct?"

Bard nodded once, his expression composed but guarded. "That's correct."

"How many felony murder cases had you handled at that point?"

"Dozens, maybe more. I've been practicing for thirty years."

"Then you'd agree that you were experienced enough to handle this case?"

"Of course."

I studied the micro-expressions flitting across Bard's face. The slight tightening around his mouth. The way his shoulders hunched forward almost imperceptibly. His posture should have been open, confident—a seasoned attorney proud of his experience. Instead, he seemed ... defensive. Like a man anticipating a blow.

Most attorneys I knew would have seized the opportunity to elaborate on their credentials, to establish authority. Bard's clipped answers told me he was trying to minimize his time on the stand. That alone set off warning bells in my mind.

Hargrave stopped pacing and turned back to the witness stand. "Let's talk about David Peña."

Bard shrugged, his fingers twitching on the armrest of the chair. "Alright."

"Are you aware that Mr. Peña was a key witness—a neutral third party who provided a statement contradicting the prosecution's theory of the case?"

Bard's fingers tightened on the armrest, knuckles whitening slightly. "I'm aware."

"And yet, you chose not to call him at trial."

Bard paused, his gaze never leaving Hargrave's. "It was a strategic decision."

My pulse quickened. There it was—the defense every attorney falls back on when questioned about their trial choices. Strategic decision. The magic words that usually shield lawyers from ineffective assistance claims.

But something in Bard's delivery felt hollow. The phrase came too quickly, too practiced, lacking the conviction of genuine strategic thinking. I'd made plenty of strategic decisions in my career—some brilliant, some disastrous—but I always believed in them at the time. Bard sounded like he was reciting a line from a script.

I reached for my legal pad, scribbling a note: *Why is he so defensive about a "strategic" choice he should be confident in?*

Hargrave leaned forward, his voice even but pointed. "Explain the strategy."

Bard shifted in his seat, the leather creaking beneath him. "Mr. Peña was not the most credible witness. He had a history."

"What kind of history?"

"Prior run-ins with law enforcement."

Hargrave tilted his head. "So you're telling this court that you made a strategic decision not to call a neutral third-party witness because of his record?"

"That's right."

Hargrave nodded, his expression subtly transforming. The practiced nod of a predator who's spotted weakness in its prey. "We'll revisit that in a moment. Anything else you included in this strategy of yours?"

"We had to weigh his potential impact."

"You mean the impact of testimony that could have exonerated your client?"

Bard's mouth pressed into a thin line. "That's not what I said."

"No, but it's what you're avoiding saying."

I watched Bard closely, the pieces clicking together in my mind. The nervous gestures. The clipped answers. The defensiveness that seemed disproportionate to the questioning. These weren't the reactions of a lawyer standing by a difficult but principled decision. This was something else—something that raised the hairs on the back of my neck.

I leaned toward Holloway, keeping my voice low. "Bard's hiding something."

Holloway kept his gaze locked on Bard, studying him with the focus of a chess player calculating five moves ahead.

Then, without looking at me, he murmured, "You should take cross."

I blinked. "What?"

Holloway finally turned to me, his voice barely above a whisper. "If you think you can draw something out, I'm not going to stop you from trying."

My pulse skipped. This wasn't just offering me a chance to participate—this was Holloway entrusting me with one of our few opportunities to salvage this hearing. The weight of that responsibility settled on my shoulders, equal parts terrifying and exhilarating.

I nodded once. "Alright."

Hargrave turned back to Bard, pacing before stopping at the podium, his hands resting on either side. His voice remained steady, calculated, each question peeling away Bard's weak defense.

"You've said that not calling Peña was a strategic decision," Hargrave said. "One based on credibility. Let's break that down. Did you, at any point, meet with Peña yourself?"

Bard hesitated before clearing his throat. "No, I did not."

"So you never personally evaluated his credibility?"

"No, but I reviewed his statement and—"

Hargrave held up a hand. "Just so we're clear—you, the lead defense attorney, never actually sat down with a witness who had potential exculpatory information in a felony murder trial?"

Bard's jaw tightened. "That's correct."

Another ripple of murmurs from the press row. I resisted the urge to turn around, but I could practically feel the reporters leaning forward, scribbling frantically. The headline was writing itself: *Defense Attorney Never Met Key Witness.*

Every law student learns the fundamental rule of witness preparation: never put someone on the stand without meeting them first. Bard had just admitted to violating that cardinal principle with potentially the most important witness in his case. It wasn't just bad practice—it was professional negligence.

Hargrave let that sit for a moment before continuing. "Let's move on to what you did do. You mentioned his criminal record earlier. Did you, at any point, investigate Peña's background?"

"Of course." Bard straightened, as if grasping at a more confident answer. "We looked into his record and found a history of interactions with law enforcement."

Hargrave paused, then turned toward the gallery as if inviting them to pay attention.

"Could you define 'interactions with law enforcement' for the court?"

Bard hesitated again. "He had previous citations."

"Citations." Hargrave raised an eyebrow. "You mean traffic violations?"

"Among other things."

"*Things...* such as?"

"A parking ticket," Bard admitted, his voice clipped.

Hargrave blinked, feigning surprise. "A parking ticket." He turned to the judge. "Your Honor, for the record, I'd like to clarify that Mr. Bard's reason for dismissing a key exculpatory witness was that he once failed to feed a meter."

A soft chuckle rippled through the gallery. Even Judge Pritchard's lips twitched as if fighting back amusement.

I watched Bard's composure crumble in real time. A flush crept up his neck, spreading to his ears. His right hand formed a tight fist, then relaxed with visible effort. This wasn't just embarrassment—it was the panic of a man whose professional justifications were being systematically dismantled in open court.

And suddenly, I understood. Bard wasn't defending a strategic choice—he was scrambling to rationalize a mistake. One he'd likely buried and justified to himself for years. I'd seen it before: attorneys who convince themselves that their failures were actually calculated decisions.

Hargrave pressed on. "You stated that Peña's testimony would not have benefited your client's case."

"That's correct."

"And yet, the prosecution's entire case hinged on one cooperating witness—a witness who had a vested interest in testifying against Mr. Ortega to secure his own deal. But a neutral third-party witness—one without a deal on the table—wasn't good enough?"

Bard clenched his jaw. "We made the best decision with the information we had at the time."

Hargrave nodded, as if considering the answer. Then he delivered the final blow.

"Tell me, Mr. Bard," he said, voice casual but razor-sharp. "If you had the chance to do it again, would you call Peña to the stand?"

The courtroom seemed to hold its breath. The scratch of pens stopped. The air conditioning faded to white noise. All eyes locked on Bard.

His face froze, color draining from his cheeks. His gaze darted briefly to Ortega, then back to Hargrave. The silence stretched, becoming its own kind of testimony. I could almost see the internal battle playing out—professional pride versus the crushing weight of hindsight.

Finally, Bard exhaled, his shoulders sagging forward in defeat.

"Yes."

That single syllable fell like a gavel. In that moment, he'd admitted everything: that his decision hadn't been strategic at all. That he'd made a mistake. That a man had spent years in prison, possibly because of that mistake.

Hargrave turned toward Judge Pritchard, eyes gleaming with triumph. He didn't need to say anything more—Bard's admission spoke volumes.

"No further questions, Your Honor."

The words hung in the air, heavy with implication. Hargrave had methodically dismantled Bard's defense, exposing the fatal flaw in Ortega's original trial. If that testimony stood unchallenged, the petition would almost certainly be granted.

I straightened in my chair, my mind already racing through potential lines of questioning. Hargrave might have drawn blood, but the witness was still on the stand.

And now it was my turn.

CHAPTER
THIRTY-ONE

"THE RESPONDENT MAY CROSS-EXAMINE THE WITNESS," Judge Pritchard announced, his voice cutting through the tension.

I rose from my seat, my mind racing with possibilities. Holloway's nod of encouragement followed me as I approached the podium, the weight of responsibility settling on my shoulders. The courtroom felt unnaturally quiet, as if everyone was holding their breath.

One of the things I appreciated about federal court—unlike the theatrical freedom of state courts—was the structure. You stayed at the podium, maintaining a certain formality and decorum. Even Hargrave, for all his showmanship, had mostly respected this unwritten rule. The solid wood beneath my fingertips provided an anchor as I gathered my thoughts.

Adjusting the microphone, I met Bard's gaze directly. His eyes darted away briefly before returning to mine—a small tell that strengthened my resolve. There was something beneath the surface of his testimony, something that didn't add up. The practiced answers, the defensive posture, the shifting attribution of decisions.

"Mr. Bard," I began, keeping my voice measured but firm, "let's talk about your trial strategy—more specifically, the decision not to call David Peña."

Bard exhaled through his nose, already bracing himself. "I already testified to that, Counselor. It was a strategic decision."

"Right. You said he wasn't credible."

"Correct."

"But you never actually interviewed him, did you?"

A beat of silence filled the courtroom. The scratch of reporters' pens paused, waiting.

Then, a reluctant, "No, I did not."

"So, to clarify—you made the strategic decision not to call a witness whose testimony could have directly contradicted the government's case, without ever actually speaking to him."

A murmur rippled through the press row, the sound of whispers and shuffling notepads.

Bard's jaw tightened, but he nodded once. "That's correct."

Gripping the edges of the podium, I leaned forward slightly. "Why?"

"Because—because we didn't think he'd hold up under cross-examination."

I caught it immediately. *We*. Not *I*. After spending his entire testimony taking sole responsibility for the decision, the slip was revealing. My pulse quickened as I sensed a crack in his carefully constructed narrative.

"We? Or you?"

His mouth pressed into a thin line, the skin around his eyes tightening. He recognized his mistake.

"Tell me something, Mr. Bard. A witness list is part of standard trial preparation, correct?"

"Yes."

"And typically, a defense attorney will investigate every potential witness who might help their client's case?"

"Yes."

"But in this case, you didn't." I paused, watching as he shifted uncomfortably in his seat. "Was that your call?"

Bard's fingers tapped once against the armrest of the witness stand. "Yes."

"So you're telling this Court that you alone decided not to even interview Mr. Peña?"

"Yes."

"Then who told you they didn't think Peña would hold up on cross?"

His eyes flickered to the gallery for a split second, then back to me. The pause stretched just long enough to be noticeable.

"I can't remember."

"You can't remember who said it, but you remember it being said?"

"Yes."

Now I felt it—the electric current that runs through a courtroom when testimony begins to unravel. Bard was hiding something crucial, and each question brought me closer to uncovering it. His discomfort was palpable now, his composure cracking at the edges.

"Did the Court appoint another Federal Public Defender to represent Ortega?"

He furrowed his brow. "No, just me."

"Did you usually work with another attorney on cases like this?"

"No. We don't get the resources that some other offices get."

That was a clear dig at the USAO. And he wasn't wrong. The Federal Public Defenders did some of the most important work in this nation and often were given some of the least resources. But I still wanted to know why he'd said "we."

"Did anyone else influence your strategy on this case, Mr. Bard?"

His Adam's apple bobbed, his face now tight with discomfort. My instincts hummed with certainty—I was closing in on something significant.

"Mr. Bard," I said, my voice steady but sharp. "Did someone influence you not to use David Peña's testi—?"

"No."

He'd already answered before the question left my mouth. Too quick, too defensive. The interruption itself was telling.

If he'd worked with someone else, if his decision had been part of a genuine strategic collaboration, Hargrave's ineffective assistance claim would weaken. All I needed was proof that the decision not to call

Peña had been reasonable—that it had been discussed, evaluated, and determined to be the best approach for Ortega's defense.

"Are you sure?" I asked. "There was no one else?"

His fingers gripped the edge of the stand. "Yes."

"Lying under oath is perjury, Mr. Bard."

The tension in the room thickened, tangible as a gathering storm. The press scribbled furiously behind me. Judge Pritchard leaned forward with heightened interest, and even Hargrave, seated at the petitioner's table, looked intrigued.

I lowered my voice. "So I'll ask you again—did someone instruct you not to introduce Peña's statement?"

Bard's jaw twitched.

His eyes flickered between me and some point behind my shoulder. "I—" he started, then stopped, his breathing shallow.

I waited, letting the silence work for me. Sometimes the most powerful tool in cross-examination isn't the next question, but the space between questions—the pressure of expectation that builds until the truth spills out.

The silence was heavy, suffocating.

Finally, Bard let out a shaky breath, his shoulders slumping as if a weight had been lifted.

"I was bribed."

The words landed like a thunderclap.

Judge Pritchard's eyes snapped up, his pen freezing mid-note. Hargrave stood, his expression a mix of shock and calculation. The courtroom erupted with whispers, the sound building like an approaching wave.

I stood perfectly still, my hands gripping the podium for support as the implications crashed over me. I'd been looking for a strategic explanation, a collaborative decision—not outright corruption.

My throat went dry.

I'd just handed Hargrave exactly what he needed—ironclad proof that Ortega's representation had been not just ineffective but criminally compromised. After weeks of searching for the truth, I'd found it—only to realize it undermined our entire position.

For a moment, I felt disoriented. When I'd first started digging into

Ortega's case, I'd been driven by the belief that he might be wrongfully imprisoned. I'd wanted justice for him. Now I'd uncovered evidence that might free him, but while representing the government's opposition to his release.

The ethical and professional lines blurred before my eyes. Which side was I on? What outcome was I fighting for?

Hargrave cleared his throat. "Your Honor, given this revelation, I would request an immediate recess."

Judge Pritchard, still staring at Bard, sighed sharply. "I think that would be best," he muttered, rubbing his forehead. "Court is in recess for the next fifteen minutes."

The gavel struck, and the courtroom erupted in whispers.

I remained frozen at the podium as Hargrave turned to speak with Ortega, their heads bent close together. The look on Ortega's face wasn't the vindication I'd expected, but something more complex—relief mixed with what almost looked like concern.

Holloway touched my arm to get my attention. "Come with me."

I followed him out of the courtroom, bracing myself for his reaction. I had just torpedoed our argument in one swift stroke, potentially destroying any chance we had of winning. But instead of confronting me in the hallway, he pushed open the door to a side conference room and motioned me inside.

I set an alarm on my phone for fifteen minutes, determined not to lose track of time amid the chaos.

"Look, before you say anything—"

"That was impressive as hell."

I blinked. "What?"

The corners of his mouth turned up slightly. "I didn't think you'd get him to break that fast."

I gawked at him. "I just handed Hargrave his victory on a silver platter."

Holloway shrugged, leaning back against the table. "The truth is the truth. That's why we're here, right?"

I stared at Holloway, still expecting him to reprimand me for my courtroom revelation. And yet, he wasn't angry. In fact, he was smiling like I had just executed a brilliant legal strategy rather than potentially losing our case.

I narrowed my eyes. "You're not mad?"

He shook his head. "Nope."

I scoffed. "I just got a federal public defender to admit on the stand he was bribed—in a case that we're supposed to be arguing *against* overturning."

But even as I said it, I realized the contradiction in my own position. Weeks ago, I'd been outraged at the idea of Ortega remaining in prison if his conviction was tainted. I'd wanted to uncover the truth, to right whatever wrong might have been done. Now that I had, shouldn't I feel vindicated rather than defeated?

And Holloway—he'd brought me onto this case precisely because he sensed something wasn't right. He'd wanted me to dig deeper, to question everything. This revelation was exactly what he'd been searching for.

Holloway crossed his arms, amusement flickering in his eyes. "Alex, this isn't about winning a case. It's about finding out what went wrong and making it right." Holloway tilted his head, watching me. "You got to the truth, Hayes. That's what matters."

Something about the way he said it sent a shiver through me. He wasn't looking at me like someone who had just sabotaged our position. He was looking at me with genuine admiration—like he saw me as more than just a competent attorney, but also as someone who understood what justice truly meant, even when it was complicated and messy.

Suddenly, my pulse sounded too loud in my ears. The room felt smaller than it had a second ago.

Holloway was still leaning against the table, his posture relaxed but purposeful. His sleeves were pushed up, revealing muscular forearms. The dim lighting accentuated the strong lines of his jaw, the quiet intensity in his eyes, and the slight smirk tugging at the corner of his mouth.

"This is a problem," I muttered, looking away from him and beginning to pace.

His smirk widened. "What is?"

"The fact that you're not furious and I'm the one spiraling."

Holloway let out a low chuckle, but his eyes never left mine. "If it helps, I can pretend to be mad if that's what you need."

"You're impossible."

"You like that about me."

As I opened my mouth to fire back the alarm on my phone buzzed. I jerked back, blinking as the reality of where we were came crashing back. Recess was over.

Grabbing my phone, I silenced the alarm as I exhaled, trying to steady myself.

Holloway grinned like he knew exactly what had almost happened between us—what I'd almost admitted to myself. He pushed off the table, rolling his sleeves back down as if nothing had happened at all.

I cleared my throat. "So, what now? Now that we know Bard was bribed?"

Holloway exhaled, tracing his fingers along his jawline. "We play this by ear. See what Hargrave does next."

"You don't think we should—"

"There's not much we can or should do at this point," Holloway said, voice low. "Hargrave has what he needs. If I were him, I'd be pushing for the judge to vacate the conviction outright. And if that happens, we're done here."

I nodded, still reeling from the last fifteen minutes. The case had just shifted completely and so had something else—something between Holloway and me that I wasn't quite ready to name.

CHAPTER THIRTY-TWO

WE MADE it back to the courtroom just as the bailiff's voice rang out, calling the court back to order. Judge Pritchard adjusted his glasses and looked directly at both counsel tables.

"Counsel, in my chambers. Now."

Hargrave shot us a brief glance. Neither Holloway nor I reacted as we gathered our things and followed behind as Pritchard swept out of the courtroom, his black robe billowing as he moved.

The courtroom buzzed with low murmurs from the press, but no one dared speak too loudly as the heavy wooden doors shut behind us.

Pritchard turned on Hargrave the moment the door shut. "Did you know?"

Hargrave blinked. "Excuse me, Your Honor?"

"Did. You. Know?" Pritchard repeated, stepping forward. "Did you know your client's public defender was bribed?"

Hargrave straightened his suit jacket. "No, Your Honor. I did not. And surely, if I did, I would have brought it up in my opening statement."

Pritchard exhaled, rubbing his temple. "This is turning into a goddamn circus."

He turned and paced briefly, his displeasure radiating in waves. "I run a courtroom, not a goddamn media frenzy. And right now, I have reporters out there scrambling to write headlines about a bribed public defender and a case that should have been cleanly litigated over a decade ago."

Neither Holloway nor I spoke. We weren't about to draw the judge's attention to us while he was still tearing into Hargrave.

But after a moment of tense silence, Pritchard's sharp gaze swiveled toward us anyway.

"And what the hell do you two intend to do now?"

I stiffened, glancing at Holloway, expecting him to answer first.

But he didn't. He looked back at me, leaving the door wide open.

I swallowed, then took a breath.

"Your Honor," I said carefully. "The U.S. Attorney's Office intends to bring charges against Mr. Bard for obstruction of justice under 18 U.S.C. section 1503, as well as honest services fraud under 18 U.S.C. section 1346."

Pritchard's expression didn't change, but I could see his jaw tighten.

I continued. "However, the petition before the Court still requires a ruling. We don't dispute that. But given these unexpected developments, we request time to prepare our response."

Pritchard leaned back against his desk, considering.

The room was dead silent.

Hargrave folded his arms, watching Pritchard closely, as if trying to gauge which way he'd lean.

Pritchard let out a slow exhale and pushed off his desk. "You'll get your time," he said, pointing a look at me. "But not much. Be ready tomorrow morning."

I nodded. "Understood, Your Honor."

Pritchard sighed, rubbing his temple again. "Jesus Christ," he muttered under his breath. "Should never have listened to Leland."

That last sentence gave me pause, but there was nothing I could say. I knew it was my involvement that caused Leland to pressure Pritchard in the first place.

The judge straightened and motioned toward the door. "You're all dismissed. Get out of my chambers."

He didn't need to tell us twice. The moment the door clicked shut behind us, I let out a long breath, glancing up at Holloway. He was watching me with the faintest hint of a smile.

"Nice work, Hayes," he said, his voice low.

I shook my head. "I have no idea how we're supposed to spin this tomorrow."

"Yeah," he said, rolling his shoulders as if shaking off the weight of the conversation. "We'll figure that out. For now, let's just get out of here."

We made our way back to the courtroom, knowing that tomorrow we'd have to fight a case we were not prepared to argue.

We took our places at counsel table. I chanced a glance over at Hargrave and Ortega, but both seemed calm as ever. Judge Pritchard took his seat at the bench, rubbing his temple before exhaling, like he was already regretting every decision that led him here.

Glancing over the room, his steely gaze landed on the press row, where reporters sat with pens poised against their notepads. With thinly veiled reluctance, he reached for his gavel.

"This Court will be in recess until tomorrow morning at 9:00 a.m. At that time, the respondents will present their case."

I stood, taking a measured step forward.

"Your Honor, I would like to request that this Court issue a warrant for the immediate arrest of Gregory Bard."

A hush fell over the courtroom.

Pritchard's eyes flicked to me, his expression shifting into something between curiosity and amusement. "Right now?"

"Yes, Your Honor. Based on the sworn testimony that was just heard in open court, Mr. Bard admitted to accepting a bribe in connection with a federal trial. That alone constitutes obstruction of justice under 18 U.S.C. section 1503 and honest services fraud under 18 U.S.C. section 1346. Given that he is now aware he will be charged, he presents a flight risk."

A beat of silence followed.

Then Pritchard let out a slow, begrudging chuckle.

He leaned forward, eyes sharp with something almost like approval. "You're a bold one, Ms. Hayes."

I kept my expression neutral, but my pulse kicked up. I could have asked for this in chambers, where it would have been handled quietly and the judge wouldn't have felt the pressure of an audience. But I wanted to ask in open court.

Yes, it could have pissed him off. Judges didn't like being put on the spot. But Pritchard was the kind of judge who cared about optics, about being on the right side of the law in front of a room full of reporters. And judging by the furious scribbling of pens in the press row, my gamble had paid off.

Pritchard finally nodded. "Alright, Counselor. You've got my attention. Draft the warrant."

I grabbed a legal pad from my table, flipping to a clean page and writing quickly, laying out the probable cause based on Bard's own testimony.

Holloway's gaze bored into me, but he didn't interrupt. Within a few minutes, I ripped the page from the pad. I stepped forward and handed the paper to Judge Pritchard's clerk, who handed it to the judge. He scanned it, then reached for his pen, signing his name with deliberate finality.

He handed it to the clerk, who then handed it back to me, and I caught him exhaling, shaking his head again. I took a steadying breath, then turned toward the back of the courtroom, where Gregory Bard sat still, pale and rigid with tension, clearly realizing his morning had taken a turn for the worse.

The U.S. Marshals were already waiting along the side of the courtroom. I stepped forward and handed one the signed warrant. He looked at it and nodded before turning towards Bard.

"Mr. Bard," he said, "I am placing you under arrest for obstruction of justice, pursuant to 18 U.S.C. section 1503, and honest services fraud under 18 U.S.C. section 1346."

A murmur erupted among the press row.

Bard stiffened. "This is ridiculous," he muttered, shaking his head. "I was just doing my job."

"Sir, please stand up," the Marshal instructed. The command hung in the air, leaving no room for debate.

Bard hesitated, but eventually pushed himself up from his seat, his expression flickering between defiance and panic.

The blood roared in my ears as the Marshal recited the Miranda warnings. "You have the right to remain silent. Anything you say can and will be used against you in a court of law. "You have the right to an attorney. If you cannot afford an attorney, one will be provided for you."

The Marshals stepped forward, taking positions on either side of Bard.

"Do you understand these rights as I have read them to you?"

Bard's jaw tightened, his breathing shallow. "Yeah. I understand."

Bard was quickly placed in handcuffs. The reporters erupted into a frenzy, shouting for statements as the Marshals led him away.

The weight of the moment settled over the courtroom like a heavy blanket.

A federal public defender had just been arrested—in open court, in front of an audience, in front of the press—and the warrant had my name all over it. My throat tightened at the magnitude of what had just happened.

Turning toward our table, my eyes met Holloway's. His expression shifted from unreadable to decidedly impressed.

Then his lips curved into that familiar smirk. "Well, that'll make the headlines."

Adrenaline thrummed beneath my skin as we gathered our materials and headed toward the courthouse doors.

The second we stepped outside, reporters immediately surrounded us. Camera shutters clicked rapidly, voice recorders thrust forward, and a barrage of questions hit us from every direction.

"AUSA Hayes, do you have a comment on the arrest?"

"Does this change the government's position on the petition?"

"Was Judge Pritchard aware of the bribery before today?"

"Did you suspect Bard was compromised from the start?"

I barely had a second to adjust before Holloway stepped in line behind me, giving me space to address the press corps. The subtle positioning wasn't lost on me—he was deliberately ceding the spotlight, letting me take credit for what had just happened in that courtroom. Interesting. The Holloway I thought I knew would have jumped at the chance to be the face of such a dramatic moment. Instead, he was handing me the microphone. The realization sent an unexpected warmth through me even as the cameras continued to flash.

I paused my stride, squared my shoulders, and looked head on at the gathered press around us, no longer wincing from the twenty cameras pointed in my direction.

"As you all witnessed today in open court," I said, "Mr. Bard admitted under oath that he was bribed in connection with Gabriel Ortega's case. Based on his testimony, Judge Pritchard issued a warrant for his arrest, and he is now in federal custody."

A flurry of questions followed, but I raised a hand, cutting through the noise.

"I cannot comment on the specifics of an ongoing investigation, but I can assure you that the U.S. Attorney's Office is committed to upholding the rule of law. When we discover misconduct—regardless of where it originates—we will act accordingly."

More voices shouted over each other, but I didn't stop to engage. I turned to Holloway, who gave me a nod of approval before we pushed through the journalists, making our way down the steps.

As soon as we reached the bottom, he leaned in. "That was a hell of a moment."

I huffed out a breath, my pulse still racing. "You could've jumped in, you know."

"Nah," he replied, unlocking his car. "You handled it just fine."

CHAPTER THIRTY-THREE

"BACK TO THE OFFICE?" Holloway asked as we reached his car in the courthouse parking garage, finally escaping the swarm of reporters who'd followed us halfway down the block.

Leaning against the passenger door, fatigue hit me like a physical weight. The thought of returning to that building—with its harsh lighting, curious stares, and Erin's lingering disappointment—made my shoulders tense.

"I don't think I can handle that right now," I admitted.

Holloway nodded, unlocking the doors with a beep. "We could find a coffee shop, go over our strategy for tomorrow."

I winced. "I've had enough time in public for one day."

He glanced at me over the roof of the car. "Fair point."

As we slid into our seats, the quiet of the car was welcome respite after the chaos of the courtroom. I stared at the concrete wall ahead of us, mind racing through options. My house wasn't an option—my father was way too nosey, and the last thing I needed was to explain this case and our working relationship to him.

"What about your place?" I asked, gaze fixed firmly on the windshield, trying to keep my voice casual.

Holloway turned to me, one eyebrow arched. "What *about* my place, as opposed to yours?"

I cleared my throat. "I'm living with my dad right now."

A hint of a smile played at the corners of his mouth as he started the engine. "My place it is, then."

The car pulled out of the parking space, our exit from the garage mercifully reporter-free. As we merged into downtown traffic, I wondered briefly if I'd just crossed some invisible line. But the thought of being somewhere quiet, somewhere neutral yet private, outweighed any concerns about propriety.

The drive was mostly silent, punctuated only by the occasional navigation instruction from Holloway's phone. Houston's familiar landscape slid past my window—glass office buildings giving way to residential neighborhoods, palm trees casting long shadows in the late afternoon sun.

I watched Holloway's profile, the sharp line of his jaw, the way his fingers tapped against the steering wheel at red lights. The events of the day left us both wired despite our exhaustion, the adrenaline still coursing beneath the surface.

Twenty minutes later, we pulled into the driveway of a modest Craftsman-style house in the Heights. Not what I'd expected from Holloway at all.

"This is you?" I asked as we got out of the car.

He shrugged, keys jingling in his hand. "Temporary rental. The USAO keeps it for visiting attorneys."

I followed him up the walkway, taking in the neatly trimmed hedges and wrap-around porch. It was charming in a way I wouldn't have associated with Holloway, whose sharp suits and precise mannerisms had always suggested high-rise living.

Inside, I set my bag by the door, surveying the space as Holloway pulled out his phone. The house was nice—modern, but not sterile. Well-kept but impersonal, no framed photos, no clutter. Corporate accommodations more than a home.

It made sense. Working out of D.C., this was just a temporary setup, a place to sleep between assignments. The decor was neutral but stylish, with warm lighting and dark wood furniture that gave it a quiet, understated charm.

Not far from the U.S. Attorney's Office, maybe a fifteen-minute drive, but it felt like a world away from the chaos we'd left behind.

"What do you want?" he asked, already scrolling through the menu for a nearby Thai place.

"Pad see ew," I said. "Extra spicy."

Holloway arched a brow. "Didn't peg you for a spice person."

"Didn't peg you for a guy who lives in an actual house. Figured you'd be a penthouse apartment type."

"Nah. Too predictable."

Rolling my eyes, I stepped into his kitchen. It was surprisingly well-equipped for someone who didn't live here permanently—gleaming appliances, a knife block, even a small herb garden on the windowsill.

Holloway moved past me to a small wine rack in the corner, selecting a bottle with practiced ease. The gentle pop of the cork echoed in the quiet kitchen as he poured two glasses, sliding one across the counter to me.

"For the record," he said, gesturing at me with his glass, "this is me being a responsible boss. You flipped an entire federal case on its head today. That earns you takeout and a drink."

I smirked, taking the glass. "That's very generous of you."

"Some say I'm a giver."

Shaking my head, I scoffed, but there was a warmth behind it. For the first time all day, I felt like I could breathe. The tension that had coiled around my spine since morning finally began to loosen. I perched on a stool at the counter as Holloway leaned against the opposite side, swirling his wine in slow, thoughtful circles.

"Let's talk strategy for tomorrow," he said, his tone shifting to something more serious.

I ran a hand through my cropped hair. "We're at a dead end with the bribery angle."

Holloway nodded. "Right. We don't know who paid him or why."

Reflexively, I tapped my nails against the counter. "If this was just about throwing a case, we'd see some obvious pattern. But this was targeted. Someone needed Ortega to go to prison."

"So whoever paid him off was either directly involved in what Ortega was wrongfully convicted of—"

"Or they needed to make sure he didn't talk."

Holloway nodded in agreement, but there was no immediate solution, no clear lead to chase. It left an itch under my skin.

"Where does that leave us?"

Holloway took a long sip of wine, considering. "We have no case."

I frowned. "You mean—"

"I mean we can't, in good conscience, continue fighting against Ortega's petition when we know his attorney was bribed to sabotage his defense."

I closed my eyes briefly, letting that settle.

We had no legal foot to stand on anymore. Ortega had been screwed over—there was no denying it now. Whether he himself was innocent or not, didn't matter anymore.

I stared into my wine glass. "So that's it? We're just going to lose this one?"

Holloway tilted his head. "You say that like it's a bad thing."

"Isn't it?" I met his gaze directly. "Don't get me wrong, I want justice for Ortega if he was wrongly convicted. That's why I started digging in the first place. But we still don't know who bribed Bard or why. There's something bigger happening here."

His eyes lit up with understanding. "So it's not about winning or losing the hearing. It's about finding the truth."

"Exactly." I took another sip of wine. "I hate walking away with half the story."

Holloway studied me, a slow smile spreading across his face. "You really can't let go once you've got your teeth into something, can you?"

"Not my style," I admitted.

He grinned, but there was something more behind it—not just amusement, but genuine respect. Like he saw the relentless, unyielding lawyer I had fought to become.

And for once, I wasn't being told to calm down or let it go. He appreciated it.

And that? That threw me off completely.

Before I could overanalyze the moment, there was a knock at the door.

Our food.

Holloway went to grab it, the door opening and closing within seconds. He returned to the kitchen and set the bags on the island. We pulled out the containers of steaming Thai food.

"This place is the best," he said. "So quick." He slid mine over before opening the lid to his dish.

I popped open the container of pad see ew and grabbed a pair of chopsticks, shoving them between the noodles and taking my first bite. The heat hit immediately, settling warm in my chest.

Holloway sat across from me, watching as I chewed. "Good?"

I nodded, still swallowing. "Really good."

He dug into his own food. "You keep surprising me, Hayes."

Before taking another bite I peered up at him. "How?"

"Most people in your position don't push like you do. They don't dig this deep. You see something wrong, and you go after it, consequences be damned."

I swallowed, my chest tightening at the unexpected compliment.

The way he watched me—eyes intent, focused completely on what I was saying—made me feel truly seen. Not as a problem to manage or a junior attorney to mentor, but as an equal whose drive and determination he genuinely admired.

I set my chopsticks down, holding his gaze. "That's not something I'm used to."

"What?"

"People not being angry at me for standing up for what I believe in."

He rested his forearms on the counter, his eyes locked on mine.

"I'm not angry at you," he said. "Not at all."

There was a beat of silence, thick and charged. The space between us felt smaller, the pull between us undeniable. My heart picked up speed.

Holloway reached for his wine glass, but instead of picking it up, his fingers brushed against mine.

I sucked in a sharp breath, my pulse pounding, but neither of us moved away.

This was bad.

This was dangerous.

This was not where my head needed to be. And yet—

His eyes flicked down to my mouth, and before I could even think, before I could convince myself this was a terrible, terrible idea—

I leaned in.

And so did he.

CHAPTER THIRTY-FOUR

THE NEXT MORNING, the courtroom buzzed with tension as we walked in. Reporters were already settled in the back rows, murmuring amongst themselves, their pens poised for whatever chaos today would bring.

I kept my gaze straight ahead, acutely aware of Holloway's presence beside me. The memory of last night—his lips on mine, the way his hands had framed my face, how quickly we'd both pulled away after that initial, electric moment—lingered between us like an unspoken question.

We'd spent the rest of the evening in awkward professionalism, discussing the case while carefully avoiding any mention of what had just happened. When I'd left his place, the air still crackling with unresolved tension, we'd agreed to deal with one crisis at a time. The hearing first, then ... whatever this was.

So now I compartmentalized, filing away the memory of his touch in favor of the legal battle ahead—or rather, the battle we weren't going to fight. After a sworn confession of bribery in open court, there was no argument left for us. We weren't here to oppose the petition anymore. We were here to let justice take its course.

I prepared to walk to the counsel's table, but someone caught my attention before I could take my seat.

"Alex."

I jumped and turned to find Erin standing beside me. Her expression was hard to read, but her eyes were sharp, scanning me with a mixture of concern, anger, and something else I couldn't quite place.

"Can we talk?" she asked, her voice low.

I glanced at Holloway, already settling in at the table, and sighed. "Sure."

We stepped off to the side, near the hallway leading to chambers.

The second we were out of earshot, Erin didn't hold back. "Everyone in the office is furious."

I crossed my arms. "Yeah, I figured as much."

"You didn't just make waves, Alex. You took a goddamn wrecking ball to everything. You had an arrest warrant issued in open court—as the most junior AUSA in the office—without even consulting anyone first. Do you have any idea what kind of political mess you just made for all of us?"

I stared at her, my frustration boiling over. After weeks of digging for the truth, of fighting against resistance at every turn, of finally uncovering a genuine miscarriage of justice, *this* was what concerned her? Office politics?

"So I'm supposed to apologize for arresting someone who confessed to corruption on the stand?" My voice came out sharper than intended. "A man who admitted to accepting a bribe to deliberately tank a defendant's case?"

"I'm not saying he didn't deserve to be arrested, Alex." Erin let out a sharp breath. "I'm saying there's a process. You don't just go rogue like that!"

"I didn't go rogue. I consulted with Holloway—who, may I remind you, was specially assigned to investigate this case. And I informed the judge before taking action." My hands clenched at my sides. "What was I supposed to do, Erin? Ignore it? Pretend I didn't hear it? Let him walk out of court and give him a chance to disappear before anyone could act?"

"You should have gone through the chain of command. This isn't the state system anymore. This is the feds. There are protocols, and you burned right through them."

"If they want to fire me for doing the right thing, then they should feel free to do so."

Erin's expression flickered for half a second, like she wasn't sure whether to be frustrated or impressed. "I don't know what's going to happen to you after this."

"Then I guess we'll find out."

Without another word, I turned on my heel and walked back toward the counsel's table, my heart hammering against my ribs. Between Holloway and now Erin, I was beginning to wonder if any relationship in my life would survive this case intact.

Holloway looked up from his legal pad as I sat down.

"That looked intense," he said, raising a brow.

"That was about how I'm probably not going to have a job after this." I reached for my pen just to have something to hold onto, trying not to notice how his cologne still lingered in my senses from yesterday.

"I'm not worried about that for you."

I scoffed. "I'm glad someone isn't."

He leaned in, lowering his voice. "You did the right thing, Hayes. And if they don't see that? They're the ones who should be worried."

I held his gaze for a beat longer than necessary, searching for any hint that he was thinking about what had passed between us. His eyes held the same intensity as when he'd looked at me across his kitchen counter, but now carefully masked by professional concern. We were both playing the same game—pretending last night hadn't shifted something fundamental.

Then the bailiff's voice rang out. "All rise."

Judge Pritchard entered the room, his expression unreadable as he took his seat on the bench.

As the courtroom settled, I caught a flicker of movement from the corner of my eye. Erin stood near the back, arms crossed, watching. Then she turned and walked out.

Turning back toward the bench, I forced myself to lock in on what was happening in front of me. Judge Pritchard let out a slow breath, looking toward our table.

"Counsel for the respondent, you may present your case."

Holloway and I stood in tandem. I kept my shoulders squared, my pulse steady, even though what we were about to do felt foreign. Holloway buttoned his suit jacket and stepped toward the podium, his voice calm and unwavering.

"Your Honor, given the totality of the circumstances and the information that came to light yesterday in open court, the United States cannot argue that the petitioner has failed to meet the standard required for post-conviction relief."

A ripple of whispers moved through the gallery, but Holloway continued without pause.

"As such," Holloway continued, "we withdraw any and all objections to the petitioner's request for relief."

Pritchard's brows lifted, but he nodded once before shifting his gaze toward Hargrave.

"Mr. Hargrave, do you have anything further before I issue a ruling?"

Hargrave shook his head, rising to his feet. "No, Your Honor. The petitioner stands on the record before you."

Pritchard leaned forward, lacing his fingers together.

"Very well. While the federal government has withdrawn its opposition, the Court is still required to determine whether the petitioner has met his burden."

Just because we didn't contest a petition doesn't mean the petitioner automatically wins. The burden of proof in habeas proceedings remained with the petitioner. Even without opposition, the Court had to make an independent finding that Ortega's constitutional rights had, in fact, been violated.

Judge Pritchard continued, his voice measured.

"A petitioner seeking relief under 28 U.S.C. section 2254 must demonstrate that their conviction or sentence resulted from a violation of their constitutional rights. The standard, as established in *Strickland v. Washington* requires the petitioner to prove both that: counsel's performance was objectively unreasonable; and this deficient performance prejudiced the outcome of the trial."

He paused, glancing down at the case file before him.

"In light of the testimony presented in open court, the record establishes that Mr. Bard, the petitioner's trial counsel, accepted a bribe that resulted in his failure to investigate or present key exculpatory evidence on behalf of the defendant.

"By doing so, trial counsel deprived the petitioner of his Sixth Amendment right to the effective assistance of counsel. Given the nature of the evidence withheld, the Court finds that, absent counsel's deficient performance, there is a reasonable probability that the outcome of the trial would have been different. As such, the petitioner has met his burden under Strickland."

Hargrave remained still at his table. Beside him, Ortega sat motionless, his face a careful mask of restraint, though I caught the slight tremor in his clasped hands. After years of fighting for this moment, he seemed almost afraid to believe it was happening.

I gripped the edge of the table, my stomach tightening. This was what I'd wanted from the beginning—justice for someone who hadn't received a fair trial. And yet, the victory felt complicated, weighted with questions about who had orchestrated this miscarriage of justice, and why.

Judge Pritchard looked up, his expression unchanging.

"Accordingly," he said, "the petition for a writ of habeas corpus is granted."

A murmur of voices erupted from the gallery, but Pritchard continued speaking.

"The petitioner's conviction is hereby vacated. The respondent shall immediately coordinate with the Bureau of Prisons for the petitioner's release."

Another gavel strike.

"Court is adjourned."

The sound of the gavel echoed through the courtroom, final and decisive. Justice had been served—at least in this narrow sense. Ortega would be freed, his conviction overturned. But the larger questions—who had bribed Bard, and why they'd wanted Ortega silenced—remained unanswered.

As the courtroom erupted into movement around us, Holloway's hand brushed against mine under the table, a brief, deliberate touch that sent electricity up my arm.

"Good job, Hayes."

CHAPTER THIRTY-FIVE

THE LEGAL CHAMBER exploded into motion the second Judge Pritchard struck the final gavel. Reporters scrambled to their feet, trying to capture quotes, reactions, anything.

Voices overlapped in a chaotic chorus.

"AUSA Hayes! Do you have a comment?"

"Mr. Holloway, will the government appeal this decision?"

"Ortega, how do you feel about your release?"

The press row buzzed with urgency. A story had just exploded before them, and the race to publish it had begun. I turned toward Holloway, who already looked like he was calculating the fastest way out of here.

"Side witness room," he muttered. "Now.

I nodded, already moving. Slipping through the side door, we left the chaos behind as we stepped into the quiet, dimly lit room.

Holloway shut the door, muting the sounds of the press frenzy outside. I leaned against the table, exhaling slowly, the adrenaline still humming under my skin. The air between us felt charged, weighted with everything that had happened since yesterday—the case, the kiss, the careful distance we'd maintained this morning.

Holloway watched me for a moment before finally speaking. "So."

I glanced up at him. "So?"

He folded his arms. "I'm trying to figure something out about you."

His expression wasn't harsh, but my pulse quickened anyway. Were we finally going to address what had happened in his kitchen? I tried to quell the butterflies in my stomach.

"And what's that?" I asked, leaning into the conversation.

"This isn't just about the law for you, is it?"

"What do you mean?"

He stepped in closer. "I've worked with a lot of lawyers, a lot of prosecutors. People who say they're in it for the right reasons—justice, fairness, the Constitution." He tilted his head. "But I've never met anyone as unshakably moral as you."

"That sounds like a nice way of saying I bulldoze my way into trouble."

"There's that too. But it's more than that." His expression turned curious, almost searching. "Where does it come from? Why are you like this?"

The question caught me off guard. I'd expected him to bring up our almost-moment from last night, not dive into my psyche. But somehow, this felt more intimate—him wanting to understand not just what I did, but why I did it.

I let out a slow breath, staring at the dark wood grain of the conference table. I'd never really talked about this—not to anyone at the office. But something about the way he asked made me want to answer.

I met his gaze. "My mother."

Holloway's brow furrowed in question.

"She was a prosecutor. A damn good one. She worked cases involving organized crime, corruption, human trafficking. And one day, she vanished."

Holloway's expression shifted, his casual stance straightening slightly. "Vanished without a trace?"

I swallowed, forcing the words out. "She was investigating a trafficking ring—one with powerful connections. As far as I can tell, she knew they were pulling strings at high levels—judges, politicians, law enforcement. She left me a voicemail the night before she disappeared, saying she'd uncovered something big."

Holloway said nothing right away. His eyes rested on me, his usual smirk absent, replaced by something more solemn.

I crossed my arms over my chest. "For years, I thought I'd never get answers. Then last year at the DA's office, I stumbled across a case file that connected to her investigation—names, locations, patterns that matched what little I knew about what she'd been working on."

The overhead fluorescent light flickered slightly, casting momentary shadows across the room. Outside, the muffled voices of reporters still echoed in the hallway. The scent of old paper and furniture polish hung in the air—the unmistakable smell of justice processed and filed away.

"Erin had always been trying to recruit me to work with her. Never actually thought I'd take her offer, but the federal connections might lead somewhere. Coming here wasn't just about advancing my career—it was about finding answers. I know she's gone, but I don't know how or why or who's responsible. I thought this job might help me figure it out." I let out a short, humorless laugh. "Instead, I got stuck reviewing habeas petitions all day."

A long silence stretched between us. Finally, Holloway spoke, his voice lower than before. "You really think that trafficking ring is behind your mother's disappearance?"

"I know they are. I just don't know how."

Holloway exhaled, running a hand through his hair.

"That's a lot bigger than you, Hayes."

"I know."

"And you're still chasing it?"

"Wouldn't you?"

For a second, he studied me. "Yeah," he replied. "I would."

A small, tired smile tugged at my lips. "Then I guess I won't be in this alone."

Holloway shook his head. "I guess you won't."

The chaos of the courtroom was still waiting for us. But in that moment, standing in the quiet, I felt something I hadn't felt in a long time. Like I wasn't fighting this war alone anymore.

Holloway leaned against the edge of the conference table, arms crossed, watching me carefully. "Maybe the best place for you to do this sort of research isn't at the U.S. Attorney's Office."

My chest tightened, the words hitting me harder than I expected. After everything that had happened with the case, with Erin, with the office at large—was he suggesting I should leave?

"What do you mean?" I asked, straightening my posture defensively.

"That's not the kind of case where you can just sit at a desk and wait for answers to fall into your lap." He tilted his head, considering his words. "You need to be able to get out there, talk to people, track down sources that aren't going to show up in a case file."

"And you don't think I can do that at the USAO?"

Holloway shrugged, but his eyes stayed sharp and assessing. "You want to find out what really happened to your mother? You're not gonna solve that sitting in one place. You need flexibility."

Holloway wasn't just talking about investigating my mother's death. He was talking about me—my career and future. Like maybe I wasn't meant to be chained to a desk litigating cases, but out in the world chasing the things that mattered. My chest tightened at that thought. I wasn't sure if he was wrong.

I sighed, shaking my head. "For the time being, I have a job to return to."

"For now."

I shot him a look. "And before I go burning more bridges, I want to talk to Gregory Bard. If he was bribed, I need to know by who, how, and why. And once we see what comes back from that, then we'll figure out what's next."

Holloway studied me for a moment longer, then nodded. "Let's see what he has to say."

A silence fell between us, the elephant in the room growing larger by the second. We'd still managed to avoid any mention of last night—the way we'd leaned toward each other, the brief touch of his lips against mine before we'd both pulled back, startled by our own actions.

"About last night," I finally said, unable to let it hang between us any longer.

His eyes locked with mine. "I was wondering when we'd get to that."

"It was—"

"A mistake?" he offered, his expression carefully neutral.

"I was going to say 'complicated.'"

The corner of his mouth twitched upward. "Complicated works too."

"I'm not sure what it meant," I admitted. "Or what happens next."

He took a step closer. "It meant that there's something here," he said, gesturing between us. "But the timing is ..."

"Terrible," I finished for him.

"Epically bad," he agreed.

I couldn't help the small laugh that escaped me. "So what do we do?"

"We focus on Bard. Figure out who was behind this. And then—" his eyes met mine, serious now, "—we see where things stand."

Relieved to have it acknowledged, even if we were essentially agreeing to put it on hold, I nodded.

After about an hour of secluding ourselves in the witness room, discussing potential angles for questioning Bard and strategizing our next steps, Holloway finally checked his watch and let out a breath.

"Think it's safe to leave?" he asked.

"Only one way to find out."

Standing and stretching from the long, tension-filled hearing, we cautiously cracked the door open.

The noise from the courtroom had died down, the press presumably scattered to file their stories. But just as we were about to step out, Sarah Grimes, Judge Pritchard's clerk, who I'd met during my first week, spotted us.

Her lips twitched in amusement. "Are you two hiding from the reporters?"

Holloway and I exchanged a look before turning back to her.

"Yes," we said at the same time.

As I adjusted the stack of files in my arms, trying to balance them with my bag, Sarah reached over and grabbed one off the top. "Let me help," she said.

"Thanks," I muttered.

Sarah laughed under her breath, gesturing us toward a side exit. "There's a back way out."

We followed her through a small, nondescript hallway, down a narrow staircase, and through a service exit that led directly to the parking lot.

As soon as we stepped outside I inhaled deeply, the fresh air filling my lungs.

"Remind me to send Sarah flowers," I muttered as we made it to the car.

"Or a bottle of whiskey," Holloway added.

We loaded into the car, but before I could even think about dodging the office for the rest of the day, reality sank in.

Sighing, I rubbed the bridge of my nose. "I can't stay away any longer. I need to go back. Face the music."

Holloway exhaled, nodding. "Yeah. Me too."

I looked over at him. "You don't have to, though. The case is over for you, isn't it?"

Hesitating, he shook his head. "Not quite."

I frowned. "What do you mean?"

Holloway exhaled, running a hand over his jaw. "We still don't know who bribed Bard. And until I can definitively rule out that it wasn't someone at the prosecutor's office, I'm not ready to give my status report to Main."

"You think it could have been someone from inside?"

He didn't answer right away. "I think until I know for sure, I'm not closing this out."

"I guess that means I still have a job for a little while."

Holloway glanced at me, his tone gentle but firm. "I meant what I said about your job being safe. If anyone tries to push you out because of this, we can get the judge involved."

I smiled faintly, but shook my head. "No, it's okay. I don't want anyone fighting my battles for me."

His gaze softened. "I get that."

I took a deep breath. "I'm just ... trying to find a place where I don't have to sacrifice my own morals to fit in and do the work. If this isn't that place, then I'll figure out where it is."

Holloway studied me for a moment, before he finally nodded. "I respect that," he said quietly.

The car hummed to life as Holloway turned the key, the afternoon sun glinting off the windshield. We'd weathered a storm together—one neither of us had anticipated when we first met. Whatever happened next, something fundamental had shifted between us.

"When all this is over," I said, my voice softer than I intended, "do you think we can …keep in touch?"

"Yeah," he said, his eyes meeting mine with unexpected warmth. "I'd really like that."

CHAPTER THIRTY-SIX

THE U.S. ATTORNEY'S Office was quieter than usual when we walked in. Most people had either gone home for the day or were buried in their work, trying to catch up on whatever wasn't related to the chaos we had just unleashed in court.

For a second, I thought maybe I could just sneak in, grab my things, and slip out before anyone decided to corner me. That fantasy shattered the second we stepped into the main hall.

Nathan Callahan stood near the entrance to the hallway leading to his office, arms crossed, his expression unreadable.

The second he saw me, his voice was low and firm. "Hayes. My office. Now."

Holloway took a step forward, his posture shifting, but I cut him off with a look before he could say anything.

"I've got this."

Holloway didn't look convinced. "Alex—"

"I'm not afraid to stand up for what I did."

Holloway's jaw ticked, but after a beat, he nodded.

I turned back to Callahan, who was still watching me impatiently.

"Let's go," I said, keeping my chin high.

As I followed Callahan down the hall, I braced myself. This was it. I was going to get fired. Actually fired this time. But I had already accepted it.

I had gone into that courtroom knowing what I was doing. Knowing that my actions might have consequences. At the same time, a small voice in my head kept reminding me that I'd been working directly with Holloway, a special prosecutor assigned to investigate potential issues within our office. That had to count for something, right? His entire mission was to find problems, and we'd uncovered a major one.

Still, I'd acted boldly and publicly. I'd taken steps that sent shockwaves through the entire legal community. No matter how justified, there would be fallout.

But I had also known that it was the right thing to do. And if that meant losing my job, then so be it.

Callahan opened the door to his office, motioning for me to step inside. Though he'd been in and out over the past weeks, with Wexler often taking point on day-to-day operations, Callahan was still the ultimate authority here. I sat down, my spine straight, already preparing myself for the inevitable speech about how I had been reckless, insubordinate, irresponsible—

But then I looked up.

And Callahan was smiling. "For the official record, you totally acted insubordinate by getting that warrant and arrest done without official permission from the office."

I swallowed. "Right."

His smile widened.

"But off the record?" He let out a low chuckle, shaking his head. "That was completely badass."

I gawked at him. "What?"

Callahan let out a short laugh, standing upright.

"Look, Hayes. I knew exactly who you were when we hired you." He gestured toward me. "You come with a certain reputation."

I groaned, rubbing my forehead. "Great."

"No, not like that." Callahan stopped, looking at me. "Some people might not like it—but I'm not one of those people."

I frowned. "So, you're not furious?"

He grimaced. "Don't get me wrong, I'm still going to have to deal with the fallout from what you did."

I winced.

"But I do think you should stand up for what you believe in. You did the right thing."

Callahan wasn't mad.

I wasn't getting fired.

If anything—he *respected* what I had done.

"And it doesn't hurt that you basically got the office cleared of misconduct."

I let out a short laugh, shaking my head. "Almost. Holloway is still investigating where this bribe came from. If someone in the original prosecutor's office was involved in paying off Bard to tank Ortega's defense, that's a whole other level of corruption."

Callahan waved a hand. "I'm not really concerned about that angle. I've known everyone in this office for years, and I'd stake my reputation on their integrity."

I studied him for a second. He seemed genuine in his defense of his colleagues, but the certainty in his voice still made me pause. How could anyone be that sure?

Callahan nodded, his expression turning more serious. "Look, Alex. There are going to be people in this office who don't like you for this. Some of them are going to hold grudges. That's just the way it works."

"I figured."

"But here's the thing." Callahan leaned forward, resting his hands on the desk. "If you keep playing the long game, keep doing your job the way you just did it in court, you're going to be just fine."

For the first time all day, I actually believed that.

I nodded, but hesitated before standing. "There's something I need to ask."

Callahan sighed, leaning back in his chair, as if already anticipating my next move.

I pressed forward anyway. "Why did Richard Langford even file the reply brief in the first place? And why was Wexler giving me so much extra work?"

Callahan studied me for a beat, then let out a dry chuckle. "As I said—you have a certain reputation that people are aware of."

"What do you actually mean by that?"

"It means the more someone tells you no, the more you're going to dig in." He shrugged. "I think Wexler figured if he kept you loaded down with other petitions and steered you away from Ortega, you'd get the hint and leave it alone. Obviously, he underestimated your persistence."

I exhaled sharply. "So he was deliberately trying to distract me from Ortega's case? That's not exactly comforting."

"It's not right," Callahan admitted. "But habeas petitions *are* usually meritless. That's drilled into us early. I think that mindset impacted his judgment. He didn't want you wasting time on something he assumed was nothing."

I shook my head, still feeling a nagging unease. "And what about Langford? Why would he file that reply brief defending our position when there was no basis for it?"

Callahan's expression shifted slightly, something careful in the way he answered.

"That was a surprise to me too," he admitted. Then, lowering his voice, he added, "And—this doesn't leave my office—but it's being looked into."

My stomach tightened. "Looked into by who?"

Callahan gave me a pointed look. "Not something you need to worry about right now, Hayes."

Reading between the lines, I nodded slowly, standing. "Thanks."

"One more thing, Hayes."

"What's that?"

"How did you figure out the bribe? Did you already know, or did you just get lucky?"

Pausing, I thought back to that moment in court, when Bard sat on the stand, squirming under pressure. "I didn't know," I admitted. "I just...got a feeling."

Callahan raised a brow.

"The way he was avoiding my questions—he wasn't outright lying, but he wasn't telling the truth."

"It was damn impressive." Callahan leaned forward, sunlight from the window catching the silver in his hair as he tapped his fingers thoughtfully on the desk. "I'm not keeping you on habeas cases any longer."

My brows shot up. "Wait, what?"

"You've got good instincts, Hayes. That whole thing in court? That wasn't just good lawyering—that was a sixth sense for knowing when someone was full of shit." He tilted his head. "That's not something you can teach. And I'd be an idiot not to make use of it."

"So what exactly are you offering me?" I asked, hardly daring to believe where this was going. "A different position?"

"I want you in the courtroom as much as I can get you. No more drowning in post-conviction petitions."

I exhaled slowly, a small smile tugging at the corner of my lips. That sounded pretty damn good.

Callahan nodded once, like that was that.

But then I hesitated. "Look," I said, "I really want to see the case through on Bard. If you'll let me."

Callahan gave me a measured look, but he didn't dismiss it outright. "Why?"

"I want to find out who bribed him and why." I shook my head. "It just seems so odd—committing a federal crime just to put someone like Ortega in prison. Why bother?"

Callahan's lips dropped, replacing his expression with something more serious. "You think it's bigger."

"I do."

"This is gonna give me a headache, isn't it?"

"Probably."

Callahan let out a reluctant exhale. "You've got the green light."

A surge of satisfaction went through me, but before I could fully enjoy the victory, Callahan held up a finger.

"But."

I waited, bracing for whatever was coming.

"You're not working on this alone," he said. "You're going to work on this with Erin."

I blinked. "With Erin? Why not with Holloway?"

"James is a special prosecutor ordered to investigate misconduct within our office specific to the Ortega petition. That would be outside the scope of the court's directive."

I suppressed my groan of frustration. Erin and I were barely speaking. After the confrontation in the courtroom hallway, I was pretty sure she wanted nothing to do with me. And now we were being forced to work together on a high-profile corruption case—one that I had created in a way she fundamentally disapproved of.

It was like Callahan was deliberately throwing gasoline on an already raging fire.

I didn't let my irritation show, but Callahan gave me a pointed look. "I know you two are friends," he said, "or at least, you were. And she's one of the best AUSAs we have. If you're going to move up the ranks here, she's exactly the person you should be learning from."

I exhaled through my nose, keeping my expression neutral. "Understood."

Callahan studied me for a second longer, and then his lips quirked slightly.

"And," he added, with entirely too much amusement, "I think this will help clear the air between you two."

I shot him a look, but before I could stop myself, I muttered, "So, I guess you have that sixth sense, too."

Callahan scoffed, shaking his head. "Nah, you two just yell really loudly at each other."

I huffed out a laugh as I pushed the door open. "Glad to know how that looks from the outside."

"Like a damn headache," he called after me.

I didn't argue.

CHAPTER
THIRTY-SEVEN

THE NEXT MORNING, I sat at my desk, flipping through Bard's case file while my eyes glazed over. I was struggling to figure out where to begin when the door to my office swung open without warning. I glanced up just as Erin stepped inside, her expression flat and unimpressed, a manila folder tucked under her arm.

"I heard I have to help you on the case that you created for yourself."

"Morning to you too, Erin," I muttered, setting my pen down.

Ignoring that, she stepped closer and crossed her arms. "So, what's the plan? We take down a public defender together? Burn more bridges?"

I stared at her for a beat, then sighed. "I really want to clear the air between us."

"Yeah?" Erin let out a short, humorless laugh. "Well, I really don't."

"Erin—"

"Let's just get this over with, Alex. You do your whole thing, I'll help where I need to, and then we can go back to pretending to like each other."

A surge of anger crashed through me. Heat rose from my chest to my neck, my pulse hammering against my temples. After everything—after she'd brought me here, after we'd been friends, after all we'd been through—this was how she wanted to play it?

Shoving my chair back, I stood, facing her fully. "We're not going to *pretend* to like each other. We're either going to fix this, or we're not."

Erin narrowed her eyes. "There's nothing to fix."

"Bullshit."

She crossed her arms tighter.

"You're still angry at me," I told her, "and I get that. But I need to know—what exactly are you mad about? That I got Bard arrested? That I didn't go through the right channels?" I shook my head. "Or are you just mad that I didn't listen to you?"

"You really don't get it, do you?"

"Then explain it to me."

Erin's eyes flashed, and she paced for a second before turning back to me.

"This isn't just about Bard or the warrant," she said, her voice tight. "It's about how you've approached everything since you got here. You—who spent years telling me you wanted to take down trafficking rings and corruption at the highest levels—suddenly act like you're the only crusader for justice in this entire office."

I felt my shoulders tense. She was bringing up our history, the late-night conversations about my mother's disappearance, the promises I'd made to fight the system from the inside.

"That's not—"

"It is, Alex! You don't trust anyone. You think *you* have to be the one to fix everything. You had Holloway, a special attorney whose entire job was to look into office misconduct, but when you decided to get Bard arrested, you didn't even consult me or Nathan or anyone who's been here for years—people who might have helped you handle it properly."

"What was I supposed to do, Erin? Ignore it? Let a guy walk free after admitting to taking a bribe?"

"No, but you could have gone through the right channels!"

"And if I had? How long would that have taken?"

She let out a sharp breath. "That's not the point."

"It is to me."

We stared each other down, each heaving with deep breaths from adrenaline. The silence thick with tension.

Finally, Erin exhaled. She ran a hand through her hair, fatigue etching dark circles under her eyes.

"You're a pain in the ass," she muttered. "You know that?"

"Yeah," I said. "I've heard."

Another tense beat passed, and then Erin sighed. "I'm still angry about how you handled things. But I'm also not going to keep fighting you on it."

I nodded, accepting the compromise for what it was. A tentative peace. Not perfect. But enough to move forward.

"For what it's worth," I said, "I get it. I have a bad habit of just going—charging ahead without thinking about the rules or how my actions reflect on you." I met her eyes. "I'll try to be more mindful of that in the future."

Erin exhaled, something softening in her expression. "That would be appreciated."

"So, are we doing this or what?"

"Yeah," she muttered. "We're doing this."

With the tension between us somewhat diffused, Erin dropped into the chair across from me, flipping open the case file while I pulled up trial transcripts on my laptop.

Flipping a pen between her fingers, she asked, "What do we know about Bard?"

"So far, just his sworn testimony that he took a bribe to throw Ortega's case."

"Right. And now we need to figure out who paid him and why."

"I don't buy that this was just a random bribe." I frowned, clicking through the notes I'd taken. "Ortega wasn't some major player—there's no obvious reason to go to this level of fraud just to put him in prison."

"What if Bard just needed the money?" Erin asked.

"No attorney is going to risk their law license—their entire career—just to take a few thousand dollars."

"What if it was more?"

I considered it. "He's still working at the FPD, or at least he was until all this blew up. If it was life-changing money, he wouldn't still be defending federal cases on a government salary."

"Fair point." Erin tossed her pen onto the desk and stood. "There's only one way to start unraveling this."

"And that is?"

"We go talk to him."

I blinked, caught slightly off guard. "You want to go down to holding and just ask him?"

"Yeah." Erin grabbed her blazer from the back of the chair and shrugged it on.

I hesitated for a second, then said, "Should we bring Holloway in on this?"

Erin gave me a pointed look. "His investigation is focused on potential misconduct within our office. Ours is a criminal case against Bard."

"I know. But I still feel like we should include him, since he's been part of this from the beginning."

"I don't want to miss this opportunity to catch Bard now, before he closes up."

"I get that, but I'm not convinced he's going to talk to us, anyway. He's an attorney. He knows better."

Erin reached for the case file and turned toward the door, motioning for me to follow.

"Attorneys are the most conceited of all," she said. "They always think they can represent themselves."

"Fine," I muttered, standing and grabbing my bag. "But when he lawyers up immediately, I'm going to say I told you so."

Erin grinned. "Yeah, yeah. Let's go see if he's as arrogant as I think he is."

The holding facility for federal detainees in Houston was located within the Federal Detention Center—FDC—Houston, a high-rise correctional facility downtown that housed individuals arrested on federal charges awaiting trial, sentencing, or transfer.

Erin and I flashed our credentials at the security checkpoint, signing in with the Marshal's Office. A stoic correctional officer led us down a secured hallway to the interrogation rooms, the heavy metal doors clanging shut behind us with each checkpoint we passed.

Inside, sitting at a metal desk with his sleeves rolled up, was Special Agent Logan Elliott, a seasoned investigator with the FBI's Houston field office.

Elliott was in his early forties, built like someone who still hit the gym daily, with sharp blue eyes and a close-cropped beard that was just starting to show gray at the edges. He wore a dark navy suit, no tie, and had the exhausted-but-alert expression of someone who'd spent too many hours trying to get a witness to crack.

He leaned back as we walked in, tapping a pen against his notepad.

"Took you two long enough," he said, giving us both a once-over before sitting forward. "Figured someone from your office would be down here eventually."

I took the seat across from him, while Erin perched on the edge of the desk beside me, arms crossed.

"What's he given up?" I asked.

Elliott huffed a laugh, shaking his head. "Not a damn thing." He picked up his notepad, flipping through his scribbled notes. "Hasn't denied anything, hasn't confirmed anything." He looked back up at me. "Hasn't asked for a lawyer, either."

I exchanged a glance with Erin, who furrowed her brow.

"Either he's waiting for something," Elliott said, "or he actually thinks he can talk his way out of this."

Erin nodded. "Then let's give him something to think about."

Elliott exhaled sharply, rubbing his jaw. "I'll let him know you two want to chat. If he agrees, we'll take him to an interrogation room. If not, he can sit in there and enjoy the silence."

I nodded. "Sounds good."

Elliott stood, grabbing his badge and notepad before stepping toward the door.

"Give me five minutes," he said before walking out.

As soon as the door shut behind him, Erin turned to me, looking smug.

"Told you," she muttered. "Attorneys always think they can represent themselves."

She had been right about that, just like she had been right when she first told me she'd finally found time to help me look through those files—right before Ortega's petition landed on my desk and everything changed. It seemed like a lifetime ago now, that moment of hope that quickly turned to frustration.

Maybe Erin was right more often than I gave her credit for.

CHAPTER THIRTY-EIGHT

THE METAL DOOR CREAKED OPEN, and Gregory Bard stepped into the interrogation room, escorted by a federal marshal.

Even in an orange jumpsuit and his wrists cuffed in front of him, he still carried himself with an air of confidence, like this was just a temporary inconvenience rather than a federal indictment.

His graying hair was disheveled, but he'd still tried to slick it back. He walked with measured steps, his expression set in neutral arrogance, like he was assessing the situation, trying to determine how much control he still had.

His gaze landed on me first.

Tilting his head, he looked almost amused. "It's you."

I kept my face impassive. "Good to see you again too, Mr. Bard."

His amusement didn't fade as he took a seat at the metal table, the chains clinking as he adjusted in the chair. He sat casually, as if we were about to discuss motions in chambers rather than his own corruption case. Then he turned his attention to Erin, eyes narrowing as he scanned her face.

Erin introduced herself, pulled out a chair across from him, then set a case file on the table.

Bard snorted. "Yeah, I know who you are."

"Then you know I don't play games."

"I'm sure you don't."

He glanced between us, crossing his arms as best as the cuffs would allow. "What can I do for you ladies today?"

Erin folded her hands on the table, her expression cool and unbothered. "We need to talk about what happens next."

"I already know what happens next, Mitchell. I sit in this uncomfortable chair, you try to squeeze a confession out of me, and then you throw me in front of a judge and hope I roll over."

Erin's lips twitched, but not into a smile. "Actually, I was thinking more along the lines of what you can do to help yourself."

Bard's eyebrows lifted in amusement. "Now we're talking."

"That depends, though. Are you willing to tell us who paid you off?"

"I've seen your office cut the best deals for the worst people. So how about one for me?"

Erin tilted her head. "Would you consider yourself the worst person?"

"If it gets me the best deal? Sure." He damn near grinned.

"Not happening."

"Come on, Erin. Can I call you Erin?"

"No."

He held up his hands in mock surrender. "Mitchell it is, then. I know what you're doing. You think you can just wear me down, get me to say something for free."

Erin scoffed. "You want blanket immunity? A reduced sentence? What exactly do you think is on the table here?"

"How about my release?"

"Not a chance."

"Then there's no sense in us talking."

The air between them grew tense, the interrogation shifting from a negotiation to a standoff.

Erin's jaw ticked, frustration flickering in her eyes. And before she could snap back, I stepped in.

"Let's back up," I said, redirecting the conversation. "You said you know how this works. So tell us—why take the bribe in the first place?"

Bard's gaze flicked to me, his amusement returning. "The money was good."

I tilted my head. "That's it? No hesitation? No questions?"

His smirk didn't waver, but there was something guarded beneath it. "You'd be surprised how easy it is to turn off your conscience when someone's waving the right number at you."

Erin scoffed under her breath, shaking her head.

But I wasn't buying it.

Bard was a seasoned defense attorney. He'd seen plenty of dirty money flow through the legal system, but I didn't believe for a second that he'd risk his entire career for just a bribe.

There had to be more to it. I watched Bard closely, my mind working through everything he was saying, and everything he wasn't. His confidence was too polished, his cocky demeanor too practiced.

"You think I just took a bag of cash from some guy off the street?" he said, his mask still in place but the edges a little tighter. "Please. I'm not some rookie idiot. I knew exactly what I was doing."

Locking onto his words, my pulse kicked up.

"Say that again," I said, keeping my voice neutral.

Bard's expression faltered. "Say what again?"

"You knew exactly what you were doing," I repeated. "Because it wasn't just some guy off the street."

His jaw tensed.

"That's the thing. If this was *just* a bribe, if this was *just* about money, you wouldn't have cared who it came from. You'd take the cash, do the job, and walk away."

Bard tilted his head, his expression carefully blank. "Your point?"

"My point is that you didn't just take money from some random fixer trying to rig a case. You took it from someone connected to the case itself."

His fingers twitched slightly against the table.

"That's why you're sitting here," I continued. "That's why you're still playing games and haven't asked for a lawyer—because you know that if you talk, if you say the wrong name, you're not just selling out a corrupt deal. You're exposing something much bigger. Maybe some*one* much bigger."

His jaw clenched, but he didn't deny it. He stayed silent.

Erin and I exchanged a glance.

I stood first. "We'll be right back."

Bard let out a slow exhale as we stepped out of the interrogation room, the heavy door clicking shut behind us.

Erin leaned against the wall, arms crossed, her gaze flicking toward me. "You're thinking this goes beyond Ortega's case, aren't you?"

I nodded, mind racing through the connections. "Did you see his face when I mentioned someone connected to the case? He didn't even try to deny it."

"Do you think Delacroix might have bribed him?" Erin asked, referring to the original prosecutor. "That would explain why you couldn't find the discovery disclosure at first."

"No," shaking my head, my mind piecing things together. "I don't think it was Delacroix at all."

"How do you figure?"

"Delacroix was already a suspect in our investigation. If it were him, Bard would just come out and say it—he'd have nothing to lose by naming someone we were already looking at. But he's clearly afraid to give over the name."

"What are you getting at?"

"Whoever bribed him is an unknown. Someone powerful enough that Bard is still afraid of them, even from inside a federal detention center."

Erin nodded slowly, thinking. "So whoever it is, he's worried about exposing them."

"And, if he exposes them, they'll know it was him who squealed."

"But he's a lawyer. He knows we could do witness protection. Why not try to cooperate?"

I stared at the closed metal door, my pulse steady but sharp. "Because someone with real power gave him the money. Someone who could reach him even in witness protection."

Erin frowned. "You're talking about someone with serious connections. Government? Law enforcement?"

"Possibly. Whatever it is, it's bigger than we initially thought. Bard wouldn't be this scared of an ordinary criminal. I'm going to see if I can get anything else out of him, but let's be honest—we're not getting much more."

Erin sighed, pushing off the wall. "He already knows he's screwed—he's just trying to find a way to dig himself out."

I nodded once in agreement, then reached for the door handle, stepping back into the room with Erin right behind me. Bard stared down at his cuffed hands, his jaw tight, his earlier cockiness completely evaporated.

"You ready to talk?" Erin asked, voice neutral but carrying an edge of impatience.

Bard let out a slow breath. Without looking up, he muttered, "I want my lawyer."

Erin and I exchanged a glance, both of us recognizing the predictable pivot. He'd finally realized he couldn't handle this alone.

"Yeah, yeah," Erin muttered. "Should've said that twenty minutes ago."

"You'll get your lawyer, Bard," I said evenly. "And when you realize they can't save you, you know where to find us."

He didn't respond, his gaze remaining straight ahead like we weren't even there.

Erin gestured toward the door. "We're done here."

Without another word, we walked out, the door locking behind us as we exited. We'd barely made it back outside when my phone buzzed.

"Hello?" I answered.

Lisa's voice came in frantic and fast on the other end of the line.

"Alex, I followed your advice—I listened to the prison calls. You definitely want to hear this."

My pulse spiked. "What is it?"

Erin glanced over at me, sensing the shift in my posture, my tone.

Lisa let out a breath, like she was so excited she could barely contain herself.

"Ortega."

My heart skipped a beat. "What about him?"

"He was involved in the calls. The ones I've been tracking—the prison calls tied to the gun trafficking ring."

I blinked, my mind stuttering for a second.

"Lisa, what exactly did you find in those calls?" I demanded, gripping the phone tighter, my voice dropping to an urgent whisper.

Lisa let out a short, almost breathless laugh. "Ortega wasn't just some low-level criminal who got caught up in the system. He's connected to a major gun trafficking operation that stretches from Houston all the way to Central America. And Ortega? He's a key player."

My pulse hammered in my ears. All this time we'd been fighting to free a man who might actually deserve to be behind bars—just not for the crime he was convicted of.

I locked eyes with Erin, who read my expression and mouthed, "What?"

"I've got the transcripts here at my office," Lisa said. "You're gonna want to read these for yourself. There are names, dates, drop locations —everything."

I nodded, even though she couldn't see me. "Don't show those to anyone else. We're coming to you now."

I hung up, my mind already working through the implications. If Ortega was part of a gun trafficking operation, suddenly the mysterious bribe to his attorney made perfect sense. Someone powerful wanted him locked up—not to punish him, but to silence him.

"What is it?" Erin asked, her expression tense.

"Everything just changed," I said, already heading for the exit. "Ortega's connected to a gun trafficking ring. And we just set him free."

CHAPTER
THIRTY-NINE

I WALKED through the hallways of the DA's office, the familiar scent of stale coffee and printer toner wrapping around me. It felt surreal being back here—like stepping into a previous chapter of my life.

Erin walked alongside me as I led the way, our conversation about Ortega's trafficking connections continuing in hushed tones. When we reached my old office, I paused at the sight of Lisa's nameplate on the door. Inside, she'd completely transformed the space. Gone were my case files stacked in orderly towers; instead, she'd created a web of evidence pinned to a large corkboard. A sleek desk lamp replaced my utilitarian one, and photos of what must have been her family decorated the once-bare walls. Even the furniture had been rearranged to maximize the window view I'd never properly appreciated.

Lisa looked up as we entered, grinning. "Welcome back, stranger."

Smiling, I glanced around. "You got my old office."

Lisa leaned back in her chair, hands folded behind her head. "Damn right, I did. Fought tooth and nail for it."

"It suits you. I guess you couldn't get the cigar smoke out of here, either?"

"I think it's been baked into the walls at this point. Some traditions die hard in the DA's office."

Lisa motioned for us to sit down, then pulled out a file of transcripts and flipped through them.

"I already filled Alex in on the basics during our call," she said, looking at Erin, "but you need the full picture. These prison calls change everything."

She slid a stack of papers across the desk. "I've been monitoring the calls as part of my gun trafficking investigation for months. What I didn't realize until now was that Ortega's been a central figure all along."

Erin nodded, already briefed on the general premise during our drive over. She leaned forward, eager to see the concrete evidence. "Show me the worst of it."

Lisa flipped to several highlighted sections. "He's not just mentioned in passing—he's giving orders, coordinating shipments, managing routes. The transcripts make it clear: Gabriel Ortega is a key player in an international gun trafficking operation."

Picking up the top page, I studied the transcript more carefully now that I had it in front of me. The name ORTEGA stood out in bold, alongside several other names—some I recognized from other cases, others completely new to me.

The conversation was coded but unmistakable—they were discussing routes, shipments, drop points.

And Ortega was definitely in charge of coordinating them.

"I need to take these with me," I said, gathering the papers into a folder. "We'll need to cross-reference every name, every location, build a comprehensive picture of his operation."

Lisa nodded. "Those are copies—I've got the originals secured. Take whatever you need."

I tucked the folder into my bag, my mind already racing through potential legal strategies. How quickly could we get a new arrest warrant? What charges would stick most effectively? Would we need to coordinate with ATF or DEA?

"What else can you tell us about your gun trafficking case?" I asked, looking back at Lisa. "Any details that might not be in these transcripts that we should know about?"

"You're not going to like it." Lisa flipped through her notes before looking back up at Erin and me. "Here's how I connected Ortega to all of this."

She pulled out a few more transcripts and tapped the top page.

"At first, I was just monitoring random calls from known players in the gun trafficking ring. The ATF flagged a few repeat contacts—guys on the inside still coordinating shipments on the outside. So I started digging deeper."

She slid a highlighted section toward me.

"This guy—Luis Montoya—he's been on our radar for months as a mid-level distributor in the operation. We knew he was connected, but we didn't realize who he was reporting to."

I skimmed the transcript, my stomach tightening as I recognized Ortega's name.

Montoya: *We got everything lined up, same as before?*

Ortega: *Yeah, the shipment's gonna move the same route. Tell 'em no surprises.*

Montoya: *Good. No screw-ups this time.*

Ortega: *Won't be. You got my word.*

"Ortega wasn't just involved," I said. "He was coordinating."

Lisa nodded. "That was the first clue. The second came when I started tracing some of the money movement. There's a financial component to this ring—we're talking dirty cash being laundered through shell companies, run by guys who don't even show up in most federal databases."

"And you think Ortega was in on that, too?"

"I do. He wasn't just a courier or some random foot soldier in this operation. He was a middleman. A facilitator. And that means—"

"He's a lot more valuable than we thought."

Erin, who had been flipping through one of the transcripts, finally looked up, brows furrowed. "But I'm still not seeing how this connects to the FPD arrest. Who bribed Bard to throw Ortega's case, and why? I don't see the link."

"It's obvious now that Ortega isn't just some low-level criminal," I said. "He was connected to a major trafficking operation. That means whoever wanted him locked up wasn't just worried about a single conviction—they were worried about whatever else he knew."

Erin leaned back, considering. "So you're saying the person who bribed Bard—"

"Is likely involved in the trafficking ring, too." I exhaled, the pieces starting to form in my head. "Think about it—if Ortega was this connected, then it stands to reason that someone very powerful didn't want him talking. They wanted him convicted and buried in the system."

Lisa nodded. "And you just got his conviction overturned."

A heavy silence settled between us.

Erin frowned. "Which means—"

"Ortega's walking free," I said.

Lisa exhaled, shaking her head. "This just got a lot bigger, didn't it?"

And a whole lot more dangerous.

I turned to Lisa, my pulse pounding in my ears. I had just helped Ortega walk free, and now we had to scramble to put him back behind bars.

"Do you have enough?" I asked, my voice tight with urgency. "To get a warrant?"

Lisa flipped through her notes one last time. "I think I do. Let's go get with the magistrate and I'll try to get a warrant issued as soon as possible."

The pit forming in my stomach was hard to ignore.

Did I make a mistake?

"I shouldn't have looked so closely at Ortega's petition," I muttered, the weight of it all settling over me. "I should've just let it go."

Both Erin and Lisa snapped their heads toward me. To my surprise, Erin—who had initially told me to leave Ortega's case alone, who had warned me about digging too deep—was the first to speak up.

"Stop," she said firmly. "You did the right thing."

Her response caught me off guard. After weeks of tension between us, after all the arguments about my methods, this sudden support was unexpected.

Lisa nodded in agreement. "You exposed a corrupted trial. Bard threw the case for a bribe. You couldn't ignore that."

Erin rubbed the back of her neck. "I know you and I don't see eye to eye on how you did it—"

"Yeah, no kidding."

She leveled a glare at me. "But I do think you did the right thing standing up for your morals. Ortega shouldn't have been behind bars if his own lawyer sabotaged his defense."

"But if that was the intent all along," Lisa added, her voice lower now, "if Ortega was involved in bribing his own attorney—then yes, he should be behind bars."

The words hung between us, heavy with implication.

Swallowing hard, I suddenly saw the case from an entirely new angle. What if this wasn't about someone trying to put Ortega in prison? What if it was about keeping him safe?

A prison like the one where he'd been serving time was the perfect cover for running an operation. It provided protection, a network of criminal contacts, and a plausible excuse for communicating in code. If Ortega had orchestrated his own conviction through a bribed lawyer, he could continue managing his trafficking operation from the safety of a controlled environment.

And I had just dismantled his entire setup.

"We need to move fast," I said, the realization making my skin crawl. "If Ortega was running his operation from inside, he'll either be looking to disappear or reestablish his position on the outside."

Because if that was true, then Ortega wasn't just a pawn in this game. He was the main player.

CHAPTER
FORTY

BY THE TIME I made it home, I was exhausted.

My brain had been running on overdrive for days. Just this morning, I'd been in court for Ortega's hearing, then watched as Bard was arrested, then discovered Ortega's trafficking connections—all within the span of hours. Even now, even after the day ended, I couldn't shake the feeling that something wasn't finished.

But the moment I walked inside, the smell of garlic and marinara hit me, wrapping around me like a warm blanket. Dad had already set the table, two plates of pasta steaming in front of our chairs. He had started pouring two glasses of water when I walked in.

"Hey, kiddo," he said, glancing me over. "Rough day?"

I dropped my bag by the door and slid into my usual chair.

"You could say that."

He took our glasses to the table and sat across from me. Dad picked up his fork, but his gaze rested on me. He waited.

Waited for me to talk. To spill everything. He set the fork back down and rested his forearms on the table. "Fill me in, kid."

Twirling some spaghetti around my fork, I stared at it for a second before finally speaking.

"I've been pretty convinced I was going to get fired."

Dad raised a brow as he took a bite. "And?"

I sighed, setting my fork down. "Turns out, I'm not."

"You almost sound upset about that."

"It's not that I want to get fired," I said. "It's just that everything is happening so fast. When I first started at the USAO, Erin said the habeas petitions would give me a chance to breathe while I settled in. But it's been non-stop chaos since day one."

I took a bite of pasta, realizing how hungry I was after barely eating all day.

Dad leaned back, studying me. "But then you find yourself right back in it."

"Every time."

He sighed, taking a sip of water, before cutting a piece of garlic bread.

"What's going on now? You're clearly not done with it yet."

I leaned forward, propping my elbows on the table.

"Remember the Ortega petition?" I asked.

Dad nodded, chewing thoughtfully.

"It got granted."

"Hey, that's okay. You're allowed to lose one case. Besides, I thought you believed Ortega was in the right anyway, right?"

"Yeah, well … we're trying to get him arrested again."

Dad blinked. "Okay, you're gonna have to break that down for me."

I ran him through the basics—how we found out that Bard was bribed, how Judge Pritchard had granted the petition, and how we had thought Ortega was a low-level criminal who got screwed by the system.

And then how Lisa had found the prison calls.

"Turns out," I said, exhaling sharply, "he wasn't just a nobody. He was involved in a gun trafficking ring. Coordinating the shipments."

Dad let out a low whistle. "Damn. And Lisa has enough to get a warrant?"

"She's working on it," I said. "She was getting with the magistrate judge tonight to try to push it through."

"And this bribe? The one that got his case thrown in the first place—you think it's tied to the trafficking ring?"

"I think it has to be. Someone wanted him locked away for a reason."

Dad nodded, but gave me a pointed look. "And now, he's free."

"And whoever put him away in the first place isn't gonna like that."

The table went quiet for a beat, both of us letting that sink in.

Dad tapped his fingers against his glass thoughtfully. "So what does that mean? 'The enemy of my enemy is my friend' kind of thing?"

I frowned, considering that. "I really don't know."

But it was something to think about. Finally, I sat up and pushed my half-eaten plate away.

"I gotta get to work."

Dad arched a brow. "Work?"

I gestured to my bag of files. "I have prison phone calls to review."

He gave me a knowing look, the same Dad look I had been getting since I was a kid.

"You know what I'm gonna say."

I rolled my eyes. "Don't stay up too late."

He pointed at me. "Exactly."

I chuckled, shaking my head. I had work to do—but at least, for a few minutes, I could pretend like I had a normal life outside of all of this. Even if I knew I'd be up until midnight chasing answers.

After dinner, Dad retreated to his room to watch TV, leaving me alone with my thoughts. I sat back down at the kitchen table, a fresh cup of coffee in front of me, my laptop open, and the stack of transcripts Lisa gave me spread out across the table.

Lisa had highlighted sections she thought were important, but as I skimmed through the pages, I quickly realized this wasn't going to be as simple as I had hoped.

The calls were layered—interspersed with mundane chatter, inside jokes, and casual conversation—but buried within them were coded phrases, subtle references that hinted at something deeper.

I flipped to the first highlighted transcript.

[PRISON CALL TRANSCRIPT] Participants: Gabriel Ortega (Inmate), Luis Montoya (Outside Contact) Monitored Call ID: #47921

Ortega: *You check in on our friends yet?*

Montoya: *Yeah. Everything's still moving. Same route, same drop. But you know we got to be careful. Lot of people watching now.*

Ortega: *You worried?*

Montoya: *I ain't worried. Just saying. Word is, they want to make sure the lawyer stays quiet.*

Ortega: *Hah. Yeah, well. He already took the package. Ain't much he can say now.*

Montoya: *Sure about that?*

Ortega: *Man's got no choice. You take from the Bishop, you're on the board. Simple as that.*

I paused, my heart skipping. "The Bishop." The phrase stood out like a flashing sign. In chess, the bishop moves diagonally across the board—never in a straight line, always at an angle. Like someone who operates in the shadows, controlling pieces without directly engaging.

This wasn't random terminology; it was deliberate. Someone was being referred to by a code name, someone Ortega and his associates were careful not to identify directly.

I flipped through the other transcripts, scanning for other highlighted sections.

[PRISON CALL TRANSCRIPT] Participants: Gabriel Ortega (Inmate), Unknown Male (Outside Contact) Monitored Call ID: #48672

Unknown: *You hear anything inside about what's happening?*

Ortega: *Not much. Just that they're still keeping things moving. But I think the Bishop is getting tired of cleaning up messes.*

Unknown: *Yeah?*

Ortega: *Yeah. If it keeps up like this, I wouldn't be surprised if he decides to take his piece and disappear.*

Unknown: *And the lawyer?*

Ortega: *Like I said, he already took from the Bishop. No way out of that now.*

I sat back in my chair, mind racing through the implications. The same reference to "the Bishop" appeared again, this time with even more ominous overtones. Whoever this person was, they weren't just involved in the trafficking operation—they were overseeing it, managing it, and apparently had the power to "disappear" when necessary.

And they had a direct connection to Bard, the "lawyer" mentioned in both calls.

The pieces were starting to align, but the picture they formed was disturbing. This wasn't just about a corrupt public defender taking a bribe. This was about a trafficking operation with someone powerful at its center—powerful enough to arrange for Ortega's conviction to be secured through bribing his counsel.

I flipped to the final transcript Lisa had highlighted, my hands tightening around the pages.

[PRISON CALL TRANSCRIPT] Date: 3 weeks ago Participants: Gabriel Ortega (Inmate), Unknown Male (Outside Contact) Monitored Call ID: #49715

Unknown: *You think he'll talk?*

Ortega: *He won't.*

Unknown: *Yeah, but if he does —*

Ortega: *Then it's a problem. But like I said, the Bishop don't like problems. The lawyer knew what he was doing when he took it. Ain't no one coming back from that.*

I leaned back in my chair, the implications sinking in like a stone in water. The timing of this call—just three weeks ago—coincided with our discovery of the missing evidence in Ortega's case. They were worried about Bard talking, about what might happen if the truth about the bribe came out.

But even more chilling was what wasn't being said. The subtle threat in Ortega's words: *Ain't no one coming back from that.* It wasn't just about money changing hands; it was about leverage, about keeping Bard in line through fear.

The Bishop. The lawyer who took the money. The person powerful enough to make sure Ortega stayed convicted until I started digging. *Who the hell fits that description?*

I racked my brain, running through every judge, every prosecutor, every major player who could have possibly been involved. Someone with significant influence in the legal system, someone who could ensure Bard's compliance, someone who operated with enough authority to make these arrangements without drawing attention.

I rubbed my eyes. It was late. Too late to make sense of any of this tonight. I needed to get some sleep, clear my head, and run through everything again with Erin tomorrow. I started packing up, stacking the transcripts neatly, organizing the files from the evidentiary hearing, making sure everything was in order before I called it a night.

But as I reached for my briefcase I noticed a small crease in the folder, a tiny gap where the papers didn't sit quite right.

A single slip of paper, folded neatly, was tucked into the file.

My breath caught as I pulled it free, my fingers tightening around the edges.

The handwriting was neat, deliberate—almost old-fashioned script.

Judges shouldn't be trusted.

The note fell from my fingers, landing on the table as a chill ran through me. Someone had slipped this into my files—a warning, or perhaps a threat. The reference to judges coupled with the mysterious "Bishop" mentioned in the transcripts was too specific to be coincidental.

Someone knew I was investigating. Someone wanted me to look in a particular direction.

Or someone wanted to throw me off the scent entirely.

CHAPTER FORTY-ONE

I DIDN'T WASTE any time the next morning. By the time I got to the office, I'd already spent the entire commute dissecting every detail of the transcripts in my mind—names, dates, conversations—hoping something would finally click into place. But no matter how I looked at it, nothing quite fit.

Frustration simmering, I grabbed the folded note from my bag, tucked it into a case file, and headed straight for Erin's office. She glanced up from her desk, halfway through a sip of coffee, eyebrows raised in expectation as I walked in.

She set down her mug. "What now?"

Placing the file in front of her, I flipped it open, tapping the note with a finger. "Someone left this in my files last night."

She picked it up, unfolding the paper slowly. Her eyebrows lifted as she read the scripted words. *Judges shouldn't be trusted.*

She looked up at me, expression guarded. "Any idea who might have done this?"

"None," I said, crossing my arms. "It was tucked in my briefcase. Whoever left it clearly wanted me—and only me—to find it."

Erin set the note back down. "What do you make of it?"

"It feels like a warning—or at least a clue. Especially considering what I found last night."

I handed her the stack of transcripts, pointing at the highlighted sections. "This name, 'The Bishop,' keeps showing up. Based on these conversations, he's likely the person who bribed Bard."

Erin frowned as she skimmed through the pages. Then she paused, tapping a particular line thoughtfully.

"Are we sure this 'lawyer' they're talking about is Bard?"

"Who else would it be?"

She lifted the transcript, reading aloud. "'The lawyer took from the Bishop. No way out of that now.

And if he talks?

Then it's a problem. But the Bishop don't like problems.' They don't specify which lawyer or what type. Could be any attorney connected to the case—prosecution, defense, maybe even someone unrelated to the trial."

I considered it. "It still makes sense, right? Bard admitted taking a bribe. It fits."

"Maybe. But something else doesn't add up. If Ortega was coordinating this gun trafficking operation, why would anyone bribe his attorney to throw his case? It's like they wanted him in prison."

I leaned forward, the pieces slowly shifting in my mind. "That's exactly what's been bothering me. From these transcripts, Ortega wasn't just aware of the bribe—he was almost pleased about it. Like being in prison was part of the plan."

Frustration rising again, I rubbed the back of my neck. "But if that's true, why wait twelve years to suddenly try to overturn his conviction?"

Erin tilted her head. "He didn't exactly wait twelve years, did he? Hasn't he filed petitions before?"

"Multiple. They all got denied."

"So what changed this time?"

I leaned back in the chair. "For starters, he suddenly had the money to hire someone like Hargrave."

Erin scoffed softly. "And he probably just made a fortune getting an actual criminal back on the street."

I let out a slow breath, my mind spinning through the implications. Ortega hadn't just waited around—he'd tried and failed to leave prison multiple times. But this time, somehow, he knew he'd succeed. And the only reason he'd have that kind of certainty was if someone else was pulling strings from behind the scenes.

"You know," Erin said, "you're starting to sound a little cynical. Be careful, Alex. Next thing I know, you'll be telling me the whole system is rigged."

"I mean, isn't it?"

She pointed her pen at me. "See? Cynical."

I rolled my eyes but couldn't help a small laugh, the tension easing slightly. But then I grew serious again, eyes drifting back to the note on the desk.

"So, who do you think left this?" I asked quietly.

She frowned. "You said it was tucked into your files from the evidentiary hearing?"

"Yes," I explained, lowering my voice. "Which means whoever left it had access to my bag during or after the hearing."

"That means someone at counsel table. Maybe even Holloway."

The suggestion sent an unexpected twinge through me. Holloway, with his sharp intelligence and that infuriating smirk that somehow still managed to disarm me. I hadn't allowed myself to think about our almost-moment in his kitchen, how close we'd come to crossing a line. The case had provided a convenient distraction, but now...

"No," I said firmly. "It definitely wasn't James."

Her eyebrows rose. "We're on a first name basis now, are we?"

I cleared my throat. "Let's stay on topic."

Erin gave me a pointed look. "We can't rule anyone out yet."

I sighed. "Fine. We need a list of everyone I interacted with that day and work through it."

She nodded. "Start from the top."

I tapped my pen against the desk, opening my legal pad to jot down names. "Court staff, opposing counsel, clerk, judge, reporters in the gallery—anyone who might have had opportunity."

"And we should probably ask Holloway first if he noticed anyone approach the table when you stepped away."

"Good idea."

I pulled out my phone and dialed. He answered after two rings, voice relaxed. "Alex, to what do I owe the pleasure?"

I smiled despite myself. "I have a question. Do you remember if anyone came near our table during the hearing?"

He paused. "Not that I recall, but my attention was mostly on Hargrave and the judge."

"That's about what I expected." I looked at Erin, who watched me with intense curiosity. "Could we meet up and discuss this more thoroughly?"

"You asking me out for coffee?"

"Consider it an interrogation with caffeine."

He laughed. "Meet me at Ludlow's in twenty?"

"Perfect," I said, glancing at Erin. "Mind if I bring a third?"

He paused briefly, amusement evident in his tone when he replied, "Sure. See you there."

I hung up and slipped the phone back into my pocket. Erin raised an eyebrow, a grin tugging at her lips as we stood to head out.

We walked silently through the office hallway, the fluorescent lights humming overhead. From neighboring offices came the soft tapping of keyboards and muffled phone conversations about motions and deadlines—the soundtrack of justice being processed through bureaucracy.

When we got to the elevator, Erin couldn't hold it in anymore. "What was with that exchange?"

I shrugged. "Nothing."

She gave me a skeptical look. "Try again."

I sighed, pressing the elevator button. The doors opened with a soft chime, and we stepped inside. As they closed, separating us from the rest of the office, I found myself hesitating. Erin and I had only just started repairing our relationship. Did I really want to complicate things by sharing something so personal?

But the look on her face told me she wasn't going to let it go.

"We kissed," I admitted finally. "Once. It didn't go further than that."

Erin gawked at me. "Seriously, Alex? Another attorney?"

I groaned, leaning against the elevator wall. "It just happened. And it's not like I make a habit of this. I've barely had time for a personal life since I joined the office."

She chuckled, shaking her head. "For someone who claims to dislike lawyers, you sure have a type."

I exhaled sharply, eyes locked on the closed elevator doors. "Maybe I'm punishing myself."

The unexpected honesty in my voice seemed to catch her off guard. She turned to me, her expression softening from teasing to genuine concern. A flicker of understanding passed between us—the kind that only happens when two people recognize the same pain in each other.

"Alex," she began softly, but the elevator doors slid open with a mechanical whirr, the moment interrupted by the bustling noise of the lobby.

The Houston humidity hit us like a wall as we stepped outside, the morning air already thick with the promise of another sweltering day. Despite that, it felt good to get out of the office and walk, even just a block. Cars honked in the distance, and the scent of exhaust mingled with the sweet smell of magnolias from the courthouse landscaping.

Turning the corner toward Ludlow's Café, its large windows offered glimpses of patrons sipping coffee inside. The smell of fresh ground beans wafted out each time the door opened. Holloway was already there, waiting at a table in the corner, sunlight streaming over him as he scrolled through his phone.

Erin studied him for a moment before leaning toward me, her voice low. "I get it, though. Those cheekbones could cut glass."

I shot her a look. "Behave."

She laughed back at me. "No promises."

CHAPTER
FORTY-TWO

LUDLOW'S WAS BUZZING as usual. The comforting aroma of roasted coffee beans and fresh pastries filled the small café as soft indie music played overhead. The place had always felt cozy and safe. Exactly the kind of spot to untangle a mess like this.

Holloway stood when he saw us, offering a polite nod to Erin and then turning to me. For a second, heat flushed my cheeks, and I looked away quickly.

We ordered our drinks—two Americanos for Erin and Holloway, a latte for me—and took our seats, away from the bustle of the main floor.

Holloway shifted his gaze between Erin and me. "Alright, spill."

Erin shot me a look, waiting for me to take the lead. I carefully pulled out the small, folded note, sliding it across the table toward Holloway.

He unfolded it slowly, reading the brief sentence silently. His eyebrows lifted. "Where'd you get this?"

"It was tucked into my file after the evidentiary hearing," I explained. "Someone must have placed it there deliberately."

He exhaled, flipping the note over and then back again. "No idea who it's from?"

I shook my head. "None. That's why we wanted to talk to you. You sure you didn't see anyone around counsel table or the files when I stepped away?"

Holloway leaned back, thoughtful, before taking a slow sip of his coffee. "No, nothing obvious. The courtroom was crowded, but the only people who came near were Hargrave and court staff. Maybe the clerk?"

Erin frowned. "Would the clerk have any reason to pass a note like this?"

"Not that I can think of," Holloway admitted.

"Could it have come from Hargrave?" I asked. "Do you think he's clean in this?"

"I've known Eric Hargrave for a long time," Holloway said, meeting my eyes. "He's ambitious, and he'll take dirty money without losing much sleep, sure. But he's not the type of person who'd knowingly involve himself in something as serious as bribing a public defender to sabotage a case."

I frowned, stirring my latte absently. "How can you be sure?"

"Because Hargrave's seen what happens firsthand when people cross that line." Holloway lowered his voice. "About fifteen years ago, his older brother Jeremy was an ADA in Dallas. Good lawyer, talented guy. But he got mixed up in a case—cartel money, bribery, corruption. Thought he could navigate the murky waters and keep himself clean." He shook his head and made a line over his throat, beneath his chin.

A chill ran down my spine. "What happened?"

"He turned informant. Tried to blow the whistle. Two weeks later, they found him dead in his own driveway."

Erin let out a slow breath. "God."

"It shattered their family. Hargrave buried himself in his work afterward—he was angry, driven. We worked together on a joint task force between the DOJ and local offices about a decade ago. That's when he told me his brother's story and made it clear he'd never touch cases with those kinds of connections."

I swallowed hard, feeling the weight of his words. "And I want to believe that."

"You can." Holloway softened his gaze. "If Hargrave was aware of what Ortega was really tied into, he never would've touched that case. He's not stupid."

I nodded slowly, but something lingered in the back of my mind. My mother had been smart, too. She knew how dangerous certain paths were, yet she'd ended up on a case that had cost her everything. Sometimes you didn't realize how deep you'd gotten until it was too late.

"Okay," I finally said. "I trust your judgment."

Erin sighed, setting her cup down with a little too much force. "The real problem is that we have pieces that don't fit together. Ortega gets convicted because his lawyer was bribed. Then we discover Ortega himself is connected to organized crime. Now he's free, and whoever is pulling the strings—this mysterious 'Bishop' character—is making sure everyone stays silent. None of it makes logical sense."

"Wait a minute," Holloway said, setting his cup down. "They're calling this person 'The Bishop'?"

"Yeah," I said, nodding. "It kept coming up in Ortega's prison calls."

"Why 'Bishop'?" He tilted his head. "You think that's symbolic? Religious?"

Erin leaned in. "It's gotta be code, right? Could be someone higher-up—someone with influence over the legal system."

Holloway nodded slowly. "Exactly. Maybe someone connected to the courts."

Historically, bishops had been trusted advisors, figures of power and protection, positioned close to the king—able to influence without ruling outright. But their role extended beyond mere counsel. Bishops in the Catholic Church oversaw the governance and administration of their dioceses, including the appointment of clergy, the management of church property, and the resolution of disputes. They were arbiters, gatekeepers, responsible for settling conflicts and shaping outcomes. Not by force, but by authority and influence.

Someone like that wasn't just a figure behind the scenes. They influenced decisions. They had the final say.

"Like a judge," I whispered.

We all exchanged uneasy glances.

Erin finally broke the silence, her voice low. "Judge Pritchard oversaw the habeas petition, granted discovery, and expanded the record."

"But why would Pritchard go through the trouble?" Holloway asked. "What would motivate him to set Ortega up, or release him after all these years?"

"That's what I can't figure out," I said. "Ortega's conviction felt deliberate, almost orchestrated. Why would Pritchard have bribed Bard to sabotage Ortega, only to let him go years later?"

Pritchard hadn't had to step in. He could have stayed quiet, denied the petition without explanation like so many others. Instead, he moved it forward, authorized discovery, and even pushed for a special prosecutor.

"Maybe the plan wasn't for Ortega to ever walk free." Holloway took a slow drink of his coffee, glancing out the window next to us. Rain pelted the surface, casting streaks down the glass. "We're assuming the habeas petition was intentional or that everyone's working for the same team, but what if we're wrong? If Ortega was part of something bigger, it's not a stretch to think someone else wanted him silenced for good."

"I don't follow," Erin said, and I nodded my head in agreement.

"Someone wanted Ortega in prison for some reason. What if keeping him there made him easier to control or monitor?"

"What?" I said. "Like the plan was for him to be killed inside?"

"But if he's in charge of the bigger scheme and had protection, even inside …"

"Getting him out might be the only way to get to him," Erin finished.

My coffee suddenly tasted bitter against my tongue. I set the cup down and pushed it away from me. "Where does that leave us?"

"Right back where we started." Erin stirred her coffee absently. "We have a note from an unknown source warning us specifically about judges, transcripts linking Ortega to a trafficking ring, and a Federal Public Defender who's too scared—or too cocky—to tell us anything else."

Holloway leaned back, slightly amused. "Sounds like a normal day at the office."

We fell silent again, sipping coffee quietly, lost in our own thoughts. I stared down at the note between us.

"We need to identify who left this note," Erin said, tapping her finger against the paper. "Let's head back to the office and make a comprehensive list of everyone at the hearing who could have had access to your files. We can work through it methodically there."

"Good idea," I agreed. "We should document everything while it's still fresh."

We finished our coffees, the determination to solve this puzzle binding us together despite our differences. I caught Holloway's gaze again. He gave me a small, reassuring nod. Warmth spread through my chest. But I knew better than to dwell on that feeling.

I tried forcing the ice back around my heart and shouldered my bag. "Let's get back to the office."

Before any of us stood, Erin's phone buzzed against the tabletop. She glanced at the screen and frowned, then lifted it to her ear.

"This is Mitchell," she answered, eyes narrowing as she listened.

I exchanged a quick glance with Holloway, whose own expression had shifted to mild curiosity as we waited for Erin to finish.

"Got it," Erin finally said into the phone. "We'll be ready."

Hanging up, she slid the phone back into her pocket.

"That was the clerk's office," she explained, grabbing her coat. "Bard's arraignment is first thing tomorrow morning."

Urgency tightened in my chest. "Already?"

Erin nodded firmly. "We've got prep work to do. Right now."

Holloway rose from his seat, giving us both a sympathetic smile.

"Guess I'll leave you to it," he said. "Good luck tomorrow."

I returned the smile. "Thanks for the help."

"Anytime," he said gently, his gaze lingering on mine just a moment longer than necessary.

From the corner of my eye, I saw Erin already heading for the door, clearly done with the moment.

Before I could say anything else, Holloway leaned in, his touch light but deliberate, and pressed a small, lingering kiss against my cheek.

The ice around my heart melted once again, and I hurried after Erin, hoping she wouldn't see the blush spreading across my face.

CHAPTER FORTY-THREE

THE FEDERAL COURTHOUSE was unusually busy for an early morning arraignment, with attorneys bustling through the halls and court staff quickly shuffling papers. Erin and I arrived early, settling at the prosecution table and exchanging brief nods with familiar faces around the courtroom. A quiet hum filled the room as people murmured, waiting for the proceedings to begin.

I flipped through my notes one last time, but my attention snapped upward when the courtroom doors swung open. Two federal marshals escorted Gregory Bard through the doorway, his wrists and ankles shackled, the orange jumpsuit stark against the formal atmosphere of the courtroom. Despite his circumstances, he maintained an air of confidence, exchanging a whispered conversation with his attorney, who had his back turned to us.

Then the attorney turned around.

"You're kidding me," Erin whispered.

Eric Hargrave stood confidently beside Bard. He adjusted his perfectly tailored suit, smoothing his tie before making eye contact with me.

"We'll talk about this after," Erin murmured.

Before I could respond, the court clerk's voice cut clearly through the courtroom chatter.

"All rise. The Honorable Magistrate Judge Marianne Fitzgerald presiding."

Everyone stood as Judge Fitzgerald entered the courtroom, her dark robes billowing behind her. A no-nonsense judge with a reputation for fairness but strict courtroom decorum, she settled into her seat and nodded.

"You may be seated," she said, picking up the case file. "United States v. Gregory Bard. Counsel, please identify yourselves for the record."

I rose and said, "Alex Hayes and Erin Mitchell for the United States, Your Honor."

"Eric Hargrave representing Gregory Bard, Your Honor," Hargrave said smoothly.

Judge Fitzgerald nodded, glancing down at Bard. "Mr. Bard, you have been charged with conspiracy to commit honest services fraud, bribery of a public official, and obstruction of justice. Have you had sufficient time to discuss these charges with your attorney?"

"Yes, Your Honor," Bard replied.

"And how do you plead?"

Bard leaned forward, his voice clear and calm. "Not guilty to all charges, Your Honor."

The judge turned to me and asked, "The government's position?"

I stood, feeling every eye in the courtroom shift toward me. "The government requests detention pending trial."

"On what grounds, Ms. Hayes?"

I took a steadying breath, conscious of Hargrave's keen gaze locked onto me. "Given the serious nature of these charges and Mr. Bard's demonstrated disregard for judicial processes, he poses a significant flight risk. Additionally, the nature of the charges suggests a likelihood he may attempt to obstruct justice further if released."

Hargrave countered. "Your Honor, Mr. Bard has no criminal history, no record of flight or violence, and substantial ties to the community. He has fully cooperated to this point. We request he be granted reasonable bail."

The judge flipped through documents, considering both arguments carefully. Finally, she turned her gaze back to me.

"Ms. Hayes, while the court appreciates the government's concerns, the Bail Reform Act requires clear demonstration of flight risk, danger to the community, or likelihood of obstruction. At this point, I do not find sufficient evidence meeting those criteria."

I felt frustration rising, but kept my composure. "Understood, Your Honor."

"Therefore," Judge Fitzgerald continued, "bail is granted. Bond is set at two hundred fifty thousand dollars. Mr. Bard must surrender his passport, remain under home detention, and will be subject to electronic monitoring until trial."

Hargrave gave a slight, satisfied nod, patting Bard on the shoulder as the marshals moved to escort him out.

Laughter and conversation filled the courthouse hallway as Erin and I stepped out into the bustling corridor. Attorneys and court staff moved around us, already absorbed in their next cases. But as I glanced toward the far end of the hallway, I spotted Hargrave leaning close to Bard, exchanging final words before the marshals led him away toward processing.

"Let's catch him before he leaves," I muttered, quickening my pace.

Erin hesitated then fell in step beside me. "You sure that's a good idea right now?"

"Probably not," I said, "but I need to hear what he's thinking."

Hargrave noticed us approach and offered a slick, confident smile. "Hayes, Mitchell. Impressive argument today. Almost thought you'd convince the judge."

I resisted the urge to roll my eyes at his sarcasm. "Surprised to see you on this case, Hargrave."

"Client needed representation, and I was available."

"And you don't see a conflict of interest here?"

"The Ortega case is over, Alex. We secured his release. Time to move on."

I narrowed my eyes. "Still, interesting timing."

"Just good business." Hargrave held my gaze, his expression neutral. "It's all about referrals."

Erin shifted beside me, crossing her arms. "And your new client? Not concerned about his potential for flight or obstruction?"

Hargrave waved a hand. "Bard is no threat. He's made mistakes, certainly. But who hasn't?" His eyes lingered on me. "Besides, I'm confident we'll resolve this quickly."

There was something calculated in his eyes. I opened my mouth to respond, but he spoke again first.

"And Alex, my dinner invitation still stands. When we're not opposing counsel, I'd love to continue our conversation from before all this started."

My jaw tightened, cheeks heating as Erin shot me a sharp look, clearly confused and curious. I forced a neutral expression. "Noted."

Hargrave flashed a quick smile, turned on his heel, and strode confidently down the hallway and out of sight.

Erin stared after him for a long moment before shaking her head. "What a charmer."

CHAPTER
FORTY-FOUR

PUSHING open the courthouse doors into the cool outside air, Erin was a step behind me, still muttering about Hargrave under her breath.

"You know what this makes it look like?" she asked.

I shook my head. "What?"

"Like Hargrave's involved in all of this."

"Holloway seemed convinced Hargrave is clean—at least when it comes to the bribery scheme."

Erin stopped and turned to face me with a skeptical look. "Are you sure Holloway has clear judgment about his old colleague? And are you sure you do?"

"Yes, Erin. I trust him." I crossed my arms, meeting her gaze with a firmness that made her eyebrows rise slightly. "I think Holloway's right about Hargrave. Ambitious? Absolutely. Maybe ethically questionable about money. But directly involved in trafficking or bribery? I doubt it."

"We just can't afford to dismiss anyone. Especially not someone who's now representing Bard."

"I get it. But I genuinely believe Holloway wouldn't mislead me. Still"—I looked across the bustling courthouse square, watching attorneys and clients hurry up the steps, my thoughts tangling as I hesitated—"representing Bard this openly is either incredibly bold or incredibly stupid."

"Or both."

We walked in silence before stopping by Erin's car. She glanced at me when I didn't move to get in.

"Are you okay?" she asked.

I glanced back toward the courthouse. "Do you mind if I hang back for a bit? I want to retrace my steps from the evidentiary hearing. Maybe walking through it again will help me figure out who left that note."

Erin nodded. "Sure. You want company?"

"I appreciate it, but I think I need to do this alone. Clear my head."

Smiling faintly, she pulled open the car door. "Alright. Call me if anything shakes loose?"

"You'll be the first to know."

Erin climbed into the driver's seat but didn't shut the door right then. She leaned out and said, "Be careful, Alex. Everyone's still a suspect."

"Trust me," I said. "I won't forget that again."

She gave a tight nod, and I watched her pull away, the sound of her car engine fading until I stood alone in the vast parking lot. The courthouse loomed before me, a monument to justice that suddenly felt cold and impersonal without her beside me. Turning back toward the imposing structure, I steeled myself, preparing to retrace my steps, determined to shake something loose from my memory. Whoever left that note in my files had to be close enough to know my every move.

The courthouse was quieter now, the mid-morning rush fading as the day's cases settled into their routines. As I stepped inside, the familiar hum of fluorescent lights mixed with the faint scent of old paper and polished wood. The marble floors beneath my heels echoed as I approached the security checkpoint.

The same guards from earlier looked up as I approached. One of them—Officer Grant, judging by the name on his badge—gave me a curious tilt of his head as he scanned my ID.

"Back so soon, Ms. Hayes?" he asked.

I placed my bag on the conveyor belt. "Just took a quick break after the Bard arraignment. Need to follow up on something."

"Forget something?"

"More like trying to remember something."

Grant let out a low chuckle as he waved me through. "Let us know if we need to arrest your memory for trespassing."

I laughed as I grabbed my bag. "I'll keep that in mind."

Ambling my way through the hallways, I let my footsteps slow as I took it all in again. The courthouse corridors transformed throughout the day, like a living organism shifting with the rhythm of justice.

In the morning, they felt crowded and urgent—lawyers rushing between rooms, clerks balancing stacks of motions, defendants slouching in hard plastic chairs, waiting for their names to be called.

Now, the rush had passed, leaving behind the lingering quiet that made these halls feel impossibly vast. Footsteps clicked distantly down the corridor, the occasional murmur of conversation slipping from half-open doors. The scent of brewed coffee and legal stress lingered in the air.

Where had I been when someone had the chance to slip the note into my files?

Pausing outside of Courtroom 3C, I glanced up at the dark wooden doors. Most courtrooms stayed open unless they were in session. I reached for the brass handle, pushing it open gently. The room was empty.

The benches sat vacant, the judge's bench towering over the silent chamber, the massive seal of the United States District Court carved into the wall behind it. The air inside was stale and still, as if the energy from the last hearing had been absorbed into the wood.

As I walked slowly up the center aisle, my eyes scanned every familiar detail. The jury box, untouched. The clerk's desk, tidy. The flag in the corner, motionless.

Then I reached counsel's table, placing my hand on the smooth surface. This was where I had stood, where I had argued.

I scanned the area for anything out of place, any forgotten item or sign that might provide a clue. But there was nothing—no stray papers, no missed details—just an empty table waiting for the next case.

I turned my attention to the judge's bench, letting my gaze linger. I let out a quiet breath and turned away, pushing open the courtroom doors and stepping back into the hallway.

Whatever I was looking for, I hadn't found it yet.

I wandered through the quiet corridors, letting my mind turn over every detail, searching for something—anything—that might spark a memory. Eventually, my feet carried me toward the small conference room where Holloway and I had hidden from reporters after the evidentiary hearing.

The door was unlocked, and I stepped inside, scanning the space. It was just as we'd left it—sterile and unremarkable. A long mahogany table in the center, a few chairs, a whiteboard along the far wall with remnants of someone's erased notes. The faint scent of coffee lingered, probably from a meeting earlier in the day.

I walked around the room, running my fingertips along the back of a chair as I let my mind retrace that moment. No one had come in while we were here. It had been just Holloway and me, both of us trying to process what had happened in the courtroom.

I stepped back out into the hallway.

A small group of law clerks were walking toward me, engaged in quiet conversation, their voices creating a soft counterpoint to the distant sounds of ringing phones and closing doors. They carried stacks of files, gesturing as they spoke, clearly wrapped up in their own world.

I almost didn't pay them any attention—until one of them locked eyes with me.

A flicker of recognition passed between us.

Judge Pritchard's law clerk, Sarah Grimes.

The woman held my gaze for just a second too long, her expression flashing before she quickly looked away.

She'd run into Holloway and me after the hearing. She'd helped me with my folders.

The note burned a hole in my pocket. The note that contained Sarah Grimes' handwriting.

I straightened. "Hey!"

Sarah didn't stop.

I took off after her, weaving through the handful of attorneys and court staff navigating the corridor. She heard me—I could tell—but she didn't slow.

"Excuse me!" I called out again, my voice firmer this time.

Pausing in her tracks, she pulled away from the group of clerks. When she turned to face me, her lips were pressed together in a thin line.

I stopped in front of her, catching my breath. "Can I have a moment?"

A beat of hesitation.

Then, with a sigh, she nodded. "Fine."

CHAPTER
FORTY-FIVE

SARAH GLANCED up and down the hall before grabbing my arm and pulling me into the women's restroom. The door swung shut behind us, muffling the distant echoes of footsteps and conversation.

"What are you—"

Quickly she lifted a finger to her lips, then hurried to each stall, pushing doors open. Once satisfied we were alone, she turned back to me with eyes wide and tense.

"We're safe here," she whispered, her voice barely audible over the drip of a leaky faucet.

"Safe from what?" I asked, confusion tightening my chest.

Sarah leaned against the sink, her knuckles white as she gripped the porcelain edge. "People who listen. People who report back."

"To whom?" I stepped closer, lowering my voice. "Judge Pritchard?"

Her eyes widened slightly. Bingo.

"You left that note in my file, didn't you?" I pressed.

She nodded once, a quick, nervous gesture. "I did. I had to."

"Why? What's happening, Sarah?"

She let out a shaky breath, checking the door once more. "I've been clerking for Judge Pritchard since he took over Judge Leland's docket." Her voice trembled slightly. "No one ever notices law clerks. We're like ghosts, drafting opinions, researching precedents, essentially writing the final rulings that judges claim credit for. But judges get all the attention, while they barely even read half the pleadings."

"Okay," I said, trying to follow her train of thought. "Are you saying Judge Pritchard is corrupt?"

Sarah's eyes darted toward the door again. "I think something is going on with him. I don't know how deep, but I know something isn't right."

"What makes you say that?"

"He takes phone calls. Lots of them. Always behind closed doors. And every time he does, something changes."

"What changes?"

"Rulings. Draft opinions. The way he approaches certain cases. Sometimes I finish drafting something completely in line with how he originally wanted it, and then—after one of those calls—he tells me to start over. Completely rewrites his position."

My skin prickled with goosebumps as the implications sank in. "How often does this happen?"

Her lips pressed together before she answered. "Enough that I started keeping track."

"Do you know who's on the other end of those calls?"

Sarah shook her head. "No. But whoever it is, it matters. It's like ... he's not actually the one making the decisions. He's just following instructions."

I tried to piece together what this meant. A federal judge taking orders from someone else—potentially someone connected to Ortega's case. The bishop on the chessboard, moving diagonally through the legal system.

"I don't know how far it goes," Sarah said, her expression urgent, her voice dropping even lower. "But what I do know is that this goes beyond just bad judgment. Someone is pulling Pritchard's strings, and it's affecting real cases with real consequences."

I nodded, my mind already racing through the implications. Who could have this kind of influence over a federal judge? What kind of leverage or power would they need? And most importantly—why use it to first put Ortega in prison, then get him out?

"Thanks," I finally said, voice tight. "You did the right thing by coming forward."

She swallowed, her eyes pleading. "Please—just don't let this come back to me. I can't lose my career over this."

"I promise. No one will ever know."

Sarah exhaled. "Be careful," she warned softly as I turned to leave. "People like Pritchard ... they don't play fair."

"Believe me," I whispered, my mind flashing to my mother's empty desk, her case files left unfinished, her life cut short for getting too close to the truth. "I learned that lesson long ago."

CHAPTER
FORTY-SIX

BY THE TIME I got back to the office, my mind felt like it had run a marathon.

Erin was already waiting for me, flipping through a file.

"Hey," she greeted, glancing up. Her eyes narrowed slightly as she took in my expression. "Everything okay?"

I shut the door behind me and leaned against it before stepping forward to drop my bag onto the desk. "I don't even know anymore."

Erin straightened. "What happened?"

"It was the clerk," I said quietly, sinking heavily into my chair. "Sarah Grimes. She's the one who left the note."

"How'd you find out?" Erin asked, her pen frozen mid-twirl between her fingers.

Hesitant, I was still processing everything Sarah had told me. The faint scent of the courthouse—old paper and furniture polish—seemed to cling to my clothes, a reminder of what had just transpired.

"I confronted her after court," I said finally. "Pritchard takes phone calls—private ones, behind closed doors. After those calls, his rulings change. Sarah's had to rewrite opinions, reverse decisions. He just flips, no explanation. She's been keeping track."

Erin's pen stilled completely, her expression hardening. "That's ... not normal."

"No, it's not."

Erin sat forward, her gaze sharp. "Does she know who's on the other end of those calls?"

I shook my head. "No. But it's got to be someone important. Someone who gives orders."

A tense silence settled between us, broken only by the hum of the fluorescent lights overhead.

Erin sighed heavily, rubbing at her temple. "A sitting federal judge has been taking outside influence on his rulings?"

"Yes," I confirmed. "And Sarah seems absolutely certain."

"That explains a lot." Erin tapped a pen against her lips. "But it doesn't answer why Pritchard went out of his way to order a special prosecutor and push this habeas case through."

"He had to. Whoever is on the other end of that phone call wanted Ortega out."

"But why? This person had also wanted Ortega convicted over a decade ago. Why undo it after all these years?"

"I don't know," I admitted, sinking further into my chair. "Ortega had something that got him locked away."

Erin drummed her fingers against the desk. "If Ortega was involved in gun trafficking, he could've threatened to expose whoever helped put him away."

"Getting Ortega released was damage control."

"But why go through all this trouble just to silence him? He was already in prison."

I stared at the ceiling for a moment, counting the tiny gray spots splattered against white tile directly above me. "Maybe it *is* what James said ... they couldn't get to him on the inside. He'd become more of a liability behind bars."

Erin's expression darkened. "So getting him out was how they did it?"

Slowly, the realization settled uncomfortably in my chest. "If Ortega had protection in prison—someone watching out for him—then the only way to eliminate him was to make sure he wasn't in there anymore."

Erin gasped. "So they fought to get his conviction overturned ... just so they could kill him on the outside."

My stomach twisted into a knot. "And we handed it to them on a silver platter."

Erin tapped her pen against her thigh. "So what now? What's our next move?"

"We have to prove Pritchard is compromised. That these rulings weren't just bad judgment, but manipulation. And we need to figure out who the hell he's been talking to."

"Do you realize what you're suggesting here, right?" Erin watched me closely. "Pritchard is a sitting federal judge. If we're right about this, it goes way beyond us. We can't handle something this big alone."

I ran my hand over my face. "Are you suggesting we take this to Callahan?"

Erin nodded firmly. "Yes. This is above our pay grade. He's going to need to know."

"Fine. Let's do it."

We gathered our files and headed to Callahan's office. The carpet muffled our footsteps as we approached his glass-walled corner office where Callahan—a wiry man in his early fifties with salt-and-pepper hair—looked up, startled, as we approached.

He set his pen down. "Something's wrong."

"We need to talk," Erin said, stepping inside and closing the door behind us.

"I'm listening." Callahan folded his hands on the desk, his wedding ring glinting under the overhead lights.

I glanced at Erin, then took a deep breath. "We think Judge Pritchard is compromised."

Callahan's brow furrowed. "Explain."

"Sarah Grimes—Pritchard's clerk—came to me. She's the one who left the note. She says Pritchard takes private phone calls all the time, and after those calls, his rulings change. She's had to rewrite opinions, reverse decisions—it's like he's taking orders from someone."

Callahan sat up straighter. "Do we know who's on the other end of those calls?"

I shook my head. "No. But whoever it is, they have enough power that Pritchard just falls in line."

Erin leaned forward. "It also means Pritchard didn't push this habeas petition forward on his own. Someone told him to do it. And, maybe it was done to expose Bard on purpose."

Callahan rubbed his chin, his gaze narrowing. "Do you trust this clerk?"

"Clerks usually know everything behind the scenes."

Callahan nodded slowly. "I was a clerk once. You're right—we see it all. If she says Pritchard is compromised, there's a good chance it's true."

"So, what do we do?" Erin asked, her voice tight.

Callahan considered. "We need a warrant to dig deeper. That means a sworn statement from Sarah. Without that, we don't have probable cause."

A pang of anxiety tightened in my chest. "I'm not sure she'll agree to that. She's already terrified she'll be exposed."

Callahan's gaze was firm but understanding. "I know it's a big ask, Alex. But we can't move forward on whispers alone."

I glanced at Erin, who nodded gently.

Pressure settled deep in my chest. "I'll see what I can do."

Callahan nodded, his expression grave but supportive. "Be careful with this. If you're right, the consequences will ripple far beyond this office."

As soon as Erin and I stepped into the hallway, my phone buzzed in my pocket. I pulled it out, glancing at the screen—Lisa.

"Tell me you have good news," I answered.

"We got the warrant on Ortega," Lisa said, her voice clipped with urgency, "but there's a problem—he was trying to flee. TSA flagged him at the airport, and they're holding him now."

I tightened my grip around the phone. "Where was he going?"

"Venezuela."

Randall Pierce had also tried to flee to Venezuela before his arrest.

Pierce, the defendant in my last trial—the one with ties to the trafficking ring that killed my mother.

"I'm on my way," I said, already hammering the elevator call button, willing it to appear faster.

"Let me go with you," Erin said.

I shook my head. "I need you to stay here and start investigating Pritchard. If we're right about this, we need to move fast."

CHAPTER FORTY-SEVEN

THE DRIVE to Bush International Airport felt twice as long as it should have. Every red light, every slow-moving sedan in front of me, every unnecessary turn added to the pressure building in my temples. By the time I pulled into the parking garage, my mind was racing.

I parked in the hourly lot and jogged toward the terminal, already sweating from the Texas heat. The young woman behind the TSA information desk glanced up at me as I approached, my breathing ragged.

"Can I help you?" she asked, polite but firm.

I flashed my credentials, flipping my badge open for her to see. "Assistant U.S. Attorney Hayes. I was told TSA is holding a detainee under warrant—Gabriel Ortega."

The woman's brows furrowed, but she nodded. "One moment." She picked up a phone and spoke in hushed tones.

Passengers hurried past me, dragging their rolling suitcases. Families shuffled through the security checkpoint lines. The stale, recycled air of the terminal carried the mingled scents of fast food and cologne.

A few moments later, a TSA officer stepped forward from the secured entrance, a name tag reading D. Reynolds clipped to his chest. He gave me a quick once-over before speaking.

"You're here for Ortega?"

I nodded. "I need to speak with him."

"Come with me. We've got him in a detainment room just past secondary screening."

I walked beside him as we made our way through a set of restricted doors, past the usual security lines, where barefoot travelers stepped through scanners, and a young agent ran a wand over an elderly man's outstretched arms.

"He was flagged the moment his passport got scanned," Reynolds explained as we walked. "Tried to play it cool, but when we asked him to step aside, he got real tense."

"What flight was he trying to board?"

"Nonstop to Caracas. One-way."

We moved past another checkpoint, this time flashing our credentials at a security station before stepping into a quieter hallway, separate from the main airport bustle. The walls were stark white, the air chilled by an aggressive ventilation system. I could hear low voices from other rooms—other travelers being questioned for smuggling, suspicious itineraries, or flagged documents.

Finally, we reached a steel-reinforced door with a small, frosted window at eye level. Reynolds swiped a keycard, and the door unlocked with a dull beep.

I stepped into the small, sterile room, the air stale and heavy with the weight of unspoken words. The metal table in the center was scratched from years of use, the chair opposite me occupied by Gabriel Ortega. His wrists bound in cuffs, his posture relaxed like a man who had weathered too many storms to fear another.

He looked up as I entered, his dark eyes scanning me with predatory assessment.

"If it isn't the lady who got me out of prison. Didn't expect to see you again so soon."

I pulled out the chair across from him. "I just want to talk."

Ortega scoffed. "I don't have to talk to you."

"You're right," I said, folding my hands on the table. "You don't. But you're not facing federal charges right now."

"Yeah? What's your point?"

"You're still facing state charges," I said. "But I outrank the state."

Ortega's eyes narrowed, but he was listening.

"If you talk to me," I continued, "and we can make a deal, I can bring the weight of the federal system into play. Which means I can trump whatever the state has lined up for you."

I leaned forward. "So, it's up to you. You can wait for the state to bury you, or you can start talking to me now."

"This whole thing is bullshit," Ortega replied, sneering. "How are you gonna fight to get me out of prison just to turn around and try to put me back in on something else?"

His tone grew more agitated. "I didn't do anything wrong. You all act like I'm some big player, but I'm just trying to get the hell out of here. You're gonna arrest me for trying to leave? That's a crime now?"

"Depends. Why were you trying to leave?"

"Because I don't wanna stick around and see what happens next."

I filed that response away.

"Why don't you talk to me about this?" I pressed, keeping my tone casual. "Help me understand why you're running. Maybe I can help."

"Like you helped me last time?" Ortega let out a bitter laugh.

"Man, this whole thing is rigged. One minute, I'm getting my ass locked away for something I didn't do. Next thing I know, I'm miraculously free because of some technicality, and now you all want to pin something *else* on me?"

"That 'technicality' was your public defender being bribed to throw your case," I said, watching him. "Do you know who paid him?"

Ortega's jaw tightened, his casual demeanor faltering.

I leaned in. "You knew your own lawyer was bought to betray you. That's why you pushed for the petition."

He didn't answer, but the flicker in his eyes said plenty.

I pressed on.

"You're not stupid, Ortega," I said. "You knew you had an argument. But why now? Why wait twelve years before making a move?"

His fingers twitched against the cuffs, his jaw shifting as he stared at the table.

"You were protected in prison, weren't you? They wanted you silent from the beginning, but you found allies inside. But you weren't safe on the inside anymore. Is that it? Or did someone want you out because you were *too* safe?"

Ortega exhaled sharply, shaking his head. "You think you're real smart, don't you?"

"I am smart. And I think you're scared."

The smirk dropped completely from his face.

Ortega leaned forward slightly, his eyes narrowing.

"You think this was just about me? You think some nobody public defender decided to take a bribe on his own?"

I kept my expression neutral, but my heart was hammering in my chest.

Ortega let out a sharp breath, shaking his head. "Leland."

The word hung in the air between us, thick and suffocating.

I frowned. "What about Leland?"

Ortega gave me a pointed look. "Put it together. You went to Leland for answers—he gave you the push you needed. But tell me, why do you think he helped you?"

I swallowed hard, the pieces slamming into place all at once. Leland wasn't just some retired judge looking to do the right thing. He was the one pulling the strings all along. And I had walked right into his hands.

"You had something on him," I murmured, more to myself than to Ortega. "Something big enough that he made sure you got locked away."

Ortega smiled—cold, bitter. "And what's the best way to make sure someone never talks?"

"The charge," I whispered, my pulse skyrocketing. "Felony murder carries the death penalty."

Ortega sat back, arms stretching against the cuffs. "They thought the state might do their dirty work for them."

Leland had been pulling the strings from the beginning—manipulating the case, the trial, and maybe even Delacroix. And I had gone right to him, had asked him for guidance, had let him lead me exactly where he wanted me to go.

I took a slow, steadying breath. "What specifically did you have on Leland?"

"Leland's got people—but so do I." Ortega's dark eyes flicked up to meet mine. "And he couldn't get to me from the inside, no matter how hard he tried. Even though he manipulated the case, even though he tried to push the jury, they didn't give him the death penalty he needed."

I clenched my jaw, the sheer scope of it all hitting me like a tidal wave.

If Leland had gone this far to put Ortega away, he'd left a trail of corruption stretching back years, maybe decades.

"You didn't answer one thing—why fight to get out now?"

Exhaustion flickered across Ortega's face.

"They finally got to some of my guys. I wasn't safe inside anymore. I wanted out—*and* they wanted me out."

"They?" Holding my breath.

"Yeah. But I never thought you'd get Bard to admit to the bribe."

I frowned, searching his face.

"What did you have on Leland?"

For a moment, he didn't say anything.

Then, his lips curled into a slow, knowing smile.

"You're just as smart as your mother was," he murmured, voice quieter now. "But that's what got her killed."

CHAPTER
FORTY-EIGHT

MY BREATH HITCHED and my heart pounded in my ears, the fluorescent lights too bright in my vision.

I opened my mouth to demand more. What did Ortega know about my mother? About her investigation? Before I could speak, the door to the room clicked open.

Both Ortega and I looked up at the same time.

A man stepped inside, closing the door quietly behind him. He wore a dark suit, crisp and perfectly tailored, sunglasses that obscured his eyes, and a demeanor that sent an immediate chill down my spine.

Ortega's posture shifted, his whole body going rigid as he stared at the man. His fingers twitched against his cuffs.

I straightened, forcing control over the sudden tension in my chest. I kept my voice even and asked, "Can I help you?"

The man didn't answer. He turned his head—enough to acknowledge me—before his gaze shifted back to Ortega.

Then, in a deep, measured voice, he spoke. "The Bishop sends his regards."

The room turned ice cold.

Ortega's entire demeanor cracked, posture snapping upright and his hands flying up in surrender, his cuffs clinking against the metal table.

Panic flooded his features.

"Wait, wait—"

The man moved too fast.

A gun appeared in his hand, smooth and practiced.

A sharp, suppressed pop cut through the room.

Ortega's head snapped back, a perfect red hole blooming between his eyes.

For half a second, his body stayed upright, as if suspended between life and death.

Then, with a sickening thud, he slumped forward onto the table. His back was still, unbreathing.

I froze.

I wasn't sure if I screamed. I wasn't sure if I breathed.

The sound of my own heartbeat slammed against my skull, deafening in the stillness that followed.

The man in the dark suit turned his head, looking at me with an eerie sort of calm, his sunglasses still in place, reflecting nothing back at me.

And then, in that same measured voice, he spoke again.

"He's right, you know. Your mother was too smart for her own good."

My lungs seized.

I saw my entire life flash before my eyes. My mother's case. My career.

Had this man been the one to kill her? Was he here to kill me, too?

This had to be it. I couldn't move, couldn't breathe, couldn't do anything other than prepare myself to die.

Still looking in my direction, he lifted his gun. I cowered as he placed it back in the holster beneath his jacket. He buttoned it up and turned, placed his hand on the doorknob, and walked out.

Like it had been nothing.

Like Ortega's life had meant nothing.

Like I meant nothing.

The door clicked shut behind him.

Seconds, maybe minutes passed before the world snapped back into focus with the sound of rushed footsteps and shouting.

"Shots fired! Shots fired!"

The door slammed open, and two TSA agents rushed in, weapons drawn.

Their eyes landed on Ortega's lifeless body, slumped over the table. Blood pooled beneath his head, spreading across the metal surface like crimson ink. He swung his gun toward me. "Hands where we can see them! Now!"

I barely registered the command, my brain still trying to catch up.

"A man just came in here and shot him!" I gasped, my voice shaky but clear. "He—he just walked out. He—"

One of the agents stepped forward, taking my arm in a rough grip. "What man? We didn't see anyone come in."

"He was just here! A man in a dark suit—he shot Ortega right in front of me!"

"We didn't see anyone," the second agent repeated, his suspicious gaze locking onto me.

I shook my head, stomach twisting. "How could you not have seen him? What the hell were you doing out there? Who let him in?"

No answer. Instead, one of the agents reached for his radio. "We need HPD in here, now."

Seconds later, more uniformed officers flooded into the room. My brain felt disconnected from my body, barely processing the chaos spinning around me.

Cold metal snapped around my wrists.

I jolted at the feeling of handcuffs tightening, my breath catching, as an officer's firm voice rang in my ear.

"You're under arrest."

I wanted to scream. Wanted to fight.

But I knew better. I knew when to shut up.

Because this wasn't just an accident. It was a setup. And I had to figure out who in this room was part of it.

The walk to the holding cell stretched forever. The officers flanking me weren't rough, but their grips were firm, every step a deliberate attempt to humiliate me. My suit jacket was rumpled against my arms, my wrists aching from the tight metal cuffs. I kept my chin high, my face unreadable, but inside, my mind was spinning out of control.

Ortega is dead. And someone just framed me for it.

The hallways blurred as the agents led me through the secure area of the airport, past the murmuring voices of officers, TSA agents, and a few lingering passengers with no idea they were standing near the epicenter of a conspiracy unfolding in real-time.

Finally, they took me into a small, windowless holding cell, the walls a dull off-white, the cot in the corner bolted to the floor. I barely had time to take a breath before one of the officers crossed his arms and said, "You want your phone call?"

I forced myself to sound calm. "Yes."

He exchanged a glance with his partner before nodding. "You get one. Make it count."

They uncuffed one hand, securing the other to a steel ring bolted to the table, then slid a corded phone toward me. I stretched my fingers before dialing Erin's number.

The phone rang. Once. Twice.

Come on, Erin. Pick up.

The third ring. My chest tightened, the weight of everything threatening to crush me where I sat.

The fourth ring. *Shit.*

"Mitchell speaking." Erin's professional tone came through the line.

Relief slammed into me. "Erin, thank God."

Erin's voice sharpened. "Alex? What's going on? I'm seeing a call from the airport detention facility."

I swallowed. "He's dead."

Silence.

"What?"

I squeezed my eyes shut, forcing the words out. "And I've been arrested. I need you to get down here right now."

"Alex, what the actual—"

"I can't explain over the phone," I cut in, glancing toward the officer watching me from the corner. "Just get here. Please."

"You know I can't be your lawyer, right?"

"Obviously." I let out a humorless breath. "But you *can* get these clowns to pull the footage from the interrogation room and show them that I was a witness, not the goddamn trigger man. I was almost shot myself."

Erin cursed under her breath. "Okay, okay. Stay put. Don't say another word to anyone until I get there."

The line went dead, and I stared at the receiver, wondering if Ortega had been about to tell me who killed my mother before his life was snuffed out. Now we'd never know.

CHAPTER
FORTY-NINE

TIME in the holding cell crawled like a knife across skin. Each minute stretched into an eternity as I sat with my back against the cold concrete wall, the image of Ortega's final moments replaying in endless, horrific loops. The way his eyes had widened in terror. The spray of crimson. The words that haunted me: *The Bishop sends his regards.*

I barely registered the sound of the door buzzing open when an officer stepped inside.

"You're free to go," he said, unlocking the cuffs on my wrist.

I stood, rubbing my wrists as I stepped out of the cell and into the hallway.

Erin waited for me. The second our eyes met, I closed the distance between us and pulled her into a tight hug. For a moment, she felt stiff, like she wasn't sure how to handle the contact. But after a beat, she exhaled and wrapped her arms around me.

I let out a breath. "Thank you."

"No problem," Erin muttered, pulling back. Her eyes flickered over me like she was checking for damage.

I followed her gaze and spotted a familiar face standing behind her.

The FBI agent, Logan Elliott—tall, broad-shouldered, with close-cropped salt-and-pepper hair and eyes that seemed to catalog everything. I'd seen him at the courthouse during the Bard hearing, watching from the back with that same impassive expression.

I raised an eyebrow. "Agent Elliott."

Elliott gave me a small nod, his usual unreadable expression firmly in place. "Ms. Hayes."

"You here for moral support?" I asked, already knowing the answer.

"Do you mind if I get a statement from you?"

I sighed. "Yeah. Let's do this."

Erin and I followed Elliott down a hallway until we reached a small interview room. It was far more professional than the holding cell I'd just been in, but it still had that sterile, government-issue air—gray walls, a simple wooden table, two chairs on either side.

We all sat down and Elliott pulled out a recorder, setting it on the table between us.

"Let's start from the beginning," he said, pressing the record button.

I rested my arms on the table. I was tired. I was angry. And I was done playing games. So I told him everything.

Agent Elliott clicked his pen against the notepad in front of him as I explained the case from the beginning, from my coming across Ortega's habeas petition all the way down to his murder. Elliott watched me with the kind of measured detachment only federal agents seemed to perfect.

"Let's go over the shooter again," he said, voice steady. "He was wearing a dark suit and sunglasses?"

I nodded, digging my fingers into the fabric of my pants just to keep my hands steady.

"Height?"

"Six foot, maybe a little over?"

"Build?"

"Lean, but fit. Like someone trained. Someone used to moving quickly."

Elliott jotted something down before looking back at me. "Hair color?"

"I—I don't know. His hair was cut short, military-style. Could've been brown, could've been black."

Elliott gave the faintest nod before moving on. "Did he say anything before he pulled the trigger?"

"'The Bishop sends his regards.'"

Elliott's jaw tightened almost imperceptibly, but he said nothing for a long moment.

"After that, he looked at you?"

A shudder ran through me. I nodded.

"And he spoke to you?"

I nodded again, and recited the words, "'Your mother was too smart for her own good.'"

Elliott tapped his pen once against his notepad. "And then he walked out."

"Yes."

"No attempt to harm you?"

"No."

"Did he have a visible exit strategy? Did you hear anything that indicated how he left?"

I shook my head. "No. But agents barged in seconds later, so either he had someone waiting for him, or he knew exactly how much time he had to get out."

Elliott scribbled a few more notes, then set his pen down. "I don't have any more questions for now."

Erin stood and offered Elliott a tight smile. I followed her lead.

"We'll be in touch," she told the man.

Elliott nodded, standing as well. "Let me know if you remember anything else."

I didn't respond or acknowledge him before following Erin out of the room and toward her car. By the time we got outside, the weight of everything pressed down on my shoulders. My mind reeled against the memories. The gunshot replayed, the popping loud despite the suppressor. Ortega collapsing, dead before his head slammed against the table.

Your mother was too smart for her own good.

I barely made it into the car before my breath hitched.

Tears burned my eyes, spilling over before I could stop them. My shoulders shook, my breaths coming shallow and uneven, and I pressed a hand against the car door to keep myself upright.

I hadn't even cried like this when Andrews had shot me.

I didn't hear Erin move, but I felt her hand land gently on my shoulder. A quick, steadying squeeze.

That simple touch broke something in me, and fresh tears welled up. I forced them back, taking ragged breaths to compose myself. I exhaled shakily, wiping at my face with the sleeve of my jacket before turning to her, cheeks flushed from the effort of holding in the wreckage of the last hour.

"I'm really sorry this happened," Erin said, voice quiet.

I shook my head, forcing out a small, broken laugh. "It's okay." I straightened and let my gaze meet hers. She looked back at me with wide, concerned eyes.

"How did you get them to let me go?"

She rounded the car to the driver's side and slid in. I got into the passenger's seat. "I made them pull the footage from the room, like you'd suggested."

I exhaled in relief, but the moment was short-lived. Ortega had known something about my mother—something important enough that the same people had silenced both of them. Whatever information he might have shared was now lost forever.

"What did you find out about Pritchard?" I asked, turning toward her.

Erin's fingers tightened on the steering wheel. "I didn't get far. Sarah wasn't at the courthouse, and I didn't want to leave anything on her voicemail."

I nodded, my thoughts drifting back to the moments before the shooter entered. "Ortega knew something about my mother's death. He was about to tell me more when that man walked in."

"The timing wasn't a coincidence," Erin said.

"No," I said, my voice low and certain. "He told Ortega that the Bishop sends his regards."

Erin nodded. "Yeah. I heard you tell Elliott."

I swallowed. "Who's the bishop?"

CHAPTER FIFTY

THE NEXT MORNING, I stormed into Erin's office, gripping the transcript and my case notes like they held the secret to immortality. Career immortality, maybe.

She barely looked up from her screen before clocking my expression and straightening in her chair.

"Good morning to you too," she said dryly. "What are you doing here? Take a damn day off, Alex."

"I have what we need," I blurted out, shutting the door behind me. "We can get a warrant on Leland."

Her fingers froze over the keyboard. Her head snapped up. "Leland? What happened to Pritchard?"

"It was never Pritchard. He was just a puppet." I laid the transcript out between us, pressing my fingers against the paper. "It was Leland pulling the strings the whole time."

Erin frowned, flipping through the pages. "Walk me through it."

"Ortega wasn't just some wrongfully convicted guy. He had something on Leland—big enough that Leland made sure he was buried."

"Leland bribed Bard?"

"Not just that. Leland orchestrated the whole thing. The trial. The charges. He pushed for felony murder because he thought the jury would hand down the death penalty. When they didn't, he made sure Ortega stayed locked away forever."

Erin let out a slow breath, leaning back in her chair. "Jesus."

"Leland never stopped pulling strings. He'd been the one pressuring Pritchard. Leland pushed for the evidentiary hearing. He wanted Ortega out because Ortega had protection inside prison and was finally threatening to talk."

"And we played right into it."

I gave her a steady look. "Erin, Leland is the bishop. And he's just one piece on the chess board."

Realization sank into Erin's eyes. "Holy shit."

"So, what now?"

"We take this to Callahan, get a warrant. And then we bring Leland in."

She grabbed the transcript, scanning over it again. I could tell the moment she hit the part about the chessboard—her head tilted, a muscle in her jaw tightening.

"You're sure this will hold?" she asked, looking up at me.

"It should. And I'm willing to sign a sworn affidavit on everything Ortega told me. With that, plus the video, plus the call transcripts, we have enough."

Erin stood, her chair rolling away from the desk. "Let's go."

I followed her out to Callahan's office, not bothering to announce ourselves with so much as a knock before stepping inside.

Callahan glanced up, eyeing us both warily as he leaned back in his chair. "You two look like you're about to ruin someone's day."

Slapping the transcript onto his desk, I proclaimed, "We have enough for a warrant on Leland."

That got his full attention. He grabbed the pages, flipping through them with careful precision.

He looked back up at me, his expression filled with exasperation. "At this point, I'm not even surprised you want to arrest a different federal judge. But can either of you explain this to me?"

Erin took the lead, outlining the case from the habeas petition all the way to my meeting with Ortega.

Callahan's expression darkened as he listened, but he didn't interrupt. Erin finished, and he said nothing right away. After a tense moment, he set the transcript back down, steepling his fingers in thought. "It's solid. Bribery alone is enough for an arrest."

I exhaled in relief, but he held up a finger.

"*But.*"

Callahan leaned forward, his expression measured. "While we can bring Leland in on bribery, if we really think he's tied into something bigger—this whole conspiracy—we need more evidence to connect all the dots."

"I think we can get him to talk."

Callahan raised a skeptical brow. "You think Leland's going to roll?"

"The Bishop, from these transcripts. And if that's the case, he knows a hell of a lot more than he's letting on. We can play Bard against him. Then, once Bard knows Leland's been arrested, we can set up a prisoner's dilemma."

Callahan studied me for a long moment. "Pretty diabolical."

My lips twitched, but my heart hammered against my ribs. This wasn't just about a case anymore—it was about whatever had gotten my mother killed.

"Go ahead and get the warrant. Let's see this through."

As I let out a slow breath, the weight of it finally hit me like a concrete wall. We were going after Leland. And I wasn't stopping until we took everything down with him.

CHAPTER FIFTY-ONE

THE GRAY, overcast dawn blurred the line between night and day. The street was eerily quiet, save for the low hum of idling engines from the three black SUVs parked along the curb. The air outside Judge Leland's house felt thick, heavy, like a storm about to break.

A full tactical team stood poised, their Kevlar vests strapped tight, their hands resting on the grips of their weapons, waiting for the signal.

I stood beside Erin, my arms crossed tightly over my chest as we watched the scene unfold. Everything felt surreal.

I looked at the understated brick house with its manicured lawn and tasteful landscaping. Nothing about it revealed the corruption inside its walls or the lives ruined by the man who slept there.

Soon, this would no longer be a judge's house. It'd be a crime scene.

A senior FBI agent gave a silent nod, and within seconds, the team moved in.

They breached the door with precision, entering quickly, voices booming—

"FEDERAL AGENTS! SEARCH WARRANT!"

A rush of movement inside. Muffled shouting. A dog barking before a whimper.

A woman's startled scream, followed by the heavy thud of hurried footsteps.

Chaos erupted from within. Grunting and shouting; banging against the floors or walls. More yelling from a woman.

Then they brought him out in cuffs. Judge Everett Leland, once one of the most powerful names in the judicial system, now a man being led down his own driveway in handcuffs, his prestige stripped away in an instant. The agents on either side of him kept firm grips on his arms, but Leland didn't resist. He didn't struggle. He didn't even speak.

Leland lifted his head, his calm, calculating eyes locking onto mine as he passed by.

I swallowed hard, the back of my neck prickling with something I couldn't quite name.

Leland continued on with calm awareness. Like he had been expecting this.

Erin shifted beside me, her presence steady, but her fingers twisted nervously at her side, betraying her own unease at the gravity of what we'd just done.

I should have felt victorious. I should have felt like we had won. Instead, I felt like I was standing at the edge of an abyss, peering into depths I couldn't comprehend, unable to see what dangers lurked below.

CHAPTER
FIFTY-TWO

THE COFFEE SHOP was quiet for a weekday morning, the hum of low conversation mixing with the occasional hiss of an espresso machine. Sunlight streamed through the large front windows, casting soft golden light onto the wooden tables and scattered patrons sipping their coffee.

I spotted Holloway first, sitting in the back corner, a black coffee in front of him, his sleeves rolled up as he scrolled through something on his phone. Lisa was with him, already stirring sugar into her cup, glancing at her phone like she was waiting on something.

Steeling myself, I headed over.

When Holloway looked up and saw me, he smiled, setting his phone down as I slid into the seat across from him.

"Hey," he said, his voice warm.

"Hey," I echoed, mirroring his small smile.

Lisa grinned at me over the rim of her coffee cup. "Took you long enough."

"For what?"

"To show up, obviously," she said, feigning innocence. "Not for anything else."

Rolling my eyes, I dropped my bag onto the chair next to me. "Glad you two got to know each other while I was busy not getting held at gunpoint."

Lisa grinned, setting her cup down. "We had so much time on our hands, so we just talked about you."

I gave her a flat look. "Fantastic."

Holloway chuckled, giving Lisa a nod. "It was about time we met. I've heard plenty."

Lisa raised an eyebrow. "All good things, I hope."

Holloway laughed. "Of course."

Lisa shot me a look. "I like him."

I shook my head, exhaling. "Great. Now I have two of you."

A shadow crossed over our table. I looked up to see Erin standing over us, coffee in hand, a smug grin on her face. "Am I interrupting something?"

Holloway chuckled, shaking his head. "Not at all, Mitchell."

I motioned for her to sit, grabbing my bag from the empty chair. "You're always interrupting something."

Erin took the seat next to me, glancing between the three of us as if trying to read the air.

"Don't look at me," Lisa said. "I got here first."

Erin took a sip of her coffee and got straight to business. "Leland's not talking."

I sighed, not even a little surprised. "I figured."

"Seems he's already made peace with whatever comes next."

"Who's his lawyer?" I asked, not betraying the nerves pulsating through me.

Erin set her cup down. "Not sure yet. His arraignment is this afternoon, so we'll find out."

Holloway jeered. "Think it's Hargrave?"

I snorted, shaking my head. "Wouldn't put it past him."

"We'll see how it all shakes out," Erin said. She leaned back in her chair, crossing her arms. "Now, can we just take a second to count how many times Alex has been at gunpoint?"

I groaned. "Come on."

"No, really," Erin insisted. "We should keep a tally."

Holloway chuckled. "It's a fair question."

I took a sip of my coffee. "I feel like you're just trying to make fun of me."

"No, I'm just deeply concerned that this is becoming a recurring problem," Erin said dryly. "It was Andrews. The guy in the suit. Wasn't there also the time in law school when—"

"Oh my God." I shoved my chair back, standing up. "We're done here."

Erin saluted with her coffee. "Try not to get held at gunpoint before the arraignment."

Lisa agreed, lifting her cup. "Yeah, I'd hate to lose my entertainment."

"Glad to know I'm keeping you both amused."

Erin and Lisa exchanged looks like they were enjoying this way too much. I sighed, shaking my head as I grabbed my bag. "I'll see you later."

Lisa waved me off, and Erin gave me one last smug grin before taking another sip of her coffee.

Holloway pushed back from his seat and stood. "I'll walk you out."

I nodded, ignoring the knowing looks Lisa and Erin shot us, the kind friends give when they know something's brewing but are pretending not to notice. We stepped outside together, the warmth of the sun a stark contrast to the cool air inside the coffee shop.

For a few moments, we walked in silence, the buzz of passing cars and the murmur of city life filling the space between us.

Holloway cleared his throat. "I'm officially no longer affiliated with the U.S. Attorney's Office as of today."

My step faltered, pulse quickening. "That so?"

"Which means," he continued, slowing his walk to a full stop, "if we wanted this to be something more, there wouldn't be a problem with it."

My stomach erupted in butterflies. I looked at him, really looked at him—the sharp intelligence in his eyes, the way he had been steady through everything, the way he had never once doubted me, even when I doubted myself.

I let out a breath, my lips curving into something softer.

"I'd really like that."

His smile widened. When he took my hands in his, for just a

second, everything else faded—the stress, the cases, the fact that I had been arrested less than twenty-four hours ago.

But a nagging thought crept in, and before I could stop myself, I asked, "What about D.C.?"

"We'll make it work."

Studying him, I searched for any flicker of doubt in his expression. I found none. And for the first time in a long time, I let myself believe that maybe something in my life didn't have to be complicated.

CHAPTER
FIFTY-THREE

THE ECHO of our footsteps bounced off the polished tile floors as Erin and I made our way through the halls of the U.S. Attorney's Office. Leland had been denied bail at his arraignment, the presiding judge calling him "a textbook flight risk" given his resources and connections. When they'd led him away, his mask had slipped for just a moment, revealing not defeat but something calculating, as if counting moves on an invisible chessboard.

"You good?" Erin asked, glancing at me with raised eyebrows.

I exhaled slowly, forcing the tension from my shoulders. "Yeah. Just ready to move forward."

"At least you finally got one big win under your belt. How's it feel to be an official federal prosecutor now?"

"Feels more like survival than victory."

"Welcome to the show."

We turned the corner toward our offices. Callahan's voice rang out behind us before we split off. "Alex, hold up."

Erin and I faced him, watching as he strode toward us, holding a file. He gave Erin a quick nod and then turned to me.

"Got a minute?"

I glanced at Erin, who gave me an amused look and nodded. "I'll see you later."

Callahan beckoned me into his office. As soon as I stepped inside, a flutter of nerves filled my body.

"Relax," he said, his lips twitching into a smile. "You look like you're waiting for the guillotine."

"Can you blame me?"

"For once, Hayes, you're not in trouble." He chuckled, sliding a thin manila folder across the desk toward me. "I've got a case for you."

I took the folder, eyebrows raised. "Seriously?"

"It's not the crime of the century. Nothing huge, but a straightforward bank fraud trial. Consider it your warm-up."

I couldn't help but grin. "Really? No more habeas petitions?"

"Don't worry, I'm sure Wexler can save you a few if you miss them."

I grimaced. "No, thanks. I'm good. Speaking of, I haven't seen him around the office."

Callahan nodded. "He's over at the Galveston office. Wanted to follow up with Langford about the mix-up with the Ortega reply."

"Yeah. That'd be nice to get some closure on."

"Nothing for you to worry about for now," Callahan said. "Just focus on this case and try not to accuse everyone of misconduct."

I twisted my lips, but I could tell there was no bite behind his joke. "Thanks, Nathan. Really."

"Don't thank me yet," he said, despite his smile. "Federal judges run their courtrooms a bit differently than that rodeo over in state court. More rules, fewer theatrics."

"Honestly, the whole legal system feels like a bit of a circus anyway."

Nathan grinned. "Welcome to the big top. Good luck, Counselor."

I laughed quietly as I stood and headed out of his office, the file clutched firmly in my hands. As I stepped into the hall, I glanced down at the label. *United States v. Bryce Coulter.*

I barely settled back in my office when someone knocked lightly on my door. I looked up to see Cynthia, the department's administrative assistant, holding a small bundle of documents.

"Got some paperwork here," she said. "I wasn't sure if it goes to you or Erin."

I waved her over. "I'll take a look. Thanks."

She placed the stack on my desk with a quick nod. "Sure thing."

When the door clicked shut behind her, I set Coulter's file aside, curiosity drawing me to the stack of papers instead. The top page had a yellow sticky note that said "Leland."

I flipped through the pages absently at first—old financial statements, printouts of emails—until my eyes landed on something different.

A black-and-white printout of a chessboard.

I froze, fingers tightening around the page.

Squares were labeled, some marked with cryptic notations and initials. But it was the words scribbled beneath one particular piece that sent chills rippling down my spine.

Under a bishop icon—scribbled hastily in blue ink—was the name: LELAND.

Below it, on the mirrored diagonal square, another name was scrawled hastily in the same handwriting: THATCHER.

As I scanned the other pieces, my vision blurred with adrenaline.

Across the board, none of the other squares had been filled in. My pulse roared in my ears, my hands shaking as I stared at the document. For the first time, the scope of what I was facing truly hit home.

Leland was just one player. Thatcher had to be another.

I glanced around my quiet office, hairs rising on the back of my neck. The paper crinkled beneath my fingers.

A wave of dread washed over me. I was standing on the edge of something enormous—something that could change everything I thought I knew.

If Leland and Thatcher were only bishops—

Then who the hell was the King?

Continue reading for a preview of *The Bishop's Recusal*.

Join the LT Ryan reader family & receive a free copy of the Alex Hayes story, *Trial by Fire*. Click the link below to get started:

https://ltryan.com/alex-hayes-newsletter-signup-1

THE BISHOP'S RECUSAL
CHAPTER 1

Bryce Coulter was going down for wire fraud, and everyone knew it.

The jury foreman cleared his throat, paper trembling between his fingers. "On count one of the indictment, wire fraud in violation of Title 18, United States Code, Section 1343, we find the defendant, Bryce Coulter... guilty."

I kept my expression neutral even as satisfaction surged through me. The gallery behind me remained silent, but I could feel the collective exhale from the victims – dozens of retirees who'd entrusted their life savings to Coulter's investment firm only to see it vanish into his offshore accounts.

"On count two of the indictment, wire fraud in violation of Title 18, United States Code, Section 1343, we find the defendant guilty."

Coulter's face drained of color. He tugged at his collar as if it were suddenly too tight, his $3,000 suit no longer armor but a costume that couldn't hide the fraud beneath.

"On count three of the indictment, wire fraud in violation of Title 18, United States Code, Section 1343, we find the defendant guilty."

The judge thanked the jury for their service as Coulter turned to whisper frantically to his attorney. I packed my notes methodically, savoring the moment but not showing it. Federal court demanded decorum, after all. No triumphant fist pumps allowed, no matter how satisfying the verdict.

Judge Henderson denied bail pending sentencing. When the U.S. Marshals approached with handcuffs, Coulter finally lost his composure.

"This is ridiculous!" he protested, voice cracking. "I have rights! They can't—"

The cuffs clicked into place, and reality caught up with him. This wasn't a negotiation anymore. This wasn't a boardroom where he could charm his way out of trouble. This was federal prison, coming for him with cold metal and bureaucratic certainty.

As they led him away, one of the victims – an elderly woman who'd lost her entire retirement – caught my eye and mouthed "thank you." That moment meant more than the verdict itself.

White-collar crime didn't have the same visceral impact as violent offenses, but watching a man who'd stolen millions from retirees face justice still gave me a rush of satisfaction.

That feeling lasted about fifteen minutes.

Now, back at my desk in the U.S. Attorney's Office, the victory felt hollow. Another pre-packaged win for the government's newest golden child. Another case slotted into my lane because it was a sure thing.

My phone buzzed. I glanced at the screen: James Holloway.

"Heard about the Coulter verdict. Nice work, Hayes."

I smiled despite myself, typing back: *"He cried when they cuffed him."*

Three dots pulsed before his response: *"The expensive suit types always do."*

My office was different now. After the Ortega case, after exposing the public defender, Gregory Bard's corruption and bringing down Judge Leland, I'd been moved from my cramped starter office to something with an actual window. The view wasn't spectacular – just the federal building across the street and a slice of Houston skyline – but it was symbolic. A promotion without the actual promotion.

I swiveled my chair toward the wall where I'd hidden my own personal case board behind a large framed print of the Constitution. Not exactly subtle symbolism, but no one questioned it. I slid the frame aside, revealing my notes, photos, and a printed copy of the chessboard I'd discovered among Leland's papers.

Two names stared back at me: LELAND and THATCHER.

Two white bishops on one side of the board, part of something much larger – a network that had reached into the highest levels of our justice system. I'd spent three months searching for more information on Thatcher with little success.

The name "Thatcher" had turned into a research rabbit hole of judicial proportions. Four federal judges, seven state court judges, three administrative law judges, and one Supreme Court clerk all shared the surname. I'd investigated each one, looking for connections to Leland, to trafficking, to anything suspicious. Dead ends, all of them. Either I had the wrong Thatcher entirely, or whoever it was had covered their tracks with professional precision.

A knock startled me. I quickly slid the frame back into place as Callahan peered in.

"Hell of a job on Coulter," he said, leaning against the doorframe, sleeves rolled up to his elbows in his perpetual 'working prosecutor' style. "Judge Henderson mentioned you specifically. Said you presented evidence 'with remarkable clarity.'"

"Turns out financial crime isn't that complicated when the defendant emails his co-conspirators using phrases like 'totally illegal but worth it.'"

Callahan chuckled. "Still requires the right prosecutor to package it for a jury."

I offered a thin smile in return. "Thanks, Nathan."

"You've impressed a lot of people around here, Hayes." He stepped further into my office. "You've built some serious momentum. Just wanted to let you know that Beckett's noticed."

The U.S. Attorney himself. The big boss. Great.

"Appreciate the update," I said, trying to match his enthusiasm and falling pathetically short.

Callahan tilted his head, studying me with the shrewd assessment that made him an effective supervisor. "Most attorneys would be ecstatic about catching Beckett's attention."

I forced another smile. "I am. Really."

"Look, I know the Leland case hit a wall. The FBI's still working it, but these things take time."

"Three months," I said, unable to keep the edge from my voice. "And we're no closer to understanding who was pulling Leland's strings."

"These investigations move slowly. You know that."

"Meanwhile, I'm being handed slam-dunk cases."

Callahan straightened, his expression hardening slightly. "Those 'slam-dunks' are putting criminals behind bars. That's the job, Alex."

I nodded, knowing he was right but feeling the frustration bubble under my skin anyway. "I know. I'm grateful for the opportunities." The words sounded flat, even to me.

His expression softened. "Good. And there's more coming your way. You've earned it."

"More slam-dunk cases? Can't wait."

"That's the spirit," he said, tapping the door frame twice. With that, he turned and left, leaving my door open – a subtle invitation for me to rejoin the office ecosystem instead of brooding alone.

I stared at the space where he'd stood, wondering if this was what victory was supposed to feel like – being rewarded with cases just challenging enough to keep me busy but not significant enough to rock any boats.

A flash of movement caught my eye as Erin Mitchell appeared in my doorway, arms crossed, looking suspiciously pleased with herself.

"Your trophy case getting full yet?" she asked, strolling in without waiting for an invitation.

"Funny."

She settled into the chair across from me, stretching her legs out. "Three for three. The golden girl of the Houston office."

I rolled my eyes. "Sure, by batting average is perfect, but they're lobbing me beach balls underhand."

Erin deadpanned. "Alex. We're attorneys. Please don't try and talk sports. It makes it seem like you're trying too hard."

Erin and I had mostly moved past the rough patches – the tension and distrust that had nearly fractured our friendship. These days, we'd found our rhythm again, falling back into the easy banter that had characterized our relationship during law school. But there were still moments when a shadow would cross her face, when I'd catch her watching me with something like concern or calculation. Times when her answers came a beat too quickly, too practiced, like she was holding something back. I never pushed. After all, I hadn't told her everything either.

"I'll have you know that I was on the softball team in high school."

"Please just stop," Erin fake pleaded.

I rolled my eyes. "So, other than insulting me, why are you here?"

"I'm here to take you to lunch. You look like you need it." She glanced around my office. "Nice digs, by the way. Updated view, and the extra square footage probably makes your anxious pacing more comfortable."

"Oh yes, I'm very comfortable," I said sarcastically.

"And busy." Erin's voice lowered, her expression turning serious. "Word around the office is that Beckett's impressed with you."

"So Callahan just informed me."

"That's a big deal, Alex."

I leaned back in my chair, exhaling. "You know what would impress me? Finding out who the hell Thatcher is and what connection he has to Leland."

Erin glanced toward the door before leaning in. "What have you found?"

"Nothing concrete." I lowered my voice. "The FBI has Leland locked down tight. He's not talking, and his lawyer's making sure he never will. Bard's case is proceeding at a glacial pace, with continuance after continuance. And every time I try to get updates on either investigation, I hit a wall of 'not your department anymore, Hayes.'"

"Maybe that's for the best." Erin's eyes held a warning. "You took down a federal judge, Alex. That's enough excitement for one career."

"A federal judge who was just one piece on the board," I countered. "Whoever orchestrated all this is still out there. And they know I was getting close."

The image of Ortega's execution flashed through my mind – the cold precision of the gunshot, the blood pooling on the table, and the shooter's chilling words about my mother. Three months hadn't dimmed the memory or the fear it inspired.

"That's exactly my point," Erin said, her voice edged with concern. "You saw what happened to Ortega. These people don't mess around."

I dropped my eyes to my desk, fingers tracing the edge of Coulter's case file. "My mother got too close to something. Ortega knew what it was. Now he's dead, and I'm being kept busy with wire fraud cases." I looked up at her. "You don't find that suspicious?"

Erin frowned. "What I find is that you survived a situation that would have broken most people. Now you've got a window office and Beckett's attention. Maybe the universe is giving you a chance to build a normal career."

I let out a short, humorless laugh. "Normal was never in the cards for me."

"You know what your problem is?" Erin leaned back in her chair. "You have a way of telling the universe to go to hell."

I blinked. "I don't know what that means."

"Good things are being handed to you—a promotion, recognition, cases that could actually advance your career—and you're telling the universe that's not what you want. Or at least, not the way you want it." She gestured toward my office door. "Most people would kill for what you have right now."

I shifted uncomfortably. "I didn't ask for any of this."

"Exactly my point." She studied me for a long moment. "Have you told Holloway about your... concerns?"

"Some," I admitted. "But he's back in D.C. now. Our conversations mostly center around how terrible airport food is and whether long-distance relationships can survive on monthly visits and daily phone calls."

"Sounds healthy."

"It's something." I stood, grabbing my jacket from the back of my chair. "Come on. You mentioned lunch, and I'm suddenly starving."

Erin eyed me skeptically as she rose. "You're changing the subject."

"Brilliantly observed, Counselor. They teach you those deductive skills in law school?"

She rolled her eyes but followed me to the door. As we walked through the office, I nodded to colleagues – faces that had become familiar over the past three months. Some offered congratulatory smiles for the Coulter verdict. Others simply acknowledged me with a professional nod. Still, something about their gazes made me feel like I was being watched, assessed, contained.

"You know," Erin said as we stepped into the elevator, "most people would be thrilled with your trajectory. Federal prosecutor on the fast track, prestigious cases, dating a sexy DOJ attorney from Washington."

"I am thrilled," I insisted as the elevator doors closed.

"Liar."

"I just can't shake the feeling that I'm being managed. Given enough to keep me satisfied but not enough room to dig deeper."

"Did it ever occur to you that maybe you're being protected?"

I scoffed. "From what?"

The elevator slowed, and Erin's expression turned grave. "People in robes aren't the only ones with power, Alex. Sometimes the most dangerous players are the ones you never see coming."

The doors slid open to the lobby, bathed in midday sunlight streaming through tall windows. The security guards nodded as we passed, but I couldn't shake the chill Erin's words had sent down my spine.

Outside, Houston's heat made me instantly regret putting on my blazer, the humidity coating my skin as we stepped onto the sidewalk. Downtown bustled with its usual midday energy – lawyers rushing between courts, office workers grabbing quick lunches, tourists mapping out their next destinations.

"What did you mean by that?" I asked as we waited for a crosswalk signal. "About the most dangerous players?"

Erin's gaze swept the street, an unconscious security check I recognized from years working together. "Just that you might want to consider the possibility that your fast track isn't about keeping you busy. It could be about keeping you visible."

"Visible?"

"Harder to make someone disappear when they're in the spotlight." The light changed, and she stepped forward. "Come on. There's a new Thai place around the corner that doesn't water down the spice."

I followed, mind racing with the implications of her words. Was my rising profile a form of protection? A way to ensure that if anything happened to me, people would notice?

Or was it simply the easiest way to keep me distracted from what really mattered – finding out who killed my mother and why?

THE BISHOP'S RECUSAL
CHAPTER 2

The summons came through Cynthia, delivered with the kind of professional gravity that meant either someone important was dead or someone important was about to make my life significantly more complicated.

"Callahan wants to see you," she said, hovering in my doorway with a manila folder clutched against her chest. "Conference room B. Now."

I glanced at the clock. Three-thirty on a Friday afternoon – prime time for career-altering conversations. "Did he say what about?"

"High-profile case. That's all I know." She shifted her weight from one foot to the other. "But there are FBI agents in there with him."

My stomach dropped. FBI meant federal jurisdiction, which usually meant either terrorism, organized crime, or political corruption. Given my recent track record, any of those options could spell trouble.

I grabbed my legal pad and followed Cynthia down the hall. I tried to appear calm but my heartbeat was fast accelerating. Through the conference room's glass walls, I could see Callahan speaking animatedly with two people I didn't recognize – a woman in a crisp navy suit and a man whose posture screamed federal law enforcement.

Callahan looked up as I knocked. "Come in, Alex."

The woman turned first, extending her hand with the kind of firm grip that suggested she'd fought for every promotion she'd ever received. "Special Agent Sarah Chen, FBI. This is Agent Rodriguez."

Rodriguez nodded, studying me with the detached assessment of someone trying to determine if I was competent enough to handle whatever they were about to dump in my lap.

"Have a seat," Callahan said, gesturing to the chair across from him. "We've got a situation."

I settled into the chair, pen poised over my notepad. "What kind of situation?"

Agent Chen opened a thick file. "Yesterday evening, twenty-two-year-old Emily Thatcher was found dead in her apartment near Rice University. Single gunshot wound to the head, execution-style."

I resisted the urge to jump at the name, trying my best to keep my expression neutral. "Any witnesses?"

"None. But we have a suspect." Rodriguez leaned forward. "Marcus Webb, her on-and-off boyfriend for the past two years. Engineering student, no criminal record, but neighbors reported hearing them arguing frequently."

"What makes him a suspect besides proximity?"

Agent Chen slid a photograph across the table. "Security camera caught him leaving her building around the estimated time of death. His prints are on the murder weapon, which we found in a dumpster three blocks away."

I studied the photo – a young man with dark hair and a nervous expression, looking over his shoulder as he hurried down a hallway. "Has he been arrested?"

"This morning. He's claiming innocence, says he was there earlier but left before anything happened." Callahan's voice carried the weight of skepticism. "The evidence suggests otherwise."

"Where's the federal angle?"

The agents exchanged a glance before Chen answered. "Emily Thatcher was the daughter of Judge Henry Thatcher, Fifth Circuit Court of Appeals."

Everything in the room seemed to slow down, sounds becoming muffled as if I were underwater. Judge Henry Thatcher.

I thought about all the Thatchers I'd researched over the past three months. Judge Henry Thatcher, Fifth Circuit, appointed twelve years ago, confirmed by a narrow Senate margin after some controversy over his previous rulings on immigration cases. His judicial record was conservative but unremarkable – nothing that had set off alarm bells when I'd investigated him months ago.

But maybe I'd been looking at the wrong things.

Was he the missing bishop or was this all just a coincidence?

"Alex?" Callahan's voice cut through my mental fog. "You with us?"

I blinked, forcing myself back to the present. "Sorry. Federal jurisdiction because she's a judge's daughter?"

"Partly," Agent Chen said. "Under 18 U.S.C. 1114, killing a federal official or their immediate family member with intent to interfere with their official duties is a federal crime. But we also have interstate elements – the murder weapon was purchased in Louisiana, and there's evidence Webb may have crossed state lines in the days leading up to the killing."

She pulled out another photograph – Emily Thatcher's apartment, pristine except for the chalk outline on the living room floor. "Plus some of the evidence suggests this might have been targeted rather than random. Nothing was stolen. No signs of forced entry. Whoever did this had a key or was let in."

"What's the prosecution angle? Why am I the only one hearing about this?"

Callahan rubbed his jaw. "That's where it gets complicated. Judge Thatcher has been on the Fifth Circuit for fifteen years. Half the senior AUSAs in this office have appeared before him at some point. The other half have personal or professional relationships that create conflicts of interest."

Rodriguez spoke up. "We need someone clean. Someone without ties to the judge or his family."

I looked around the table, understanding dawning. "And I'm the only one who fits that description."

"You'd be first chair," Callahan said. "High-profile case, lots of media attention. It's a big opportunity."

An opportunity. Right.

"What's the timeline?" I asked, buying myself a moment to think.

"Webb's arraignment is Monday morning. We need someone ready to hit the ground running." Agent Chen gathered the photographs. "The family wants justice, and they want it fast."

I stared at the case file, Emily Thatcher's name printed in block letters on the tab. This could be coincidence – tragic timing that had nothing to do with chess pieces or conspiracy theories. Or it could be exactly the break I'd been looking for, a chance to get close to one of the bishops on that board.

"Judge Thatcher will obviously recuse himself from any related proceedings," Callahan continued. "But his influence in legal circles means this case will be under intense scrutiny."

"Have you spoken with him directly?"

"Briefly. He's devastated, as you'd expect. But he's also determined to see this through the proper channels." Callahan's expression hardened. "Which means no mistakes, no procedural errors, nothing that could give the defense ammunition for appeal."

"I'll need complete access to all evidence," I said, decision crystallizing. "Crime scene reports, forensics, witness statements, everything."

Agent Chen nodded. "You'll have it by end of business today."

"And I'll want to interview the suspect myself before we proceed."

"We'll arrange it. Tomorrow morning at the federal detention center."

Callahan leaned back in his chair, studying me. "You sure you're ready for this? High-profile murder cases are different from financial fraud. The pressure's intense, and the stakes are higher."

I met his gaze directly. "I can handle it."

The lie came easily, probably because part of it was true. I could handle the legal aspects – building a case, presenting evidence, arguing before a jury. What I was more worried about was my own conflict of interest as far as the name "Thatcher" was concerned.

"Good." Callahan stood, signaling the end of the meeting. "Agents, thank you for your time. Alex, I'll need regular updates on your progress."

Agent Chen paused at the door. "For what it's worth, the evidence against Webb is solid. This should be straightforward."

I looked up at her. "In my experience, nothing involving federal judges is ever straightforward."

She smiled grimly. "You're probably right about that."

As everyone filed out, I remained seated, staring at the case file. Emily Thatcher smiled up at me from her driver's license photo – young, bright-eyed, completely unaware that her death would become a chess move in a game I was still trying to understand.

She was twenty-two years old, a senior at Rice studying international relations with plans to attend law school. She volunteered at a local legal aid clinic and had spent the previous summer interning at the Federal Public Defender's office.

Following in her father's footsteps, building a career in public service.

Now she was dead, and her boyfriend was the prime suspect in what appeared to be a textbook case of domestic violence escalated to murder.

But the timing nagged at me. Three months after I'd discovered that chessboard, Thatcher's daughter turns up dead, and I'm the only prosecutor available to handle the case.

Either this was the universe's idea of ironic coincidence, or someone was making moves I couldn't see yet.

I closed the file and headed back to my office, mind already racing through the implications. If Judge Thatcher really was connected to the conspiracy that had killed Ortega and possibly my mother, then prosecuting his daughter's murder gave me unprecedented access to his life, his connections, his vulnerabilities.

It also put me directly in the line of fire.

THE BISHOP'S RECUSAL
CHAPTER 3

I found Erin in her office at seven-thirty the next morning, already nursing what appeared to be her second cup of coffee while reviewing a stack of depositions. Saturday mornings at the U.S. Attorney's Office were usually quiet, but Erin had always been an early riser, especially when a case demanded her attention.

She looked up as I knocked on her doorframe. "Let me guess. You couldn't sleep either."

"Something like that." I stepped inside and closed the door behind me. "Got a minute?"

"For you? Always." She gestured to the chair across from her desk. "Though if you're here to complain about your new high-profile case, I'm not sure I want to hear it."

"Actually, I'm here to ask you to join it."

Erin paused mid-sip, coffee cup hovering inches from her lips. "Come again?"

"I need a second chair. Someone I trust, someone who knows how to handle complex cases without letting politics get in the way."

She set her cup down carefully. "Alex, this is the daughter of a Fifth Circuit judge. Every move you make will be scrutinized by the defense bar, the media, and probably half of Washington. You sure you want to complicate things by bringing me into it?"

I waved a hand at her statement. "The case is already complicated.

Between who the victim is and my name as first chair, we're already maxed out on the complications scale. Adding your name to the roster isn't going to change much."

Erin leaned back in her chair, arms crossed. "How complicated?"

I glanced toward the door, then lowered my voice. "Remember the chessboard from Leland's papers? The one with the bishop positions marked?"

"The Thatcher name you've been chasing for months."

"Judge Henry Thatcher. Emily's father."

Understanding dawned in her eyes, followed immediately by concern. "Alex, please tell me you're not suggesting—"

"I'm not suggesting anything yet. But this case gives us legitimate access to Thatcher's life, his connections, his background. If he's clean, we rule him out and focus on getting justice for Emily. If he's not..."

"If he's not, then you're prosecuting the murder of a corrupt judge's daughter while investigating whether he's part of a criminal conspiracy." Erin rubbed her temples. "Do you hear how insane that sounds?"

"I hear how it sounds. I also remember watching Ortega get executed in front of me, and the shooter mentioning my mother."

That stopped her cold. Erin had been there for the aftermath, had seen me shaking in the holding cell, had helped piece together the evidence that brought down Leland. She knew better than anyone how deep this conspiracy ran.

"What does the evidence look like?" she asked finally.

I pulled out the case file, spreading crime scene photos across her desk. "Marcus Webb, the boyfriend. They found the murder weapon with his prints, security footage places him at the scene around the time of death, and neighbors heard them arguing."

"Sounds open and shut."

"Maybe. But there are details that don't fit. Emily was shot execution-style, single bullet to the head. That's not typical for domestic violence murders – those are usually crimes of passion, multiple wounds, signs of struggle."

Erin studied the photographs. "Could be he planned it. Premeditated rather than heat of the moment."

"Could be. Or could be someone wanted it to look like Webb did it."

"You think he was framed?"

"I think I need to investigate all possibilities. And I can't do that alone."

Erin was quiet for a long moment, fingers drumming against her desk as she weighed the implications. Outside her window, downtown Houston was slowly coming to life – early risers grabbing coffee, joggers making their way through the streets, the normal rhythm of a Saturday morning.

"If I agree to this," she said finally, "we do it by the book. Every procedure followed, every piece of evidence properly documented. We can't give the defense any ammunition for appeal."

"Agreed."

"And if we find evidence that Thatcher is involved in something illegal, we turn it over to the appropriate authorities immediately. We don't go rogue, we don't try to handle it ourselves."

"Also agreed."

She picked up one of the crime scene photos, studying Emily's apartment. "She was twenty-two years old. Pre-law student, clean record, no known enemies besides an occasionally volatile boyfriend."

"Which makes this either a straightforward case of domestic violence, or someone using that as cover for something else."

"And you think the 'something else' might connect to your mother's case."

I met her gaze directly. "I think it's worth finding out."

Erin set the photo down slowly. "You know, when I convinced you to come to the federal side, I thought you might get interested in white-collar crime. Maybe some nice, clean financial fraud cases."

"Sorry to disappoint."

"Oh, you're not disappointing me. You're terrifying me." She stood, grabbing her jacket from the back of her chair. "But you're also right. If there's a connection, we need to find it."

"Does that mean you're in?"

"I'm in. But we're going to need help. This case is going to generate massive media attention, and Judge Thatcher will have every legal heavy-hitter in the state watching our every move."

"What kind of help?"

"The kind that can handle forensics, witness interviews, and background investigations without tipping our hand about what we're really looking for." She pulled out her phone. "I know someone who might be perfect for this."

"Who?"

"Special Agent Logan Elliott. Remember him?"

"Remember him? He interviewed me after I watched Ortega get executed. Sort of hard to forget."

Erin shrugged. "Sorry if it triggers you, but he's thorough, discreet, and he owes me a favor."

"Thanks, but I'm not worried about that. What I want to know is whether we can trust him?"

"With this? Yes. Elliott's been chasing corruption cases for years. If there's something dirty about Judge Thatcher, he'll find it."

"And if there isn't?"

"Then we prosecute Marcus Webb for murdering his girlfriend and put a killer behind bars. Either way, Emily Thatcher gets justice."

I nodded, but something in Erin's tone made me pause. There was a finality to her words, as if she was trying to convince herself as much as me that justice could be that straightforward.

"You think I'm chasing ghosts, don't you?" I asked.

Erin gathered the crime scene photos, stacking them neatly before sliding them back into the file. "I think you've been through hell, and you're looking for patterns that might not exist. But I also think your instincts have been right more often than wrong. So we'll follow the evidence wherever it leads, even if it takes us somewhere we don't want to go."

"And if it leads us back to the conspiracy?"

"Then we'll deal with that when we get there. But Alex, promise me something."

"What?"

"If this gets dangerous – if we start getting too close to something that could get us killed – you won't try to protect me by keeping me in the dark. We're partners on this, which means we share the risks."

After everything that had happened with the Ortega case, after the times I'd charged ahead without fully considering the consequences for those around me, she was asking for honesty. Complete transparency, even when it might put her in danger.

"I promise," I said, meaning it.

"Good. Then let's get started."

Keep reading *The Bishop's Recusal* by grabbing your copy on Amazon today!
https://a.co/d/hbLA434

Join the LT Ryan reader family & receive a free copy of the Alex Hayes story, *Trial by Fire*. Click the link below to get started:
https://ltryan.com/alex-hayes-newsletter-signup-1

THE ALEX HAYES SERIES

Trial By Fire (Prequel Novella)
Fractured Verdict
11th Hour Witness
Buried Testimony
The Bishop's Recusal

ALSO BY L.T. RYAN

Find All of L.T. Ryan's Books on Amazon Today!

The Jack Noble Series

The Recruit (free)

The First Deception (Prequel 1)

Noble Beginnings

A Deadly Distance

Ripple Effect (Bear Logan)

Thin Line

Noble Intentions

When Dead in Greece

Noble Retribution

Noble Betrayal

Never Go Home

Beyond Betrayal (Clarissa Abbot)

Noble Judgment

Never Cry Mercy

Deadline

End Game

Noble Ultimatum

Noble Legend

Noble Revenge

Never Look Back

Bear Logan Series

Ripple Effect

Blowback

Take Down

Deep State

Bear & Mandy Logan Series

Close to Home

Under the Surface

The Last Stop

Over the Edge

Between the Lies

Caught in the Web

The Marked Daughter (Coming Soon)

Rachel Hatch Series

Drift

Downburst

Fever Burn

Smoke Signal

Firewalk

Whitewater

Aftershock

Whirlwind

Tsunami

Fastrope

Sidewinder

Redaction

Mirage

Faultline (Coming Soon)

Mitch Tanner Series

The Depth of Darkness

Into The Darkness

Deliver Us From Darkness

Cassie Quinn Series

Path of Bones

Whisper of Bones

Symphony of Bones

Etched in Shadow

Concealed in Shadow

Betrayed in Shadow

Born from Ashes

Return to Ashes

Risen from Ashes (Coming Soon)

Blake Brier Series

Unmasked

Unleashed

Uncharted

Drawpoint

Contrail

Detachment

Clear

Quarry

Dalton Savage Series

Savage Grounds

Scorched Earth

Cold Sky

The Frost Killer

Crimson Moon

Dust Devil (Coming Soon)

Maddie Castle Series

The Handler

Tracking Justice

Hunting Grounds

Vanished Trails

Smoldering Lies

Field of Bones

Beneath the Grove (Coming Soon)

Affliction Z Series

Affliction Z: Patient Zero

Affliction Z: Abandoned Hope

Affliction Z: Descended in Blood

Affliction Z : Fractured Part 1

Affliction Z: Fractured Part 2 (Fall 2021)

Alex Hayes Series

Trial By Fire (Prequel)

Fractured Verdict

11th Hour Witness

Buried Testimony

The Bishop's Recusal (Coming Soon)

Stella LaRosa Series

Black Rose

Red Ink

Black Gold

White Lies

Avril Dahl Series

Cold Reckoning

Cold Legacy

Cold Mercy (Coming Soon)

Savannah Shadows Series

Echoes of Guilt

The Silence Before

Dead Air (Coming Soon)

Receive a free copy of The Recruit. Visit:

https://ltryan.com/jack-noble-newsletter-signup-1

ABOUT THE AUTHORS

L.T. RYAN is a *Wall Street Journal* and *USA Today* bestselling author, renowned for crafting pulse-pounding thrillers that keep readers on the edge of their seats. Known for creating gripping, character-driven stories, Ryan is the author of the *Jack Noble* series, the *Rachel Hatch* series, and more. With a knack for blending action, intrigue, and emotional depth, Ryan's books have captivated millions of fans worldwide.

Whether it's the shadowy world of covert operatives or the relentless pursuit of justice, Ryan's stories feature unforgettable characters and high-stakes plots that resonate with fans of Lee Child, Robert Ludlum, and Michael Connelly.

When not writing, Ryan enjoys crafting new ideas with coauthors, running a thriving publishing company, and connecting with readers. Discover the next story that will keep you turning pages late into the night.

Connect with L.T. Ryan
Sign up for his newsletter to hear the latest goings on and receive some free content
➜ https://ltryan.com/jack-noble-newsletter-signup-1

Join the private readers' group
➜ https://www.facebook.com/groups/1727449564174357

Instagram ➜ @ltryanauthor

Visit the website → https://ltryan.com
Send an email → contact@ltryan.com

LAURA CHASE is a corporate attorney-turned-author who brings her courtroom experience to the page in her gripping legal and psychological thrillers. Chase draws on her real-life experience to draw readers into the high-stakes world of courtroom drama and moral ambiguity.

After earning her JD, Chase clerked for a federal judge and thereafter transitioned to big law, where she honed her skills in high-pressure legal environments. Her passion for exploring the darker side of human nature and the gray areas of justice fuels her writing.

Chase lives with her husband, their two sons, a dog and a cat in Northern Florida. When she's not writing or working, she enjoys spending time with her family, traveling, and bingeing true crime shows.

Connect with Laura:

Sign up for her newsletter: www.laurachaseauthor.com/

Follow her on tiktok: @lawyerlaura

Send an email: info@laurachase.com

Made in the USA
Middletown, DE
29 July 2025

11392043R00177